The Music Box Girl

K.A. Stewart

Also From K.A. Stewart

The Jesse James Dawson Series
A Devil in the Details
A Shot in the Dark
A Wolf at the Door
A Snake in the Grass
A Line in the Sand

The Arcane West Trilogy
Peacemaker

Second Olympus

Because of Caleb

<u>Acknowledgements</u>

First and foremost, I need to thank Caleb Malcom. It was his assertion that my "can't happen" was really a "maybe if" that made this story what it is.

As always, I have to thank everyone who supports me on a daily basis: Dr. Gita Bransteitter, Alice Loweecey, Janet Yantes, Melanie Schultz, Scott Stewart, and Aislynn Stewart. Without this group, I too would probably be some kind of insane genius, living in the basement of a building. (Probably not an opera house, though. Maybe a Chipotle?)

And last, but never least, the readers who seem hell-bent on following wherever my twisted mind takes me. You are why I do what I do.

PROLOGUE

The thick coating of dust proved that no one had been in the attic for decades. Felicia surveyed the vast expanse of the room, stretching the entire length of the enormous house, and wondered how they'd ever get through it all.

"Where do we start, Mother?" The girl at her elbow, a budding young lady of almost thirteen, had her blond hair bound up in a tight tail, a cloth tied around her face to avoid breathing in the plumes of dust that billowed up every time one of them moved.

"At one end, of course!" Casimir, his young nephew Peter thrown giggling over one shoulder, marched off under the eaves with lantern in hand.

Felicia shook her head in amusement at her brother. He was trying so hard to make this a game, and not the sad and depressing task that it was. "Start here, Josie. We'll sort out anything salvageable, and then the furniture can be hauled out by the automatons. Peter, why don't you and Uncle Cas start on that wardrobe."

Some of the things she recognized, Felicia realized. A doll that she'd long ago lost and forgotten. A picture drawn in her primary school days, lovingly kept but brittle with age. An entire crate of baby clothes, though it was anyone's guess if they'd been hers or Casimir's.

"Remember this, little sister?" A gangly clown marionette dropped in front of her face, painted face chipped and leering, and she jerked with a start. Casimir howled with laughter, joined by his little shadow, Peter. "That's just what you used to do when we were children!"

"Beast." Felicia swatted at him half-heartedly. "Throw that horrid thing out."

"No. I think I'll keep this. For memories." The tall man placed the toy in a small-but-growing pile near the stairs.

"You can't keep it all, Cas," she quietly reminded him.

He glanced her way, the playful humor washing out of his gray eyes in an instant, proving that it was only a show he was putting on for the children. "No, but I want to keep some of it. It's just not right to have it all chucked in the bin. It was their life, Felicia. Their entire life, and we're just… We're getting rid of it all."

Rising, Felicia tried to brush the dust from her skirts, with little success. Casimir took her hand when she offered it, and they exchanged the sequence of three squeezes as they'd always done since childhood. "As much as I miss them both, they're gone, Cas. We can't keep them here by holding onto these things. The buyers want to move into the house next month, we have to clear it out."

Casimir sighed, his dark bangs falling into his eyes as he shook his head. "Maybe this would be easier if it hadn't happened so close together, you know? But…three months, and both of them…"

"We should have known. He never wanted to live without Mother. Together or not at all, remember? We should be thinking about how happy they are now, together again and always."

The elder brother tried to smile, and the moisture he blinked from his eyes could just be from the dust.

"Mother?" Felicia looked over as her young daughter called out. "What's this?"

"Well I don't know, let me see."

"This" proved to be a book, of sorts, carefully stored in a piece of folded, faded silk. The pages were yellowed, brittle, and the corners on one end had the faint green tint of mildew, but otherwise, it seemed in decent condition. The spine was bound with three strips of red ribbon, the color washed out by sheer age, and the cover had been hand-written in beautiful calligraphy. "The Terrible Mystery of the Music Box Girl, by Susan Whitfield."

"Hey, that's Great Auntie Susan!" Peter bounced over, whatever game he'd been playing at not nearly as interesting as the new treasure from the trunk.

Felicia glanced up at Casimir, showing him the aged keepsake, and he shrugged. "It's not one of her published ones. Maybe something she did early on, and never finished?"

"I thought you knew all of Aunt Susan's works."

He smirked. "You found me out, sister dear, I'm not perfect."

"What's it about, Mother?" Josie sat down in the dust, wrapping her arms around her knees and looking up expectantly. After a moment, Peter joined her, mimicking his sister's position. He even tried batting his eyelashes, which earned a muffled chuckle from his uncle.

"Oh fine, you two. Just a chapter, then back to work. Bring the lantern closer, Cas." Careful not to damage the aged pages, Felicia opened the book to the first page, settling down on the dust covered floor. "Chapter one. The automaton was obviously malfunctioning. There was a lurching hitch in its gait as it moved, and even an untrained ear could hear the distinct click where the teeth on several gears had either broken or been ground off..."

ACT I

Chapter 1

The automaton was obviously malfunctioning. There was a lurching hitch in its gait as it moved, and even an untrained ear could hear the distinct click where the teeth on several gears had either broken or been ground off. The faint charred odor of long-stale grease followed the construction wherever it moved, and when something snapped like a gunshot, no one in the vicinity was surprised.

Well, no one save the draft horse attached to the coal cart, and that monstrous creature shied with a startled bellow, dragging the wagon halfway down the block and scattering pedestrians before it like a flock of pigeons. It barreled toward the busy cross-street, which would most surely cause a disaster, but a well-meaning passerby managed to snag its harness and bring the beast to a stop. Its dappled flanks heaved with the efforts of its sudden, if brief, flight.

The automaton staggered to an abrupt halt, frozen forever holding its load of coal, as its gears seized up and the snapping cables within its chest sent pulleys pinging around inside like bullets. Only the strong steel construction kept the mechanical parts from escaping and flying into the nearby pedestrians like shrapnel. A sad plume of smoke trickled from its auditory receivers, accompanied by the last plaintive whine of its mechanical voice box.

"Goddamn piece of tin-snip rubbish!" The coal master appeared, his bristling mustache broadcasting his irritation even if the stream of profanity had not been a clue. "Piece of scrapyard junk!" He kicked the automaton in the leg, eliciting no response at all from the metal creature – it was well and truly broken – but causing no small amount of damage to his own booted foot.

A small crowd gathered, drawn by the impending disaster with the cart horse, and entertained by the antics of the livid coal master. Chuckles passed amongst them as they watched him hop in circles on his uninjured foot, cursing fit to turn the air blue.

"You there!" The coal master pointed at another automaton, identical in all ways to the first except that the second was still functioning. "Take this coal to the cart, then haul this thing off to the shop. We'll break it down for spare parts."

A mechanical voice answered, "Yes sir" with a faint crackle of damaged wiring behind it. The second construct was not in much better condition than the first, and one could hear a slight ping with every step as an internal cable vibrated just a bit too hard. If one knew what to listen for, of course. That second machine would be inoperable within a month, in all likelihood. That was what became of poor maintenance practices.

The crowd dispersed after a few moments, everyone returning to wherever their lives were taking them. No doubt home to an evening meal, to stoke a nighttime fire to ward off the early autumn chill. Perhaps to curl up beneath a lantern and read to one's children, or beloved.

No one noticed the figure in the dark cloak, standing safely to the side of the hurried pedestrian traffic. She took refuge deep inside her hood, lest someone see, and stood so still that not one glance darted in her direction. Such was their way, the way of the humans. Always so frantic, always so preoccupied within themselves. It worked to her advantage.

When the throng had cleared somewhat, she stepped

from the growing shadows, gliding along in a rustle of skirts just like anyone else around her. Certainly, under the cloak her gown was much too fine for this area of the city, but it was also decades behind the fashion with a faded band around the hem where the coal dust had been washed from it many, many times. It would not attract attention, not here. Just as she wanted it.

By the time she had walked eight blocks, there was a distinct change in atmosphere as she left behind the coalworks of the city and ventured into higher class districts. The clothing here was of better quality, more recent acquisition. With the cooler weather coming on, velvets were making their return, along with collared coats and heavier gloves, and fur wraps would soon replace summery parasols. These things she noted, making a mental note to adjust her own wardrobe accordingly.

Most went about in carriages, or the new horseless conveyances, the steam pistons hissing and popping as they sped down the street, scattering those still on foot from their path. Shopkeepers were shuttering their windows for the evening, dousing their lanterns, calling out farewells to their neighbors in commerce.

Here, she crossed the street quickly, vanishing into the alleys before anyone could question why a woman would be doing such. This was not the area for doxies, and her presence would be noted and wondered at if she lingered too long.

In the alleys, with no eyes to see save vermin and inebriates, she moved faster, realizing that she would be late if she did not make up some time. The incident with the coalworks automaton had distracted her longer than she had intended, and she was behind schedule.

Four blocks north, and two east, and she found the grate just as she'd left it. The bolts into the sandstone colored brick had long since stripped smooth, and it took nothing for her to lift it away and duck into the passage within, replacing the barrier behind her with no sound at all of dragging metal. A human would never be able to lift that grate, she knew, stripped bolts or no. Only she used this entrance, even the city vagrants having long since given up the effort of moving the grate as futile.

Once inside, she only had to crouch for a few paces before the tunnel opened up into a t-shaped junction. A sewer once, long forgotten and paved over, the building atop it constructed decades after the tunnel's function was abandoned. A small trickle of water still meandered down the center of the paving stone floor, never deep enough to dampen her skirts, but enough to create an almost musical melody as it wended through the uneven stones.

Sometimes, when time permitted, she would pause here, locating a particular tone or note that was out of place, and then she would shift the stones in their beds, altering the water flow until it suited her. Tonight, there would be no such indulgence.

Taking care not to slip on the moss-covered stones beneath her boots, she traversed her own well-known path, taking her deep into the bowels of the building.

Already, she could feel the thrum at the back of her skull, the deep vibration caused by the sheer number of living beings above her. Hundreds and hundreds of voices, murmuring amongst themselves. Singly, they were nearly silent, but in multitudes, they roared at a frequency just below human hearing. Their feet, encased in polished shoes or high-buttoned boots, shifted restlessly on the wooden floor far above. In their hands, the paper of the programs rustled, crackled.

She heard the first low draw of a bow across a cello and quickened her pace. She would miss the opening if she did not hurry. The orchestra was already warming up.

The strings and woodwinds were humming at a higher pitch just behind her jaw joints as she emerged from the sewer tunnel, shifting a large prop barrel to cover the opening as she did every time. The storeroom into which she entered was covered in the cobwebs of long disuse, but she still took care to lift her skirts, leaving only the faintest of tracks through the thick dust. Her oil can, kept near the door to lubricate its hinges into silence, was still there and untouched just as she expected. She inspected the hinges before deciding that more was unnecessary. Just as well, she didn't have time anyway.

The backstage area was largely clear, the hands already scattered through the riggings above the stage, either to watch or to adjust the scenery as needed. The performers were in the wings, waiting for their cues, knowing just how much time they had before curtain by what place the orchestra was in their warm-ups. The dancers had been corralled, slippers rosined and laced, and last minute adjustments to the costumes had been given up as lost causes. The show was about to begin.

She slipped through the darkness behind the stage with the ease of long practice, finding the servants' stair that would take her to the box level. Her box would be waiting, as always, the one nearest the stairway, allowing her to slip in and out unseen.

The muted roar of many voices was almost silent by the time she found her seat in the farthest back corner of box number seven, a corner that even the stage lights could not penetrate. She would be safe there, shrouded in her cloak, motionless. No one would ever glance at the dark box. No one ever had.

The timepiece pinned to her bodice whirred softly, marking the change of the hour, and on cue, the heavy burgundy velvet curtains parted, golden cords drawing them to the sides of the stage. Like the sunrise, she always thought, the world suddenly revealed in a sweep of all-encompassing light. Nothing else existed outside of that brilliance.

The music swelled from the orchestra pit below, and she

allowed herself to be lost in it, swept away on the tide of melody and harmony, each instrument strumming a different chord inside her head. It was flawless. Well, nearly so. The third bassoon was flat, though his compatriots largely drowned out his sad efforts, and the fourth viola was missing a string, which she nimbly fingered around in a display of inspired improvisation.

No one else in the audience would ever notice. In fact, only the maestro himself would be aware of the errors, and so long as the orchestra kept on beat, he'd be unlikely to say a word. He'd become complacent, in his advancing years. He'd been there nearly as long as she, and she knew that his joints pained him in the colder weather. The oncoming winter would swell his knuckles, stiffen his knees. It wasn't as if he could simply replace a bearing or oil a gear. Humans did not repair themselves well. He had earned a small measure of respite.

The chorus took the stage, setting the scene for the night's performance. She closed her eyes, noting which voices were new, which cracked with strain, picking out one or two that were sharp on the harmony. She would have to send a note. That would have to be corrected.

The lead soprano, a young woman named Caroline, treated the audience to the pure notes of her first aria, and the silent watcher was forced to move her jaw slightly to relieve the pressure. The high notes, while technically perfect, caused an odd vibration somewhere behind her left ear, one reason that she had never enjoyed the sopranos so much. Perfect, yes, but piercing.

The next voice, though… Oh, that was the one she always came to hear. The lead tenor's melody rose above the rest, the chorus falling silent as all eyes went to the handsome, strapping young man at center stage.

Well, once he had been, at any rate. Simon LeClerc was advancing rapidly toward his mid-forties, and if he had to use a girdle to hold in his slight paunch, or use bootblack to conceal the gray in his dark hair, the audience was willing to suspend disbelief. However, while stage makeup could cover a myriad of physical ills, she could hear the hint of strain in his formerly vibrant voice. He was flat. Soundly, decidedly flat. It wasn't much, just a hairsbreadth off from his former perfection, but she could tell.

The audience was rapt, of course. Hanging on every note that tumbled from his lips. The human ear was not designed as finely as hers, would not be able to discern the tiny flaw that she detected so keenly, but it was only a matter of time.

She was sad, she realized. For decades, she had come to watch Simon, his beautiful tenor voice soothing in a way the higher pitches could never be. For years, she had chosen operas particularly suited for him, and she had basked in every bit of applause he had so rightly received. But now…

She'd noticed the faltering voice last summer, and had hoped that it was merely weariness. By the autumn production, his voice was once again all that it could be, all it had always been. But the Christmas chorale was nearly a disaster by her standards, Simon deliberately hiding his own melodic line beneath that of the weaker tenors in the chorus, hoping that no one would notice he could no longer carry the lead. The spring fete had been much the same, and though the summer season had been cancelled for extensive remodeling to the opera house, the lengthy rest had alleviated none of his problem.

She was forced, finally, to admit that Simon was aging past his prime. Soon, he would have to depart, make way for someone younger, someone who could hold their pitch. Unfortunately, there was no one in the chorus who could easily take his place. Enthusiastic, yes, but none of them had the power or purity of Simon at his greatest. He would have to be allowed to finish this run, complete the fall season. Perhaps by Christmas, she would be able to locate a replacement.

She would have to send a note.

Departing from the opera house after a performance was never as easy as arriving. There were celebrations to wait out, patrons coming back stage for tours, or to bestow gifts upon their favorites. The stage crew had to reset for the next night's show, the costumers had to gather the garments dropped negligently by the dancers. The maids had to make their way through the entire building, gathering up programs, crumpled and forgotten. They swept the carpets, and the boxes, all save for box seven, because of course when no one used it, cleaning was not necessary.

And so she sat in utter stillness, waiting until the booming echo of the last closing door had faded away. Waiting until she was well and truly alone. Only then did she make her way down the servants' staircase, through the backstage area, into her forgotten storeroom and out through the sewer. The grate slid back into place easily, and she was once again in the open street.

She drew her hood up higher around her face, and kept to the shadows. This area of the city was empty at this time of night, all the merchants closed, all the opera-goers moved on to other diversions. She would be noticed, here, and so she passed through quickly, silently. Only once did she hear the clop of a horse's hooves, the creak of carriage springs, and then she froze into her unnatural motionless state, only her eyes moving as the conveyance trotted by and off into the darkness without marking her presence.

The coalworks, now those offered a different kind of threat. The coalworks never slept, men and automatons ceaselessly shoveling the black rocks into the furnaces, generating the steam that powered most of the city. Always brightly lit, always heavily travelled, passing through the streets of the coalworks promised almost certain discovery at every turn. A woman in the coalworks at this time of night was no lady, that was a given, and could not be expected to be treated as such. She always had to be careful, returning home by that path.

The sounds were the worst part. The constant grind and rattle of the machines, the clang of metal on metal. Voices, both human and automaton, raised to be heard over the volume, dissolving into a harsh cacophony, discordant, unintelligible. It made it impossible to hear anything with any precision, impossible to detect something coming up behind.

The street lights cast prying, orange orbs about themselves, a revealing gleam that she avoided through long practice. Not even the hem of her long skirts brushed their circles of light. With one hand, she kept her hood pulled down, shadowing her face even more, her head ducked to avoid making eye contact with any stray gazes. As such, with her eyes on the cobblestones beneath her boots, she did not see the man lurching out of the alley until it was too late. He barreled into her and bounced off so hard, he may as well have walked into a wall.

"Oof!" He staggered back against the wall, blinking bleary eyes in confusion for a few moments. "Hey there… Watch yourself, girly." Coal dust covered his face, leaving his eyes like two bright points in a mask of black. His clothing was rough-spun and oft-patched. His boots were more hole than leather. A coal worker, then, and probably out of the building to sneak a belt of liquor in the back alley across the way.

"My apologies, sir." Two steps back, the shadows were deeper. She withdrew cautiously, keeping her hood tugged low.

"Here now, wait, that ain't no way to offer a proper apology." The man pursued her, and she caught the scent of bourbon strong on his breath as she'd expected. "Pretty thing like you, there oughta be something you could do to make up for almost runnin' a fella over." With a leer and a speed a man that drunk should not possess, he darted forward, grabbing at her wrist.

She could tell the moment he realized that there was no soft, yielding human flesh underneath the brushed silk of her sleeve. The confusion darted across his face, dulled with alcohol and idiocy. "What…?" He leaned forward, craning his neck at an angle almost enough to throw himself completely off balance, peering up into the recesses of her hood. His eyes went wide, shock chasing away some of the effects of the booze. "What the hell…?" His chest expanded as he gasped in a breath, surely to exclaim loudly, or to call for aid, or… Whatever his purpose, she could not allow it.

Her free hand shot out, grasped him around the throat, and his voice came out in a choked gurgle. His eyes bulged out, and his hand scrabbled at hers, grimy fingers tearing the lace trim from her glove. Lifted a few inches off the ground, his feet drummed against her legs, doing her no harm and offering him no aid. His face slowly turned purple, and the vessels in his eyes burst, staining the white red. After a few moments, he stopped struggling, hanging limply in her grip. She held on a few moments longer, then simply let go, the man falling into a heap at her feet.

She glanced around, but there was no one in sight. No one sounded alarm, there was no thunder of running boots and tweeting of police whistles. She remained unseen.

Carefully lifting her skirts, she stepped over the body on the cobblestones, and continued on her way.

Chapter 2

The opera house was everything he'd ever been told. That was his first thought. He'd always suspected that his mother had exaggerated in her descriptions, but no, every single detail could have been taken straight from her bedtime tales. Four stories high, the towering windows in the front flanked by gold-leafed statues of various Greek deities, the marble steps leading up to the doors gleaming in the sunlight.

The opera house was Detroit's crowning glory, the symbol of the power and influence the city had come to embody. In a world where automation and innovation were prized, the world's leading producer of steel had become the center of the modern universe. Immigrants flocked here by the thousands every year, hoping that they too could carve out their own tiny piece of the American dream. A rare few succeeded.

Tony stood for a few moments, just gazing up at the imposing structure, trying not to think about how shabby he would appear, walking up those very stairs. Still, there was no use putting it off. It was either walk up the stairs, or retreat back home like a kicked hound. And he hadn't any money for a return trip, so even that second option was less than feasible.

"Move, Anton, before grass grows around your feet." He could almost hear his mother chiding him, and he smiled softly to himself. Hitching his rucksack higher on his shoulder, he put one foot on the first marble stair and began to climb.

The entryway of the opera house was no less stunning, the dual marble staircases sweeping left and right, framing an exquisite statue of the muses that took center stage in the grand foyer. People scampered here and there, intent on their pre-performance duties, whatever they might be. Not one of them glanced at the stranger, and it took him a moment or two to catch someone's attention.

"Excuse me, I'm here to audition?"

The woman wore a maid's uniform, but it was still at least twice the quality of his own worn clothing, and she looked him up and down with a raised brow as if she herself would determine his fate. "The director's office is down that hallway, on the right. You can have a seat outside, if he's busy." And with a small sniff of derision, she was off again.

Well. It was a start.

Finding the office was easy, his success proven by a nameplate beside the door that read G. CHALMERS, MANAGING DIRECTOR. The door was shut, however, and before he could even raise his hand to knock, he could hear voices inside in heated discussion. With a sigh, he found himself a seat on a padded bench, and settled in to wait.

Tony rested his elbows on his knees and pretended that he couldn't hear the raised voices in the office behind him. Even with the door closed, muffling the exact words, it was very clear that one of the men inside was extremely unhappy, and just as clear that the other was trying to placate him. There was no telling how long the conversation had gone on, nor how much longer it was apt to be, but where else did he have to be, really?

And so Tony sat on the low bench, examining the hardwood floor between his feet until he had memorized the exact number of nails used in each board. His boots were worn, he observed once again. Coming on into winter, he was going to need new ones. That would require a paying job, and sadly, boots were going to be low on his priority list after lodging and food and a decent coat.

"I shouldn't have left," he murmured quietly to himself in his native Polish. "Should have waited for spring, like I promised Mother." But Mother was gone, free of the debilitating pain that had marred the last years of her life. And sometimes, you just couldn't wait for spring.

He'd promised Mother many things. First and foremost was that he would leave behind the small estate and village where he'd grown up and venture into the city to make something of himself. *"God has given you a gift, Anton. You insult him by squandering it."* Mother had believed in him from the time he was a small child with the unwavering certainty that only a mother could have. She always trusted that someday, the world would hear him sing.

The office door slammed open, putting a decisive punctuation on one man's exit. He stopped as his eyes landed on Tony, raising a dark brow that was liberally sprinkled with silver. Tony returned the look steadily, examining the stranger. He was older than Tony, easily by more than a decade, and there was a smudge of bootblack on his forehead where he'd obviously tried to hide his graying hair.

The older man drew himself up under Tony's perusal, his own piercing gray gaze travelling up and down the younger man's form and obviously finding him lacking. He wrinkled his nose and turned on his heel, stalking off in the opposite direction.

The second man emerged from the office, dabbing at his flushed face with a handkerchief monogrammed with the initials "GC". His thinning hair was in disarray, giving him the appearance of a flustered guinea hen. For a moment, it was obvious that he believed himself to be alone, until Tony cleared his throat. "Oh! Oh my, where did you come from?"

"I was told I could wait here, sir. You are the director?"

Tony hopped to his feet and offered his hand. "My name is Anton Krol."

"Oh. Oh yes." The befuddled man shook his hand more out of habit, and blinked owlishly at him. "I am Mr. Chalmers, the managing director. And you are...Mr. Krol?"

"Yes, sir. Anton, sir."

"Yes, yes...Anton..." The befuddled man adjusted his waistcoat, then wiped his spectacles on his handkerchief, smudging them beyond hope of being useful. "I'm sorry for your wait. Performers, you know, so temperamental. Now how may I help you?"

"Of course, sir." The agitated little man's face was a rather unhealthy shade of red, and seemed slow to revert to its natural color. "If you'll pardon me...are you all right, sir?"

"Hm? Oh... Oh yes, quite fine. Bit warm in there, just in need of some fresh air and all... Now then..." He adjusted his smudged glasses on the end of his nose, looking Tony up and down with none of the derision the other man had shown. "Now, let me guess, you are looking for work, yes?"

"Yes, sir."

"And what position are you looking to fill?" To his credit, the rattled fellow was doing his best to pull himself together, focusing on the task at hand.

"Anything really, sir. I have some amateur musical background, tenor of course. I would be happy to audition for you on any piece you like..."

There was no mistaking the faint grimace that crossed the older man's face. "Ah, well, yes... You see the thing is... We're not currently hiring performers. Our chorus is full, and there are really no openings..."

Tony's heart sank, but it was no more than he was expecting. What opera company would hire an unknown singer off the streets? Without a patron or a recommendation, he might as well have walked into the capitol and volunteered to be governor with the same expectation of success. But walking up the marble steps outside, seeing the sweeping parapets of the opera house high above, he'd dared to let himself hope. He should have known better.

"I see. Thank you for your time, sir." He snatched his threadbare coat off the bench, shrugging into it. Bitterly, he noticed that more threads had come loose around the cuffs, creating more fringe to droop over his hands. Soon he would look like a raggedy scarecrow, left to rot in the elements.

"Now, now wait… We don't have any positions open at this time, per se, but if you were willing to wait a bit…"

Tony turned, stopping just short of plopping his cap atop his head. "Wait?"

The manager nodded. "It happens that we have had a sudden opening in the stage crew, constructing sets, running the backstage functions of the shows and the like. If you have any skill with tools, it might be possible for you to begin there, at least for now. It would at least be a wage."

Ah. So he had noticed the shabby condition of Tony's clothing, truthfully the last decent garments he possessed. "And in the future, I would be given the opportunity to audition?"

Mr. Chalmers glanced down the hallway after the first man, paling slightly, then recovered when he was certain they were alone. "Perhaps, in time. Should a place open up. Are you interested?"

What choice did he really have? Where else was there to go? "Yes, sir. I'll take it." This time, the manager shook his hand quite happily.

~*¡*~

"This is our workshop here," the stage manager instructed, gesturing to a large room the size of a small warehouse. "Usually just doing maintenance on the existing pieces, but sometimes we get to build from scratch. Just depends on how damaged the sets get while they're in storage."

The man's name was Jack Kelly, and Tony had quite liked him from the moment they'd been introduced. An immigrant, like Tony himself, Jack had a faint Irish brogue that became more pronounced the moment Mr. Chalmers delivered Tony and fled back into the opera house proper. If he noticed the slight lilt to Tony's English that marked him also as a non-native speaker, he didn't mention it.

Jack's hands were gnarled and scarred, attesting to the hard manual labor he did on a regular basis, but his blue eyes were merry, and the lines on his face spoke of his tendency to laugh more than scowl. "Further on back, we have a few cots against the wall if you need a place to stay until you can find your own bunk, or if we're working all night or such. Rare, but it does happen sometimes."

Well, he'd slept in worse places. Recently, in fact. The workroom was dry, only a bit drafty, and under the pungent aroma of paint and machine grease was the faintly sweet aroma of sawdust. The shelves on either side of the walkway were built all the way to the ceiling, all but sagging under the weight of set pieces and props from the productions of decades gone by. There were worktables set out, each with its own complement of tools, apparently decided by what task was to be performed there.

Woodworking, he noted, and a table for small machine work. A couple of automatons were propped against the far wall, obviously designed for heavy lifting, though they had been long unwound if he was any judge. Even a steam powered sewing machine, designed to handle the yards and yards of heavy canvas that often went into set construction.

While the equipment obviously wasn't new, it had been maintained well, and used often.

"Who've you got there, Jack?" Tony glanced up in time to take a step to the side, neatly dodging the man who leapt from the rafters above, landing between the two men with a solid thump. The new arrival was a sandy blond, his head barely coming up to Tony's shoulder, but he was muscular, built square like a steam shovel.

"Stig, this is Anton Krol, new hand we just hired. Anton, this is Stig. He's been working here almost as long as I have."

Tony took the offered hand, pleased to note that this Stig didn't try to squeeze his knuckles into jelly or any other juvenile form of domination. "Tony, please. Everybody calls me Tony."

"Tony it is, then. You new in town, Tony?" Stig leaned against the shelving, fishing a hand-rolled cigarette from his back pocket.

"Yes, actually. I arrived last night."

"From where?" The cigarette hissed and sparked as Stig lit it, but the stagehand didn't seem to notice.

"Well, Poland originally. But we came over when I was very young. I grew up in Newport, but work's scarce, so I came into the city."

The two hands exchanged knowing glances, nodding. "Decent work's scarce most everywhere, lately." Jack clapped his new hire on the shoulder companionably. "Still, glad to have you. It's a bad time to be a man down, with a full production underway."

Stig muttered something under his breath, his cigarette smoke wafting in coils around his blond head. Jack gave him a sharp look, and he fell silent.

"Um… If I can ask, what exactly happened to the man I'm replacing?" Again, the two hands traded glances, but it was Jack who finally answered.

"He quit. Decided he didn't like the working

conditions." There was scorn in the stage manager's tone, but something more. Something that intimated more than Jack was saying.

"What conditions, precisely?"

Stig snorted. "He didn't like the ghost."

"Stig! Shut yer yap." Jack punched the other man in the shoulder, earning a glare from the blond.

"What? Ain't like he ain't gonna find out."

"Ghost?" Ah, so that's what this was, Tony realized. Hazing of the new man. It happened in most places, but usually not so soon.

Jack rolled his eyes even as Stig nodded enthusiastically. "This opera house is haunted, friend. Has been for longer than anyone remembers."

"It's…just old stories," Jack hastened to amend, shooting daggers at Stig with his eyes. "You know how these old buildings are. They creak, make noises as they settle. Almost have a life of their own. Some folks… Well, some folks believe they've seen…things. Stig here, he's our resident ghost hunter. Knows all there is to know."

"It's the ghost of a lady, they say," Stig interjected, grinning. "Some say she was a singer in the early years of the opera, and that she hanged herself with the curtain ropes over an unfaithful lover. Folks have seen her, swooping around back stage, always in a dark cloak. And sometimes at night, when the opera house is empty, they say you can hear her singing…"

"If the opera house is empty, how can anyone be here to hear her sing?" Stig's smile turned into a scowl, but Jack barked a laugh, clapping Tony on the shoulder again.

"Knew I liked you. You'll do just fine."

"Yeah, well if'n she's just a story, who keeps delivering those notes that got Himself in a snit?" The blond hand cast his boss a triumphant look.

"Himself?"

"Simon. Simon LeClerc, the lead tenor. Our 'ghost'

has taken a dislike to him in recent weeks. She keeps delivering notes to Mr. Chalmers, demanding that he be replaced. Says his voice has gone flat." Jack smirked slightly. "Don't know where the notes are coming from, personally, but it amuses me to see Himself with his knickers in a knot."

"Tall man, gray eyes, dark hair stained with bootblack?"

"Yup, that'd be him." Stig nodded, grinding his cigarette out under his boot. "Right prig if you ask me. But nobody does."

"'Cause you'd answer them, Stig, and then we'd both get fired." The stage manager rolled his eyes, but there was amusement in them.

Tony nodded. "I saw him, earlier, when I was asking Mr. Chalmers about auditioning. If looks could kill, I'd be a dead man right now, and that's the truth."

Stig whistled lowly. "You tried to audition? As a tenor? Zooks, man, you're lucky he didn't try to knife you in a dark alley or something. Himself doesn't take lightly to incoming talent, and that's putting it pretty."

Jack nodded his agreement. "Simon's been the lead tenor here for a long time, and he probably will be until the day he dies. I don't see him stepping aside for anyone, at least not gracefully. And what Himself wants, Himself gets. The owners are too afraid he'll leave to stand up to him."

"That explains a lot, actually." Simon had seen him as competition, that much was clear, and all without Tony ever singing a note. He'd have to watch himself. Nothing was more dangerous than a fading star's ego. "Still, singing or no, I'm not going to turn down a wage. Just…point me where you need me."

"Bah, you don't need to sing up on the stage. We need entertainment back here too! Just serenade us with that be-yoo-ti-ful voice." Stig clapped him on the other shoulder with a chuckle, almost hard enough to stagger him.

"C'mon, I'll introduce you to the rest of the boys."

The rest of the boys included a pair of brothers who went by the monikers Big and Little, a young Italian lad named Franco who wasn't even old enough to shave regularly, and a handful of others who were just as happy to see Tony as he was to have a job.

"There are more men who come in for performances, just for extra hands, but we're the only permanent crew," Jack explained. "Funds have been a bit tight these past few seasons, so they don't like paying any more than they have to. Fact is, I'm surprised they hired you on, but I'm not going to complain."

"Anything I should know about working for the opera?" He asked, after the initial introductions had been completed.

Stig smirked from his perch on one of the shelves. "The dance matron's name is Old Lady –" Jack coughed and glared, and Stig amended his statement. "Mrs. McRory. She carries a silver-headed cane, and if she thinks you've been dallying with one of the girls, she'll crack your skull right open for you. So if you're looking for a bit of fun…"

"Avoid the dancers, hm?"

"Nah. Just don't get caught." The short man waggled his eyebrows suggestively. "Unless that ain't your bent, in which case there's a few pretty boys in the chorus…" The rest of the crew chuckled and threw bits of paper and small scraps of wood at Stig. "What? Just trying to be accommodating for the new man."

"Erm, no, thank you. I'm just here for the job, nothing more."

"Got a girl at home?" Big leaned on the work table, his head tilted curiously. He was no taller than Stig, and weighed less than half what the stocky man did. Conversely, his brother Little towered over Tony and could have picked him up like a rag doll, though both men appeared to be of a jolly nature and not likely to resort to such.

"No, no girl. Nothing much left there at all, actually, now that my mother's passed." The men made general noises of condolence. "Ah, it is what it is. The last thing she made me do was promise her I'd come here and at least try to audition. So here I am."

"And yer stuck with us, you poor sad sot." This time, Tony threw a wad of grease-stained paper up at Stig, pelting him right between the eyes, much to everyone's amusement. Stig himself nearly rocked himself off the shelf, laughing uproariously.

"All right, enough of this fooling around. Big, Little, get up into the riggings and see if the rope on drop three is going to hold tonight, or if we need to replace it. Franco, go touch up the leaf on the set pieces for Act Two. Tony, come with me. I'll show you where you can drop your stuff, then we'll put you to work."

Mother would have been pleased, Tony decided, as he settled in with his new coworkers. These men had embraced him instantly and completely, and while it may not have been the employment he'd been hoping to find, it had great potential to be quite enjoyable.

What else was he going to do, anyway? The small estate where he'd grown up had no use for him, and in truth, they'd only allowed he and Mother to live there for so long because of her long-time loyalty to the family. They really should have dismissed her once Bess left, as it was foolish to have a nanny for a child who was no longer there, but Mother had stayed on as a personal assistant to the lady of the house instead, and so they'd been allowed to keep their small house on the corner of the grounds.

As always, the thought of Bess brought a smile to his lips. One of his fondest childhood memories was of her, hanging upside down from the willow tree out front, her blond curls dangling down like golden springs. It had been one of their last adventures together, before her mother had decided Bess needed to go to private school. Notably, before either she or Tony became old enough to realize they could be more than playmates.

As he often found himself doing, of late, he wondered what Bess was doing now.

Chapter 3

"Oh you did *not*!"

Bess rolled over on the bed, giving a wicked grin to her friend Susan. "I swear to you on my Auntie Regina's white cotton bloomers I did."

Susan flopped down on the bed, her eyes aglow with expectation. "And what did he say?"

If not for all of the intervening years, the pair of them could have been in college again. Susan with her raven-black hair and Bess with her mop of blond curls, as different in both appearance and personality as any two women could be, and yet they'd been best friends since… Well, since Bess had left her family's country estate for boarding school when she was eleven.

"He drew himself up very straight, cleared his throat, and announced 'Miss Elisabeth Barstow, and guest.'" Both women collapsed into girlish giggles, Susan burying her face in a fluffy pillow. "I mean, what else could he do? I had the invitation…"

Once they had regained their breaths, Susan rolled to her back, staring up at her long-time friend. "I don't know how you ever manage it. I'd have passed out from fright before I ever reached the door."

Bess sniffed, swinging her feet off the bed to stand. "If you walk around like you know where you're going, no one stops you." She paused by the mirror in the corner, looking herself over critically. Her trousers were just tight enough to scandalize proper society without being slatternly, her ruffled blouse was unbuttoned at the top, showing just a hint of cleavage. Her leather boots hugged her calves, and her vest only served to draw attention to the curves she was so very proud of. No rib-cracking corsets here, thank you very much.

The butt of the holstered gun, though, sticking out just over her left hip, that would cause a scandal and a panic all in one. She'd have to remember to take the Colt revolver off and stow it safely away while she remained in Susan's home. Thoughtfully, she piled her wealth of golden curls atop her head, wondering what it would look like with a few pins just so.

"I'm so glad you're back, Bessie. I've missed you. Andrew has too."

Bess caught Susan's eye in the mirror and smirked. "Andrew is terrified every time I come back into town, afraid I'm going to spirit you away on one of my scandalous errands."

"Oh, my gallivanting days are over, I fear. I'm a mother now, I have responsibilities." Susan pushed herself up off the bed, smoothing her dress. "Speaking of which, you must come to the nursery to meet Wallace before we put him to bed for the night."

"I still can't believe you named the poor child Wallace. It's like you don't love him at all!" She shot a wink at Susan in the mirror.

"Wallace was Andrew's father's name. I didn't precisely have a choice." The brunette lobbed a decorative pillow, hitting her friend in the back. "I tell him your stories, you know, so when he's old enough to understand, he'll know all about his Auntie Bess, the great explorer."

"Not sure I've earned the title 'great' just yet. Maybe next year." Bess turned and gave her dear friend a tight hug. "Thank you for letting me stay here, Sue. I just couldn't bear the thought of going back home to rattle around in that big empty house."

"Any time. You know that. Dinner's at seven. You

better make sure you put on a dress or Andrew's head is likely to explode. And as amusing as that might be, he is my husband." With a wink, Susan departed, drawing the bedroom door shut behind her. Not a second later, she poked her head back in. "I'll have the automatons bring your trunks up from the carriage and leave them here in the hallway, all right?"

"That's fine, thank you."

Alone at last, Bess sat down on the bed, pulling off her boots with a sigh and tossing them into the corner just to hear the satisfying thunk. With a weary groan, she fell backwards, sinking into the down comforter. It had been a long damn trip by airship, first across the Atlantic and then the several legs it took to get from New York to Detroit. Solid ground still felt a bit wobbly beneath her feet. Not to mention that her head still felt a bit light from the high altitude, and the fact that her cheeks and nose were windburned.

Of course, had she just ridden inside with the other passengers like the captain had tried to insist, that could have all been avoided. It had been worth it though, to see the look of horror on his face every time he looked out the wide window to see her perched at the portside railing. From that vantage, she could look down into the depths of Lake Erie as they flew over, watch the wakes of the steamers as they passed beneath, like water bugs on a pond. Worth every single uncomfortable moment.

Thankfully, she had somewhere to stay that wasn't some impersonal hotel room. Or even worse, some thin-walled Bedouin tent or drafty clay hovel. "Good old Sue. I'd be lost without her." However, the longer she found herself lying on the luxurious cloud of satin and feathers, the less she felt inclined to get up. Fishing the watch out of her vest pocket, she flipped it open to check the time. "It's only three, I've got time for a short nap." That was all it took for her to be fast asleep.

~*!*~

"So, Elisabeth. How long are you planning on being in town?"

"Why, Andrew, are you tired of me already?" Bess looked up from her soup to catch her best friend's husband flushing dark red.

"Well, no, that's not what I meant... I was just... Making small talk."

Andrew was a nervous man. A good man, a banker, and he doted on Susan and their new son, but he was timid. He never quite knew how to act or what to say when Bess behaved like...Bess.

Bess chuckled, and pretended that she didn't see Susan hiding a similar smile in her napkin. "To answer your question, I haven't decided yet."

"Planning on returning to Egypt, then?"

"Erm...no. The Egyptian government has politely asked that I never ever come back." Andrew choked on his chowder, and the devilish imp in Bess' mind prompted her to add, "Perhaps because I shot the ambassador in the ass."

"Language, Bess, please!"

"You did *what*?" Andrew's last word came out as a horrified squeak.

"Well, in all fairness, I wasn't *aiming* for him." She glanced up at the odd sounds her friend's husband was making. "Oh for Heaven's sake, Andrew, breathe in!"

After some vigorous back patting on Susan's part, Andrew's certain death by asphyxiation averted, they settled down to their meal again.

"Honestly, Bess, I never know what to believe when you start telling such stories." Susan shook her dark head, her locks confined in a matronly bun at the back of her head. "The newspapers blow so many things out of proportion. Is it true that you stole a golden statue out of a tomb and fought off a horde of Bedouin raiders to get away?"

"Not…entirely true." A faint smile curved her lips at the memory. The "horde" of Bedouin raiders had been one fairly scrawny street thug, and her golden statue had been a necklace of amber and twine, so old that the twine had powdered upon being handled, and she'd been left with a handful of artfully carved stones. The tomb had been a tomb, that part was true, but it had been desecrated long before she ever came upon it. No doubt the necklace had been stashed there sometime after the original treasures had been removed. It was also true that she *had* been forced to shoot the man, and he *had* meant to cause her bodily harm, but it could hardly be called an accomplishment.

"I shudder to think what else they've said about my travels. Am I still relegated to the society section, or have I progressed to the front page?"

"Not the front page yet, but they've started noting your stories in the travel section. I think Detroit society's given up on you."

"Well it's about damn time!" Bess grinned at Susan's chiding look. "Language. I know." They all paused as the servants brought the next course, a rather plump quail stuffed with herbs and grains. "Honestly, I'm still not sure why I'm making the news at all. It's not like I'm doing anything that others haven't done before."

"Because you're a woman, Bess. An unmarried woman at that, cavorting in foreign countries and having gunfights and adventures. You're scandalous, and scandal sells papers."

Bess rolled her eyes to herself, muttering "Scandalous."

"Well, if you're weary of it, you could always just remain here. Find a nice fellow, settle down…" Andrew, his eyes on his plate, missed the look of venom Bess shot his way. "In fact, there will be some parties and the like coming up, things for the bank. You are welcome to come with us, if you want. I could introduce you to a few nice chaps." He seemed rather pleased with his brilliance, and looked around the table for confirmation from either woman.

"She'd only just arrived, Andrew. Let her get settled before we marry her off." Susan's smile was gentle, and she deftly directed the conversation elsewhere. "Now, you were telling me earlier about Mr. Webber's upcoming retirement?"

Dinner ended with no further commentary on either Bess's unconventional lifestyle, or plans to wed her to the next lawyer-banker-doctor who wandered along, for which she was grateful. The advancing night found her on the balcony outside her friend's modest library, watching the city trundle on, just past the garden walls.

It was different than her usual nightly view. There were no scents of heavy spices to waft upward on the night's breeze, no oppressive heat lingering after a long day of relentless sun beating down on hard-packed earth. The railing under her hands was metal, not sandstone, and it already held a biting chill that was a promise of the winter to come. This was not Marrakesh, or Cairo, or any of the small villages she had spent time in over the last few years. This was Detroit, the steel heart of America as the country forged bravely ahead into the new century. The people here dressed in tailored coats, tall hats, lace gloves and prim gowns. No flowing robes or loose trousers to be found. Steam automobiles and horse-drawn carriages replaced caravans and camels, and those she would *not* miss in the least.

A heavy shawl draped around her bare shoulders, and she turned to give Susan a small smile. "I've been in warm climes so long, I forgot how cold autumn can be here."

Her friend slipped an arm around her waist, and the two women stood in companionable silence for long moments.

"Your gown looked lovely tonight, Bess," Susan finally offered.

Bess looked down at the brushed silk gown of pale green, fingering the lace on the heart-shaped neckline like she'd never seen it before. It felt odd, to be wearing petticoats and other proper undergarments. "Thank you. I'm sure it's woefully out of fashion by now, but it's one of the few nice ones I have that isn't wrinkled beyond all saving." It was a bit extravagant, perhaps, for dinner in with friends, but her wardrobe was sorely lacking in society-appropriate attire.

In contrast, Susan looked every bit the respectable society matron. Her gown was a deep blue velveteen, her high collar fastened up to her chin with perfectly matched pearl buttons. Even her ear bobs were quietly understated pearls, adding an air of quiet elegance that suited her friend so well. "Well, Andrew noticed your efforts, and said complimentary things."

Bess chuckled quietly. "What do you think he'd say if he knew I had a pistol in my garter?" Susan gave her a sharp look, and Bess shrugged a little. "I felt underdressed without it." The small single-shot Derringer resting against her thigh had been the only comfortable part of the evening, in fact. It had saved her life more than once, though what she thought she'd have to defend against in Susan's dining room she couldn't possibly fathom.

"Oh, Bessie…" The lovely brunette shook her head, her gaze going back out to the drowsy city. "Have you ever thought about it? What Andrew was saying?"

"What, giving it all up and finding a husband?" Bess sighed, releasing her friend so she could rest her elbows on the railing. "Only all the time."

"Really?" Susan tilted her head in surprise.

"Mhm. I think about it often. It was the one thing my mother always wanted for me. It was the one thing we ever fought over."

"Your mother loved you very much."

"She did. She also didn't understand me at all. I think

she looked at me like a cuckoo left in a nest. I climbed trees instead of playing at tea with dolls. I wanted to learn to ride and shoot instead of embroider. I got in fistfights and stuffed frogs in my pockets, instead of sitting quietly with my curls and petticoats. How could this strange wild girl be the daughter of Josephine Barstow? She hadn't the foggiest idea what to do with me."

Somewhere to the east, a lone church bell chimed the hour, starting at least ten seconds too early. Soon, all the churches in the city joined in, the bells rolling out in to the darkness before fading into silence again. On both sides of the river to the south, the coalworks belched black smoke into the night for miles, the underside of the clouds stained orange with the glow of the fires.

Past the growling, fuming coalworks, she could see the lights of the city reflected in the calm, still waters of Lake St. Clair. The opposite shore was far enough away to be invisible, and she had often thought that it seemed the world just dropped off into the depths somewhere, lost amidst the stars that had come down from the sky to dance in the water. Somewhere on the Canadian side of that unseen shore, her family had a lake house where she spent many a summer holiday. When she was a child, she'd dreamed that the lake was the sky, and somehow, if she could just swim out far enough into it, she would learn to fly. Fly away…

"Is there something wrong with me, Sue?" Bess turned suddenly, fixing her best friend with a serious look.

"What on earth are you talking about?"

"Is there something wrong with me, that I don't want all these beautiful things that you have? Andrew is so wonderful to you, and Wallace is enchanting, his name notwithstanding. Your house is perfect, you have a lovely circle of friends, Andrew has a well-paying job…" She frowned. "And I look at all this, and I just… All I see are bars on windows and walls around gardens, and things to keep me in. I've never wanted the things a good and decent woman is supposed to want, not even as a child. Is there something wrong with me?'

"No, no of course not." Susan reached out to take her hands. "You're just you, Bess. You always have been. From the time you were a small girl, from the stories you told me. Something about a willow tree, if I recall?"

That erased the frown in favor of a tiny smile. The willow tree incident. Bess had often wondered, if she hadn't fallen that day, if Tony hadn't had to carry her to the house with a broken ankle… Would Mother have sent her away?

"I mean…you do *like* men, don't you Bess?"

She swatted her friend on the shoulder. "Of course I like men. Quite a bit, actually."

"Then perhaps you just haven't found the right one. Maybe the one you're looking for isn't a banker, or a doctor, or a barrister. Perhaps he's an adventurer too, and he's out there, riding in a boat down a deep jungle river, totally unaware that you exist yet." Susan swept her hand out over the dark city, painting her image with words. "He's wearing a sweaty shirt, the sleeves torn off to bandage the wounds of his trusty serving man, and his keen eyes are scanning the shoreline, his rifle cradled in his arms as he looks for the enemies who ambushed them once already. Distant drums beat, but are they friend…or foe?"

Bess burst out laughing. "Oh listen at you! You should be a writer, Sue, penning adventure serials for one of the papers."

"Andrew would have apoplexy." Susan chuckled, slipping her arms around her friend again, giving her a gentle hug. "There's nothing wrong with you, Bess. I think you've had a fright that you don't want to talk about, and what you need more than anything right now is some rest in a safe place. When you feel better, you can move on again. You don't have to go to any parties if you don't want to."

"Oh, I don't know. Perhaps I'll go to one or two. What can it hurt, right?"

"Right." Susan patted her shoulder, tugging the knitted shawl around her shoulders a little tighter. "Don't stay out here too long, you'll catch a chill."

"Yes, mother." Susan stuck her tongue out, and Bess chuckled, looking back toward the coalworks.

Detroit never changed. No matter how long she travelled, it was always there, waiting to welcome her home. Perhaps she *would* stay for a while. Perhaps, if she truly tried to live this life her mother had wanted for her, it wouldn't seem so bad after all. And if it was, well, at least she'd know for sure then.

Funny, she hadn't thought of Tony and the willow tree in years. She hadn't seen her childhood playmate since the day she'd been shipped off to boarding school at age eleven. Winter holidays had been spent travelling to distant relatives' homes, never at the family estate, and the summer breaks were spent at other endeavors, like intensive private music lessons or exclusive riding academies. Then she'd been off to college, and then to her adventures. Tony would be a grown man by now, no doubt with a family of his own, and a passel of raven-haired children. Even as a youngster, he'd been handsome.

A small smile crossed her face as she turned to go inside. What would he think of her now?

Chapter 4

The show had been disastrous. Oh, not to anyone's ears but her own, of course, but still… Simon's decline was hastening, and his attention was clearly not on his work any longer. Where once he could lift an entire audience into the heavens with his voice alone, now it seemed he barely knew they existed, merely going through the motions of performing his role.

Even worse, it wasn't only him. Caroline had been pitchy in her aria, the orchestra had missed two cues by at least half a beat, and the chorus had somehow, in impossibly unanimous fashion, managed to skip an entire verse in the second act.

The audience had long since departed, the performers right behind them, and still she sat alone in her darkened box, mulling over her next course of action. The notes were not accomplishing anything, to her great frustration. Normally, they elicited an immediate response, and she always got the sense that the manager was grateful for the thoughtful input she'd given him. But not now. Now, there was tension in the staff, tension in the singers. Everyone was wound tightly as an eight-day time-piece, and it was leeching into their performances.

Part of it stemmed from the rumors, of course. She'd heard them whispered, amongst the crew, the dancers, the chorus. The remodeling of the opera house had only been a ploy, they said, a means to prepare the venue for sale. The owners were growing old, and wished to retire. The opera would be sold, and then who knew what would happen.

Everyone's jobs were in danger, if the rumors were to be believed.

She made her way out of the box, turning to take the main stairs instead of the servants' passage. It brought her out at the back of the auditorium, the stage spread out before her, waiting. Walking down the aisle, she let her hands run over the backs of the newly reupholstered seats. The carpets beneath her boots were new as well, as were the heavy velvet curtains and the shimmering golden ropes that would draw them back.

The orchestra pit had been refurbished, the mechanisms beneath it that would allow it to be raised and lowered freshly oiled and adapted for steam piston use. It could be raised as an extension to the stage, as they would do during the Christmas chorale, or lowered completely to reveal the passageway to the under-stage storage and trap room. Even the musicians' chairs had been replaced, cushioned and polished.

In her opinion, the opera house had never looked so fine. Regardless of the reasons for it, the remodeling had been a welcome event in her mind. And if there was a sale in the workings, Gilbert had yet to speak of it to her. Surely he'd have mentioned it. He knew how she liked to know this sort of thing ahead of time.

These rumors needed to be put to rest, she decided. It was wreaking havoc with the performances, and she'd noticed several missing faces from both the chorus and crew. If they believed their jobs were in imminent danger, they'd flee, and she just couldn't have that. She couldn't very well stage an opera with no one on the stage!

The whole situation was unacceptable. She would simply have to send another note. Perhaps word this one more strongly. Yes, that would do. Perhaps Gilbert didn't understand how detrimental this entire situation was becoming. He had good intentions, but his skill as a manager was…lacking.

Her course set in her mind, she made her way up the stairs onto the stage, pausing to look out over the seats. The opera house was so different when it was empty. Full of people, the walls themselves seemed to vibrate with their own voice, answering all of the conversations they had absorbed over the decades. But when the lights had been doused and the doors locked, the silence echoed. It was almost a roar in and of itself, a great gaping emptiness screaming to be filled.

Sometimes she would acquiesce, filling the darkened building with her own voice. The high, pure notes would soar up into the rafters before dying away into soft, downy whispers. She liked those nights. For just a moment, she could picture them, watching her. The seats filled, their conversations stilled, their breaths held as they waited for her to begin.

In a bit of foolishness, she flourished her cloak over one arm, dropping into a deep curtsy to the empty auditorium. In her mind, she could hear the applause, rising like a roaring tide up into the rafters. It went on and on, and hundreds of feet shuffled, shifted, the seats creaking as the audience stood, roaring their approval.

When she stood again, of course the place was still empty, and the silence wrapped itself around her like a smothering cloth. It was easy to imagine singing before the full house, the awed gasps and whispers turning to thundering applause… But no, not for her. It would not be allowed. In fact, if any of them ever saw her, it could be disastrous. To imagine otherwise was foolishness. Simple foolishness. Drawing her cloak around her, she made to depart.

The backstage area was neat and tidied, ready for the next night's performance. She walked idly through, examining the prop pieces and backdrops. Some of them were becoming a bit worn. They would have to repaint before they could perform this particular opera again, she decided, and added that to the list of things to go into her next note. Fortunate that there was such a plethora of shows to choose from, and they needn't recycle them more than once every few years or so. They had time to make the necessary repairs, once the fall season was over. The Christmas chorale would require considerably less work.

A costume piece had been left draped over a table, and she picked up the scrap of silk, turning it in her hands. It belonged to Caroline, she thought, something from the third act. A kerchief to go in her hair, small crystal beads dangling over her forehead to catch the lights and sparkle as she sang. It should be returned to the flighty girl's dressing room, before someone truly misplaced it.

As she was about to make her way toward the dressing rooms, a small sound broke the breathy silence of the opera house. She froze, stillness often being her fastest and best defense, but it was soon plain that the noise was not nearby. Curious, she followed it into the depths of the opera house, tucking the silk kerchief into her pocket without a second thought.

She only rarely visited the workshop during the opera season. More often, she'd spend time here during rehearsals, making certain that the sets and props were being constructed to her satisfaction, but once the performances began, she had more pressing things to attend, as did the stage crew. Thus, she was not expecting anyone to be there so late at night.

The sound that drew her, humming pleasantly just behind her eyes, was a voice, that much was soon clear. A tenor voice, pure and smooth as any she'd ever heard. This was perplexing, because of all the men in the chorus, she knew of none who could attain that level of exquisite perfection. Who, then? The men on the stage crew were chosen for their brawn, not their vocal talents, and if any of them had been able to belt out more than a drunken bawdy song, she'd bust a spring in surprise.

The door to the workshop stood wide open, spilling light into the hallway.   Shying away from that revealing brilliance, she made her way to one of the ladders built into the wall, climbing quickly into the rafters of the theater. From there, she could look down into the shop, and the shadows would conceal her from whoever was within.

The catwalks swayed at her passage, and she kept her skirt gathered in one hand lest the rustling sound of cloth betray her presence.   At first, she had trouble locating anyone below.   Only the two automatons, seldom used, were in view, and they were obviously not the source of the beautiful melody.   Most of those mechanical constructs barely had what would qualify as a voice at all, sufficient to perform their designated tasks.   Their purpose required nothing more.

A shadow crossed the floor directly beneath her, and she froze so abruptly that dust sifted down around her. Beneath, a young man emerged from the shelves, a papier-mâché horse's head laid over one shoulder.   He dropped his burden down on the paint table, brushing the dust off his shirt.   Not once did his song falter, nor did his eyes rise to the rafters to search for his unseen observer.

The song itself was simple, a country folk song that she'd heard often before.   But the voice… Oh, the voice could make one weep, if one were capable of such.   The young man, cobwebs layered in his raven black hair, smiled softly as he worked, obviously singing for no one's pleasure but his own.

He was untrained, that much was certain.   Her finely tuned ear picked out the places where he could manage his breath better, control the vibrato.   But the notes, oh the notes.   Her senses hummed with it, a haze of gold coloring the edges of her vision.

She realized at some point that she had crouched in her place on the catwalk, her cloak gaping open to reveal the pale blue gown she'd donned for the evening.   That light color would be visible against the darkness of the ceiling, if the mysterious stagehand so much as glanced in her direction. Quickly, she stood and wrapped the dark cloak around herself, sending the catwalk rattling against its moorings.

The song below faltered, and the stage hand glanced around in puzzlement. She froze again, drawing her inhuman stillness around her as tightly as the dark garment that hid her. Not once did he think to look up and after a few moments, he moved on, dousing lanterns as he retired toward the rear of the shop.

Sleeping on the cots, she realized. Something she should have been informed of. What would have happened if she'd simply walked into him, not knowing he was in residence? Disastrous.

Once the lights had been extinguished, she quietly made her escape, hurrying back through her storeroom and sewer tunnels, her legs moving her faster through the sleeping city faster than most modern conveyances could manage. It was safe, at this time of night. There was no one to see, and even the coalworks had banked down for the night, only a skeleton crew of workers hunkered down to keep the night fires burning.

Safe within her own home again, she once again pondered the enigma of the singing stage hand. Who was he? When had he come to the opera house? How long would he be staying?

It had not escaped her notice that *here* was a voice who could replace Simon, but why was he not at least in the chorus? Had Gilbert gone deaf? And why had she not been informed of his audition? She had attended all that had come before.

The solution became clear to her, and she felt a bit obtuse. Of course, Gilbert had discerned the lack of training, and had therefore found a place for him until such time could be made to instruct him properly. This was the most logical course of action. She wondered who he would choose to teach the new stage hand. Simon, of course, would be the most logical choice, but something told her the aging tenor would not be welcoming to his own replacement. There was a sense of bitterness lingering around her one-time star.

Johann, then? No, Johann had departed to sing with another company, nearly a year ago. She'd forgotten. Sometimes her memory played tricks on her, became muddled. But never mind that. Hendricks? Hm. While his voice was good, he would never be more than part of the chorus, or perhaps a secondary role if the right opera were presented.

No, there was no one left in the company who had the ability or the willingness to teach a new voice.

"I could teach him myself, of course, were circumstances different." Her voice bounced off the walls of her empty house. She often spoke aloud to herself, just to have something pressing on her senses other than silence. Sometimes, it just helped to have something else to hear.

The very idea amused her, really. Teach him herself. Wouldn't that shock them all? She had to wonder at the look on Gilbert's face if she simply introduced herself to the company and offered lessons. She had to wonder at the look on their faces.

Her gaze went to one of the many mirrors in the old manse, and she examined her own visage dispassionately. No, teaching him herself was simply not an option. Not like this. Would that things were different, that her appearance were not…as it was.

When was the last time someone had looked upon her face? Not counting the unfortunate inebriate in the coalworks, of course. When…? The Master had been dead for nearly thirty years, now. He'd been the last to truly look at her. Look at her, and smile. Gilbert… He refused to look upon her. Even when she had dealings with him now, it was either by note, or the occasional conversation, whispered from the shadows. Even he could not bear to look at what she was.

When had she last spoken to anyone besides Gilbert, come to think of it? She hadn't had an actual conversation in…when? How long ago? She shook her head a bit, as if that would dislodge the recalcitrant memories. So many things jumbled together, and time often passed without notice. It would suffice to say that it had been quite some time and she would let it go at that.

"Well…what if it wasn't necessary for him to look at me?" She paused to ponder her own question, rolling that thought over in the gears of her mind. It was not a preposterous concept. Oh, certainly, there would be no correcting her appearance to something more palatable, but covering it up? Did she not go about in public disguised as it was?

A disguise… Her hand found the silk kerchief in her pocket, the beads clattering softly as she unfolded it. Holding it before her eyes, she was pleased to note that she could see fairly clearly though the thin fabric. Perhaps a coronet, made of twisted wire. Or combs, tucked into the curls of the dark wig that sat atop her head. Something to hang the improvised veil from. Sheer enough not to impede vision, but opaque enough to hide her face.

Yes… This might work…

Chapter 5

Tony found that he quite liked the nights at the opera house when everyone else had gone home. After asking Jack for some work that he could do in the evenings, he found that he could keep his hands busy if he wished, or lay and read one of the few books lying around, or even just sing to entertain himself.

Certainly, performance nights were exciting. There was always a buzzing energy about the place as everyone rushed to take their places, the orchestra warmed up, the stage crew found their ropes and levers. Tony had been assigned to the backdrop crew, raising and lowering the heavy painted constructions for different scenes. Counterbalanced as the drops were, one man could technically have done it, but for safety's sake, there were always at least two on the ropes. Better that, than someone's grip slipping and sending the ponderous framework crashing to the stage below.

He found that he liked the others on the stage crew, a group of rough and rowdy hands to a man, but all of them good natured to a fault. They'd been quick to embrace him as one of their own, and if Stig ribbed him about his singing, well they were quick enough to answer back about Stig's ghost hunting, or Davy's bad luck with women, or… Tony finally decided this must be what it was like to have brothers.

And of course, the best part by far was being able to hear every opera performance. He'd have had to save his wages for a year just to attend once, and here they were paying *him*. Sometimes, when the orchestra and chorus were at full throat, he would sing along, quietly, to himself. Never loud enough to disturb the performers of course, but he could imagine what it would be like out there under the lights.

After they'd safely extinguished the lamps, reset the stage for the next night, swept the backstage clear of debris, the hands would retire to their respective homes, and Tony was left alone. Well, alone with an unseen spectral companion, presumably.

Thus far, he'd had no encounters with the "ghost", though more than one person had cornered him to ask if he'd seen or heard anything late at night. Apparently, the ghost's notes were becoming more demanding, and her opinion of Simon was sliding ever downward.

Though the notes were delivered by mysterious means to Mr. Chalmers, it usually took only a few hours for word of the contents to race through the entire company like wildfire. Inevitably, it would put Simon in a foul mood, which would then trickle down through all levels, performers and stage crew alike. Just yesterday, Stig had been dressed down by one of the baritones for leaving a counterweight perched precariously atop a table. It had fallen and narrowly missed crushing the singer's foot.

"*I* didn't leave it there," Stig had snarled. "I ain't stupid." It had nearly come to blows before Jack intervened, ushering Stig back to the workshop and sending the baritone back to the dressing rooms with a good chastising of his own.

"Just be more careful next time, Stig, okay?" Jack ran his fingers through his hair in frustration. "We don't need any more trouble from the cast."

"I *said*, I didn't leave it there!" Stig's temper, once sparked, was slow to fade. That much Tony had learned in his few weeks with the opera. "Tell those puffed up pansies to stop touchin' things what don't belong to them!"

So yes, the quiet time alone in the evening was a treat. Jack had promised that Tony could stay as long as he liked, at least until winter was over, so long as he didn't leave once the doors were locked. "The papers are still full of that coalworks fellow that got strangled by that rogue automaton, and they haven't found the contraption yet. Safer in here than out wandering the streets at night. And don't go prowling around the opera house at night, either. It's dangerous. Ropes and pulleys and weights and the like. You could injure yourself in the dark and no one would know until morning. Oh, and leave that one automaton alone. The aether core on that one is about plumb full, and you can't be sure what it's gonna do from one second to the next. Haven't got Mr. Chalmers to cough up the money to replace it yet."

The aether core, a glass tube of bluish gases, was located inside the metal skulls of the automatons, and it was what allowed them to retain a semblance of rudimentary memory. The problem being that, unlike humans, they could not forget. Therefore, after a certain amount of time, the core became cluttered, and the memories that were recalled were often random and disjointed. At that point, an automaton's behavior became unpredictable, and the only thing to do was replace the core with a fresh one. It was a safety issue, given that an automaton was at least twenty times stronger than the average human.

No doubt, the mysterious mechanical murderer in the newspapers was such a construction, one that had been poorly maintained and was now functioning without direction. Luckily, the thing would eventually wind down and become immobile. So long as some poor unlucky sot didn't wind it again, of course.

"Yes sir, of course sir. I'll be *fine*, Jack." The stage manager's concern was touching, and his fussing amused Tony.

Besides, leaving the machines alone was just fine with

him. He preferred to do any labor himself, as long as he could. There was a certain pride in using his own strength. The workshop wasn't precisely small, and there were things on the upper shelves that hadn't seen daylight in years. With Jack's permission, he started taking down some of the older, shabbier prop pieces and repainting them in his free time. It made him smile to see something come back to life that way, the colors renewed and vibrant.

The one he was working on now was a section of archway, adorned with artfully drawn vines and dangling grape clusters. Impossible to tell what opera it had been used for, but perhaps the touched-up paint would inspire someone to use it again. Setting it upright, he walked across the workshop to view it from a distance, finding that the touches of highlights he'd added to the grapes made them gleam from a distance, just the effect he'd been going for.

"Not bad, Krol. Not bad at all." He grinned to himself as he wiped his hands on a rag and went about tidying up for the night.

As he stowed the paints away in their cabinet, a soft sound reached his ears, one that should not have been, not in the empty opera house. He closed the cabinet gently, straining his ears to be certain he wasn't imagining things, but no, echoing in the silence were the faint plaintive strains from a piano, no doubt the one out in the orchestra pit.

"Dammit, Stig." The stocky stagehand hadn't given up trying to convince Tony of his opera ghost, and here he was, resorting to petty pranks. Snatching up a lantern, Tony went in search of the prankster, fully intending to give him a dose of his own medicine.

Rather than approach from the backstage area, he circled around through the empty halls, making his way through the deserted lobby with scarcely a boot step to be heard. The closer he got to the auditorium, the louder the music became, a piece that he recognized as one of the tenor arias from the night's show. Whoever was playing was actually very skilled. That piece had never been orchestrated for a single piano.

Stopping just outside the doors, he doused his lantern, and crouched low as he slipped through the door, catching it so it would glide silently shut behind him. Staying as low as he could, he crept down the side aisle, approaching the orchestra pit to arrive behind the mysterious piano player. Stig would think twice about playing jokes on him again.

Just as he was about to pop over the edge of the orchestra pit with a yell, the music abruptly stopped mid-stanza, and he froze in place.

"I know you are there." It wasn't Stig, that much was obvious. A woman's voice, clear and high. There was a faint squeak as the piano stool swiveled, the woman no doubt now facing Tony's hiding space. "Come out, please."

Sheepishly, he stood, now feeling like a right jackass. "Sorry, ma'am. I was expecting someone else."

She made no indication that his apology was noticed, only tilting her head to one side as she watched him. The only light came from the small lamp sitting on the piano, the glow behind her casting her mostly in shadow. He could tell that her gown was a dark burgundy velvet, the hem faintly dusty with coalworks soot and most of it concealed beneath a heavy black cloak. The hood was drawn up to shadow her face even further, but he could see raven black curls peering out around the edges. Her face remained a mystery, and apparently would even if he'd carried his own lantern in, because it was covered with a silken veil, decorated with clear crystal beads.

Wait, why should he feel like a jackass? She'd no right to be here, not at this time of night. "What–?"

"Am I doing here? I had hoped you would ask." The

strange woman stood, her gloved hands clasped primly in front of her. "I am here to speak with you."

"Well, you've succeeded." Tony frowned a little. "Did Stig send you?" It hadn't escaped him that here was a cloaked woman, like the legend of the opera ghost. It would be just like Stig to hire someone for his little prank.

"Stig. The small Swedish man on the stage crew? No, he did not send me. I came of my own accord." There was something odd about the way she held herself, her back and shoulders formally straight, and a strange clipped fashion to her words. Almost as though they were pronounced too perfectly. English was her second language, Tony decided, and something she had arduously practiced.

"Very well. What did you wish to speak to me about? You know you're not supposed to be in here, right?"

She ignored his second question, only tilting her head to the opposite side, the beads across her veiled forehead clicking quietly. "I was here a few nights ago. I heard you singing."

Tony felt heat rise in his cheeks. "I didn't know anyone was listening."

"You are very good. Your voice is superb."

"Um…thank you."

"You came here to audition, did you not? As a tenor?"

"Yes, but Mr. Chalmers said there aren't any openings, currently." It was more that Simon wouldn't *allow* anyone to audition, really, but Tony felt oddly disloyal, airing company business to this stranger. A stranger who had yet to reveal her purpose, he reminded himself.

"As long as Simon LeClerc remains lead tenor, there will be no openings. I am certain you have realized that." Well, so much for company secrets. "And truthfully, you are not good enough to challenge him. Not yet."

"So you broke into the opera house after hours to insult me?"

The tilt to her head somehow became irritated with just

the slightest change of angle. "Of course not. I have come to offer to teach you."

Tony stood in silence for a few moments, trying to wrap his mind around that unexpected offer. "If you'll excuse me… But I have no idea who you are or how you got in, and since you're covering your face, I'm assuming that you wish your identity unknown. How do I know that you've any credentials for teaching me anything?"

"Oh. Oh yes, you are right of course. I should have thought of that. Yes of course. Perhaps I should sing for you. Would that suffice?"

"I…I suppose it might?"

The woman turned on her heel, her skirts swirling around her in hushed whispers as she crossed the orchestra pit and climbed the stairs onto the stage. "Have a seat in the first row, please." Bemused, Tony moved to obey.

From the first row, looking up at her lighted by only the tiny piano lamp, Tony could easily see how a woman such as this could be mistaken for a ghost. Her cloak blended into the darkened stage, making parts of her form disappear and reappear at random intervals. Only the white veil over her face and her white gloves seemed constant, and oddly disembodied.

"Do you have a piece you would prefer me to sing?"

For a moment, he wracked his memory for something obscure and unlikely to be known, then decided that was petty and beneath him. "Surprise me."

"As you wish."

There was a brief moment where she drew herself up even straighter, if possible, then a sweet trilling voice echoed out into the auditorium. Tony recognized it immediately as Caroline's aria from that very night and knew too that this stranger was singing it with more technical perfection than the perky little soprano could ever hope to manage. Each note was almost painful in its clarity, and swung from the highest of highs to the lowest of lows in a run that would have taxed even the most skilled singer.

He realized he was holding his breath about halfway through the piece, and forced himself to breathe. She was stunningly perfect. Why in the world was she not singing with the company? No matter who she was, he'd have remembered if he'd have heard that voice before. As the last notes died away, they sat in silence for long moments, Tony unwilling to break the spell.

Finally, though, he realized that she was waiting for are response. "Who *are* you? Why are you not singing with the company?"

"I prefer to remain anonymous, and I have my reasons for not singing publically. Do my skills satisfy you?"

"You are…very talented. I can't argue with that." He stood, approaching the edge of the stage. "I guess I don't understand. Why are you doing this?"

"Because I refuse to see talent squandered because of Simon LeClerc's ego. Your voice will be heard, Anton Krol." It sounded like a proclamation from on high, the way she said it. A pronouncement from God himself, perhaps. "I can return in the evenings, after the opera house is closed. We can begin tomorrow, if you like."

"Why do you want to remain anonymous?"

"Let us just say that it would cause…problems, if my identity were known. You musn't speak of me to anyone, or let on that you are receiving lessons."

"How can I audition, if no one knows I've been training?"

"You will not audition in the traditional fashion. There will come a time, once you are trained, when you will be able to display your talents in such a manner that no one will be able to deny you. You must trust that these things will happen as I say."

Tony frowned a little, trying to find the catch, the flaw. "I can't pay you."

"I ask for no compensation."

"Why?"

"I have my reasons. Is this arrangement satisfactory to you?"

He sighed, running his fingers through his hair. "You realize this is the strangest thing I've ever heard of, yes?" He got the sense that she was amused by that, though he couldn't see her face through the veil. "All right. Tomorrow night. Do I need to let you in?"

"No, I have my own way. We will meet here at the stage as the clock chimes two."

Inwardly, Tony winced. Lessons at two in the morning would make sleep a rare commodity, but... If she could truly teach him as she claimed, this could be the only chance he had. "All right. Tomorrow then."

"Return to the workshop. I will depart once you've gone. Please do not attempt to follow me."

"Oh sure. Of course." Still a bit befuddled and bemused, he turned and made his way up the aisle. Halfway to the door, he turned to see her still standing on the stage, watching him leave. "You know my name. What am I to call you?"

She was silent so long, he started to fear that he'd angered her, but she finally said, "Perhaps you should choose a name that pleases you."

He thought for a moment, then nodded. "All right. You will be Melody."

Ever so slightly, she inclined her head. "And so I shall be."

INTERLUDE –
Christmas

Chapter 6

The opera house was decked out for the Christmas chorale with garlands and wreaths draped across the balconies and wound around the proscenium arch. Tinsel had been strewn about like silver icicles on every conceivable surface, and the muse statue in the lobby had been replaced with a life-size mechanical music box of ice skating children that twirled in magnet-guided circles to the tinkling sounds of Christmas carols.

Even in the midst of stringent rehearsals, the cast and crew went about in a state of bubbling excitement, everyone making plans to return to distant homes for the holidays or simply spend a few weeks away from the opera house.

"And what about you," he asked Melody, during one of their late night lessons. "Will you be going home to your family for the holiday?"

Her gloved hands stilled on the piano keys for a long moment. "I haven't any family."

Tony frowned. "You'll be alone for Christmas?" Christmas had long been one of his favorite times of the year, a time when he and Mother had decorated their small home and the smell of baking treats wafted through ever crevice. The thought of someone being alone at that time was unspeakably sad to him.

"I do not usually observe the holiday. There has been no need for many years."

"Well… I've been invited to go stay with Jack and his family, but if you want me to stay here… We could do something. Have dinner?"

She tilted her head, still hooded and veiled, at him, and though he could not see her expression, he got the idea that she was pleased by the offer. "That is very kind of you. But no, you should go spend time with your companions. A small respite will be good for your voice. You've been working so very hard."

He sighed, leaning on the piano, pretending that he didn't notice how she drew back away from him slightly. "I don't know. I'm still not completely comfortable with the upper part of the register."

"You will be."

"Did you hear Simon at today's rehearsal?" He still had no idea who Melody truly was, nor how she slipped in and out of the theater with such ease.

Her clothing was always very nice, though from what little he knew of fashion, it was out of date. She was always covered in the heavy cloak, which she refused to remove, and her face was ever hidden behind the silken, beaded veil. White gloves covered her hands, and she refused to take them off even to play the piano. The only thing he truly knew about her was that her hair was midnight black, and curled softly around her forehead.

Every so often, he would ask a leading question, trying to guess at who she might be. Tonight, he was trying to see if she might actually be a member of the company already, and present at every rehearsal, right under his nose. He'd already eliminated all of the brunettes in the chorus, but perhaps she wasn't a singer at all? A dancer, or even one of the maids? How odd that would be, to find that he'd been trained by a housekeeper. "His voice cracked."

The veiled woman nodded. "I heard. He is straining too much. After the chorale, he will tell Gilbert that the rest over the holidays is all his voice needs, but he will be incorrect."

It was not the first time she'd referred to the manager by

his first name. Tony filed that away in his mind as another clue to his teacher's identity. "What do you think Mr. Chalmers will do?"

"I am not certain. I doubt he will do anything, until we can present him with an alternative. Simon is too valuable. Or was."

"Well, if I can't manage that arpeggio, I'm not going to be worth presenting." He stood up straight again, resting one hand on the piano. "Let's go again."

"As you wish."

Their lessons had gone on for a couple of months now, and promised to go on for much longer. Though part of him was champing at the bit to go to Mr. Chalmers and demand an audition, he could also tell how far he'd come since they began, and how far he had yet to go. Whoever Melody was, and whatever her true motivations, she had proven to be an excellent and insightful teacher.

Tony often found himself humming as he worked, mentally going over the past night's lesson, and his efforts had not gone unnoticed by the men on the stage crew.

"I think your caterwauling is actually getting better, Tony," Stig observed one day. "You might not break glass, now." Tony had thrown a rag at him, but secretly, he was pleased.

He couldn't help but feel that Mother would be pleased as well. It was all happening as she'd wished. Slower than perhaps she had hoped, but still. It was going to be a better Christmas than he'd expected.

Being invited to spend the holiday with Jack and his wife and children had been an unexpected gift in and of itself. Tony hadn't been looking forward to his first Christmas alone, trundling about the empty opera house while everyone else was on holiday. He'd even started trying to see if his meager savings would allow some small outing of his own, though at best he'd be able to afford a small dinner at a pub, and perhaps one night in a warm inn, if it wasn't too far away.

The stage manager had informed him in no uncertain terms that his wife was expecting Tony for Christmas, and if he didn't appear, he would have to deal with her personally. Tony was more than happy to accept, and he was looking forward to it. His tiny bit of savings had gone instead to buy a windup tin car for Jack's seven-year-old son, and a few hair ribbons for his daughter, who was just nearing three.

And there had been one more gift he'd purchased, even sparing a few coins to have it wrapped by the nice lady in the shop. As Melody's playing came to an end, he fished the small box out of his pocket and set it on the piano in front of her.

"What is this?" She raised her hand to take the box, then hesitated, as if unsure that it was truly for her.

"A Christmas present. You can open it early, I don't think anyone will mind." Tony grinned, leaning his elbows on the piano.

"I…did not get anything for you." She set her hand back in her lap, clasping its partner tightly.

"You teaching me is gift enough, Melody. Please accept it. It would mean a lot to me."

After a moment, she inclined her head slightly. "As you wish." She took the box from its resting place, and unwrapped it with painstaking care, barely creasing the heavy paper. Once she had extracted it from its wrappings, and those were safely set aside, she opened the small box to reveal a bracelet of crystal charms on a thin gold chain.

Tony smiled as she drew the piece of jewelry from its case, holding it up in the lamp light. "It matches the crystals on your veil. It's not expensive or anything, but I thought you might enjoy it."

She was silent for a long time, and he started to worry that he'd inadvertently offended her somehow, until she finally replied. "It is quite lovely, Tony, and very thoughtful. I do not know what to say."

"Well…how about Merry Christmas?"

There was a smile in her voice, even if he could not see her face. "Very well. Merry Christmas, Tony."

~*!*~

As far as Christmas parties went, this one was somewhere in the mid-level of tedium. One of Andrew's direct superiors at the bank had invited all of his underlings and their spouses – and somehow by extension, Bess – to his home, and they all appeared as commanded, decked out in the finest they could afford on their respective salaries.

They chatted and gossiped and drank copious amounts of watered down wine. The host's singularly horse-faced spinster daughter performed some morose composition on an agonizingly old harpsichord, blessedly ending when they were summoned to the evening meal.

The dinner was exquisite, if a bit bland for Bess' taste, and she'd been deliberately seated in the midst of a herd of single bankers, all of whom were smotheringly solicitous of her needs. However, afterwards, when the men took themselves off to the study for cigars and brandy, her gaze followed after them longingly. It had been ages since her last good cigar, and after the awkward attempts at conversation at the dinner table, she could have used a decent drink.

In contrast, the female half of the gathering settled in the parlor, the room stifling hot and full of voluminous skirts and the deafening rustle of yards and yards of taffeta. Bess found a place in a corner and pressed her back to the wall as if she expected to be attacked from behind at any moment. She'd seen gatherings like this before. It wasn't entirely impossible.

Her own gown had been one of Susan's, hastily altered to fit Bess's more voluptuous figure, but as it wasn't technically hers, she hadn't felt comfortable slitting the skirt to get at the Derringer in her garter. Therefore, the skirt remained whole, and the Derringer remained tucked safely in her luggage back at Susan's house. Needless to say, her six-shot Colt revolver wasn't going to be the new fashion accessory of the season, and so for the first time in years, she was truly unarmed. She felt positively nude.

The hierarchy among the women was quickly established, the hostess of course holding court and a few other higher-ranking wives nodding their curled and feathered heads in agreement with everything the woman had to say, no matter how ludicrous or snide. Susan sat on the outer ring with several of the junior partners' wives, the younger clique having obviously banded together for sheer survival.

It was not, Bess mused, unlike watching a pack of African wild dogs, snapping and snarling to establish dominance. The weaker ones would be driven out, or killed, and the stronger would go on to breed the next generation of the species. The thought made her laugh, which she managed to strangle into a respectable coughing fit instead.

Unfortunately, by the time she'd recovered herself, all eyes had turned her way.

"Are you all right, Bess?" Susan's brow creased in concern.

Bess waved her off with a small smile. "I'm fine. Just…a bit parched. It's a bit warm in here, don't you think?"

The hostess, a woman saddled with the unfortunate name of Gertrude, pasted an insincere smile upon her heavily made-up face. "I would think you'd be used to warmer climes, what with your adventures in Egypt and the Africas and all."

"Bess has been back in the country for several months now, she's adjusted to the local climate quite nicely."

Susan offered her friend an encouraging smile when none of the others were looking at her. Bess could have told her it was a lost cause. The pack had her in their sights now.

"I surely would never be brave enough to venture out in such uncivilized lands alone," one of Gertrude's sycophants interjected, fanning herself with one hand as if the very thought would drive her into a swoon. "However did you manage without an escort?"

"That part is actually very simple. If you look like you know where you're going, no one stops you."

"Yes, but why would you *want* to?" This from another of the feathered toadies. "There's nothing out there in the desert but sand and bandits and heathens."

"Because it's there. Because I could." That at least was one question to which Bess knew the answer, even if she was certain that very few women in the room would understand it. "There are so many amazing things out there, things that people have forgotten, or are about to lose. The world changes every day, and before we know it, wonders like the pyramids and the deserts will be gone. They'll be cobblestoned over, and someone will erect dress shops and hatteries."

"And it will be about time!" They tittered in unison, led by Gertrude who sounded very like a mule braying. It was easy to see where her horse-faced daughter had gotten her traits.

"So…if you loved it there so much, why did you return?" The question came from one of Susan's friends this time, a young woman named Cecily if Bess recalled, and there was at least a sincere curiosity in her eyes.

The honest answer – that she'd been evicted due to errant gunshot to an important personage's derrière – would not do Susan's social standing any favors, so she improvised. "I was homesick. As wonderful as my travels are, Detroit is still home, and it had been some time since

I'd seen my dear friend Susan. She had a new baby, winter was coming on… It seemed a good time to linger."

"Yes, and how is that charming baby, Susan?" Like that, the pack turned their attention on Susan who was much more adept at handling them. With their predatory gazes distracted, Bess slipped from the room without notice.

The house was larger than Susan and Andrew's, but it seemed to Bess that all homes of this nature followed a certain pattern, so finding the library was easy enough. The room was blessedly cool and dark, shelves of books reaching from floor to ceiling. An automaton stood in one corner, dark and inactive, for the sole purpose of maneuvering the heavy ladder around on its track whenever someone needed to reach a book on an upper shelf. Bess was willing to bet the books hadn't been touched in decades, and the automaton had been unwound for most of that time.

All the same, she found what she had hoped for, a set of French doors that opened out onto a small veranda. Stepping out into the winter chill, Bess smiled to see the first delicate flakes of snow drifting about on the night air. How long it had been, since she'd seen snow. She held out a hand, watching as the tiny ice crystals landed on her palm, sparkling for a split second before melting against the warmth.

"Now what on earth would you be doing out here in the cold, Miss Barstow?" The male voice startled her, and on reflex her hand went to her waist where the heavy weight of her Colt should have been resting. It wasn't there, of course, nor should she have reason to need it, she reminded herself.

"Just getting a breath of fresh air. I could ask the same of you."

The man stepped from the shadowed library, and she recognized him from dinner, some secondary partner to the bank named Theodore Tisdale.   He'd been seated directly across from her at the table, and while he'd watched her closely, he'd said very little.   "I saw you come in here, and I was curious what would bring a woman to wander a strange house all alone."

He was taller than her, with dark hair slicked back in the fashionable style, his mustache neatly trimmed and waxed. His tuxedo was tailored, but obviously for a much younger version of himself. Years hunched over a desk had started the beginnings of a paunch, hidden cleverly behind his cummerbund.   Handsome, in a very ordinary, common way.

"Though I suppose, given your reputation, that finding you wandering around alone should come as no surprise."

It could have been just awkward small talk. Bess was forced to admit that she wasn't as adept at social niceties as she'd once been.   But there was something behind his smile, behind the words that felt…oily. Something about it put her defenses up.

"I know I'm going to regret asking this, I truly am, but exactly what reputation are you referring to?"

Tisdale put his hands up in a placating gesture. "Only that you are a woman with her own mind about things. You answer to no man, and that you acknowledge no known rules of proper society."

"On the contrary. I acknowledge all of the rules of society. I just happen to disagree with most of them, and with the definition of 'proper.'"

He leaned against the doorway, hooking his thumbs in his cummerbund, and the fact that he stood between her and a safe retreat was not lost upon her. "Then is it true what they whisper? That you've got a lover in every city between here and Cairo?"

And there it was. His true nature and intent revealed in one telling question. His interest was base at best, and his insinuations crude and clumsy. She knew his kind. She'd been dealing with them since she'd left behind pigtails and pinafores. Bess smirked on the inside, but kept her face coldly blank.

"You will find, Mr. Tisdale, that things are often whispered because if they were shouted aloud, the entire world would know how ludicrous they were." Gathering her skirts in one hand, she made to push past him. *If you walk like you know where you're going, no one stops you.*

His hand clamped down on her elbow, as she had known it would. His kind couldn't allow a mere woman to have the last word. "I think you know as well as I do that such whispers almost always arise from a place of truth." He leaned close, and she could smell the brandy on his breath, mingled with the sweet smell of fine cigars.

"I'm almost positive that what you and I know are two very different things." Slowly, she took a step back, subtly urging him to follow her into the darkness of the library. Slightly tipsy as he was, he took it for encouragement, rather than a means to escape and he stumbled along with her willingly.

"I know a woman who knows what she wants when I see her." His leer was marred by a piece of spinach stuck between his two front teeth, and Bess barely stopped herself from wrinkling her nose in disgust.

"And what exactly do I want, Mr. Tisdale?" Maneuvering backwards in the hooped skirt was a bit more problematic than she'd anticipated, and she cursed silently as it caught on the corner of an end table. One small twitch of her hips freed her, and she continued to lure him closer to the dormant fireplace against the far wall. She relaxed once she felt the bricks under her hands. *Almost there...*

"You want a man. The same thing as any woman wants." He released her arm and placed his hands against the mantle, caging her between his arms.

Her fingers found what she was looking for, and she took a firm grip. "You may be right, Mr. Tisdale. If you should happen to find one, would you let me know?"

It took the inebriated man a heartbeat or so to realize he'd been insulted, and his dark brows drew down over his forehead like two angry caterpillars. "Why you cheap –"

She never found out what she was, as she chose that moment to lift the fireplace poker and drive the tip of it down through the toe of his very nice leather shoe. Tisdale let out a howl of pain and fell on his elegantly tailored rump, scrabbling at the iron rod that held him pinned to the floor.

"A pleasure to make your acquaintance, Mr. Tisdale." With a sweep of her skirts, she left him there, writhing on the floor and shouting drunken epithets at her back.

Out in the hallway, people had appeared, drawn by the sounds of anguish issuing from Mr. Tisdale's throat. The host, one Mr. Worthy, gaped at Bess as she strode out of the library. "Good heavens, what is going on here?"

"You should summon a doctor, Mr. Worthy. It appears Mr. Tisdale has had a horrible accident with a fireplace poker." Bess spotted Susan in the gathering throng and hurried to her side before anyone could think to stop her. "I'm sorry, Sue. I'm going to take a cab home, all right?"

Susan nodded, squeezing her hand tightly for a moment. "Go on. I'll handle this here." Bess' heart swelled a bit in gratitude for her friend who never once asked what had happened, but was willing to stand with her anyway.

Bess was almost to the door before Mrs. Gertrude Worthy blocked her path, flanked by her feather-bedecked cronies. "This is what comes of poor breeding, you know. Traipsing about in unsafe environments, associating with criminals and heathens. Lack of manners, that's what it is! And you aren't even going to apologize to that poor man!" Her minions nodded and clucked their disapproval.

It was the last straw. "Mrs. Worthy, I was just thrown out of a foreign country because I shot a man in the ass. Do you really want to stand in my way just now?" The old harridan lost all color in her face, and the only way one could tell was through the cracks in her caked-on cosmetics. After a moment, one of her clique tugged her out of the way by one arm, leaving Bess free to depart.

She could feel them gathering on the front steps as she marched her way down the walk and out the front gate with her head held high. And just because she couldn't help herself, she paused on the sidewalk and turned to look at the remains of the Christmas party. "Merry Christmas, one and all!"

Surely there would be a cab stand nearby. Skirts hiked out of the accumulating snow, she went in search.

ACT II

Chapter 7

Christmas came and went, lost in a swirl of holiday doings and the culmination of the chorale that they'd rehearsed so diligently. Tony spent a wonderful holiday with Jack and his wife and children, and they gifted him with a new warm coat, for which he was eternally grateful. Once the company reassembled to begin work on the new spring production, his lessons with Melody began again, and he noticed the crystal bracelet he'd given to her dangling against the lace of her sleeve as she played the piano. It pleased him to no end.

The opera ghost, on the other hand, was not pleased. The increasingly demanding notes kept arriving for Mr. Chalmers, sometimes two and three a day, and more than one person had fallen victim to some highly suspicious "accidents". Set pieces toppled over when they should be secured, costume pieces went missing, drop pulleys were found locked and the keys misplaced. Once, the inner doorknob to Simon's dressing room was unscrewed, leaving the furious man trapped until someone heard him pounding on his door and released him from the outside. No serious injuries, thankfully, but the wariness had spread through the company, and even those who soundly scoffed at the idea of the opera ghost were starting to eye the dark corners of the stage with some concern.

Still, Simon was once again cast as the tenor lead for the spring show – a favorite of Tony's titled *The Maharajah* – despite the fact that his performance during the Christmas chorale had been notably subpar. Tony couldn't be sure if

Simon was actually getting worse, or if his lessons with Melody were simply fine-tuning his ear, but he too could tell now that the aging singer was struggling. More than once, he caught himself wincing at a slightly flat note, or a vocal run that simply didn't complete its climb the way it ought. He was starting to understand the opera ghost's pique, whoever or whatever was actually behind it.

And under it all was a growing tension as rumors of the sale of the opera house continued. Mr. Chalmers often laughed off questions, but it hadn't escaped anyone's notice that he also refused to deny them. On the day that he arrived on the stage with two strange men in tow, interrupting their rehearsal mid-scene, no one was truly surprised. More than one member of the company exchanged bank notes with the person standing next to him, proving that wagers had been placed long ago.

"Mr. Chalmers, I am in the middle of a rehearsal!" Maestro, at the head of the orchestra, cast a withering look at the manager.

"Yes, Maestro, please forgive this interruption… Everyone, if I could have your attention please! Maestro, Mrs. McRory, Mr. Kelly…everyone…" The beleaguered conductor threw his hands up in exasperation, but gestured for the manager to go on. The rest of the company wandered in from the wings, and Tony found himself in a knot of the stage crew as they left their posts on the drops to come listen.

"Everyone, I know that there have been rumors for some time that the opera house was going to be sold. I am here to tell you now that they are all true." A murmur of satisfaction went up amongst the watching crowd, and he had to wait for them to quiet before he could continue. "These gentlemen here to my left are Mr. Reginald Thomas and Mr. Frederick Strang, and they have purchased the opera house as of this morning."

Both men, dressed in fine suits and tall hats of the latest

fashion, nodded around to the gathered company. They were alike enough to be interchangeable save that one was dark and the other had hair of ruddy red, with neatly waxed moustaches and matching silver-headed walking sticks. Almost as if someone had told them this was how they must dress to be considered gentlemen, and they adhered to the instructions religiously.

"Look like a right pair a prigs, don't they?" Stig muttered in Tony's ear, and Tony choked back a laugh as Jack cast them both chiding glances.

"I would also like to announce that as Mr. Thomas and Mr. Strang would like to manage the opera house directly, I will be retiring, effectively immediately."

The murmurs that went up that time were full of shock and dismay. No one had imagined that Mr. Chalmers would be departing. He'd been with the theater longer than any person there, and to think of the place without his befuddled smile and smudged glasses was nearly unthinkable.

Again, he waved down the conversations until he could speak again. "Don't worry, everyone. I've been considering retirement for some time now, and this is just the impetus I needed to follow through. I have loved my time here at the opera house, but it is time for younger minds to take over, and I pass the torch gladly."

Whatever else Mr. Chalmers might have said, it was lost in a rush of people who crowded around the departing manager to express their goodbyes and thanks. Tony, feeling that he didn't know Mr. Chalmers as well as the others, kept his distance. While it was a pity to see the manager leaving, a part of his mind wondered frantically what this would do to his plans, and Melody's. It could work in his favor, with managers who were not already intimidated by Simon's temper, or it could be disastrous if they preferred to stick with a proven performer over taking a chance on someone new.

"Well, didn't see that coming…" Stig plopped down on a barrel next to him. "Figured Chalmers would be here 'til the day they carted him out on a plank."

"Do you think the new owners will keep us all on?" Tony glanced at the crowd, to see that Jack and Mrs. McRory were being introduced to their new employers. "Maybe even hire on a few more hands? Surely, if they bought the theater, they're wealthy."

"Scrap metal."

"Hm?"

"Scrap metal. Saw a story in the paper about that pair. They figured out some new way to reuse steel and iron, made a killing when they sold the patent. They're calling them Detroit's newest steel barons." Stig shrugged his broad shoulders. "Bet they don't have a clue what it takes to run a theater."

"They'll learn fast, then." Tony shook his head to himself as he watched Simon push his way through the throng, thrusting himself to the center of attention as always. Ah well. There went that opportunity.

"All right, everyone, back to rehearsing! Let's show Mr. Thomas and Mr. Strang just what a fabulous company they've purchased!" At Mr. Chalmer's urging, the cast and crew slowly drifted back to their marks, and the maestro resumed his place at the front of the orchestra.

Tony and Stig took up position behind a large plaster elephant on wheels, boosting Big up into his place inside the construction so that he could operate the levers that would make the beast curl its trunk and flap its ears. It was one of the few times when Tony would actually be onstage, albeit unseen, and even that small bit of exposure thrilled him. Someday, he promised himself. Someday, he'd be out there singing, instead of behind the scenes, shoving around the scenery.

From his place behind the elephant's leg, it sounded good. The chorus was in full throat, instead of the half-hearted efforts they usually displayed during a mere rehearsal, and from what little he could see, even the dancers were putting their full energy into the number. Only Simon faltered, and what should have come out as a voice full of bravado and triumph instead sounded like an old and weary man, struggling to keep up with the younger set. Tony winced on the last note, as the older tenor forced it out with a gusto that was out of place in the piece.

"Very good, everyone, now please reset for act three—"

"I will not!"

A weary murmur went through the cast and Tony poked his head out from behind the elephant to see what was happening. It was Simon, of course, as he had known it would be. The aging tenor threw down his elaborate costume headpiece, not caring in the least as pieces of the ornate decorations snapped off and went skittering across the stage. Somewhere, a costumer would be chewing their hat.

"I refuse to perform for these so-called managers when it is obvious that they're more interested in the dancing girls than in any sort of vocal talent." Imperiously, he snapped his fingers toward the wings. "Bring my coat! I'm going!"

The new owners stared at him, gaping like landed fish, and Mr. Chalmers only rolled his eyes at the ceiling with a sigh.

"Oh for Pete's sake," Stig muttered, and Tony was inclined to agree with him.

When no one moved to obey his orders, Simon obviously decided that more emphasis was necessary, and he turned on his heel, marching off the stage in the opposite direction.

"What do we do?" The dark-haired man, presumably Mr. Thomas, looked to Mr. Chalmers for guidance.

"Grovel." When neither man moved, the departing manager gestured for them to hurry. "Grovel! Grovel!"

Belatedly, they scampered after their temperamental star, and Mr. Chalmers used that moment to make his escape, disappearing in the direction of his office.

Big, from his perch inside the elephant, smirked. "What he needs is a good pop in the mouth." Tony waved at him to hush, lest Simon overhear and turn his temper on the stage crew. It would not be a good way to get noticed by the new owners.

"We'll be stuck with him now for sure. Betcha those two idiots wouldn't know a good voice if it walked up and bit them in the—"

"Stig!" Jack, from across the stage, leveled a glare at the stocky stagehand, who looked not at all abashed.

"Well, they wouldn't."

From the wings, Simon and the new owners reappeared, both of the strangers with their fine hats in their hands as they did whatever was necessary to get the tenor to return. "We would consider it a personal favor, if you could…"

Simon gave them a magnanimous smile that nearly oozed smug satisfaction around the corners. "If my managers wish. Maestro! I'll be singing the first part of act two, if you will please. Per the request of our new managers." The words sounded like a request, but the tone sounded like an order. Making little shooing motions at the rest of the cast, he cleared himself a good portion of the stage until he was standing alone.

With a sigh, Tony and Stig quietly wheeled the elephant back into the wings as the orchestra began the first bars of Simon's aria. Inwardly, Tony winced at the first flat notes. It was awful. Truly awful. His vibrato was all wrong, and what should have been a heart-wrenching emotional piece describing the character's loneliness and grief came out instead as a shaky, warbling mess.

Just as Simon's voice rose to what should have been a masterful crescendo, the dancing girls standing to stage left gave shrieks of alarm, and Tony whirled in time to see one of the drops plummet from the ceiling.

"Look out!" It was too late for warning, though, and the drop came crashing down on the stage in a billow of painted canvas. Simon, struck from behind, collapsed under its weight.

"Out of the way! Tony! Big, Little, get it up off of him!" Jack immediately jumped into action, rallying the stage crew to lift the heavy piece of scenery off of the singer, who was making entirely too much noise to be badly injured.

Between the three of them, they managed to lift the yards of heavy canvas up enough for Simon to scoot out from under the drop. Tony found the top bar, and examined the ropes that should have been holding it to the pulleys in the rafters. They'd been sliced neatly through. Holding one in his hand, he showed it to Jack, who frowned darkly.

"Goddammit Stig! What the hell is going on up there?"

A few moments later, Stig's round face appeared over the edge of the catwalk. "There's no one up here, sir! I swear, I was down below, helping with the elephant!"

"He's telling the truth, he was standing next to me when the girls screamed." Tony brushed his hands off as he stood up, eyeing the rafters warily. That had been no accident.

"It musta been the ghost!" Stig announced, barely hiding the glee in his voice. The dancers, an easily frightened lot as it was, squealed and huddled together until Mrs. McRory silenced them with a loud thump of her cane upon the stage.

Mr. Thomas, very studiously helping Simon brush the dust off his clothing, snorted in disdain. "A ghost? You truly believe in such superstitious nonsense?"

"There, there, no harm done. These things do happen. Such is the thrill of working in theater." Mr. Strang offered the tenor a smile that wilted at the edges when it was returned with a look of absolute fury.

"These things do happen? Truly? For the last six months, these things have been happening all too frequently!" Simon drew himself up to his full height, yanking his clothing into some sort of order. "I have been mocked, belittled, repeatedly harassed, and now outright attacked, and not one of you has done a thing to stop it!" He leveled an accusing glare at the entire company, pinning each and every one of them under the heat of his ire, until finally his gaze made its way back to his new managers. "And you two. Until you figure out who is doing this, and put an end to it, you can find yourselves a new star! Good day, sirs!" Turning on his heel, he marched off the stage, leaving the two new owners to look at each other helplessly.

Finally, after long moments that proved Simon was not indeed going to reappear and be mollified, Mr. Thomas looked at the maestro. "Is he…going to come back?"

"Does it *look* like he's coming back, sir?" The frustrated conductor threw his hands up in defeat. "And we've no understudy! He's never allowed an understudy."

"What are we going to do, Reg?" Mr. Strang lowered his voice, but on stage, everything carried quite nicely. "The opening show is sold out already! We'll have to refund a full house!"

Muttering amongst themselves, the cast began drifting offstage, removing costumes and preparing to give up for the day. Inside, Tony's heart sank. He'd been so looking forward to opening night, and the lights and music and excitement. Damn Simon and his temper. Damn the ghost too, whoever it was. The alleged specter had driven them to this point. He aimed a petulant kick at a faux boulder nearby, and immediately felt childish.

"Sirs? If I may make a suggestion…" Jack's voice rose over the general din. "Anton Krol could sing that part."

Suddenly, it seemed that the entire world turned its eyes

on Tony, and he blinked in surprise, certain that he'd heard wrongly.

"Who?" Mr. Thomas looked in the direction Jack pointed, spotting Tony dressed in his worn shirt and pants, raven hair peppered white with plaster dust from the workshop. "A stagehand? You can't be serious."

"He's been taking lessons, sir. Let him sing for you, at least." When Jack spotted Tony's look of surprise, he smirked at his friend. "I've heard you. You don't get better like that without lessons. Just didn't feel like prying if you didn't want to talk about it."

Mr. Strang gestured impatiently. "Well, step forward, come now. Who is your teacher?"

"I, um... She prefers to remain anonymous, sir. I intend to respect her wishes." He'd never felt so drab, so shabby, as that moment when he stepped out to the front of the stage, flanked on either side by the two finely dressed gentlemen who now held his fate in their hands.

With a sigh, Maestro resumed his place at the head of the orchestra, obviously finding this an exercise in futility. Tony wasn't sure that he was wrong. "From the beginning of the aria then, sir."

You know this, Anton. You can do this. He did know it. He could have sung it in his sleep, and most likely had. Straightening his shoulders, he drew in his breath as Melody had instructed him. *Remember what she taught you.*

His first note came out strong, true, and his doubts vanished in the joy of simply singing. The watching crowd disappeared, the orchestra melted away, leaving only the music behind, wrapping itself around him and carrying him away in a tide of emotion. He lost himself in the song, in the story, pouring his heart out as sincerely as he could. *Honest emotion will often excuse a faltering note or unsteady transition.* But there were no false notes, no stumbles, no mistakes.

When the last notes died away, he stood there in silence for a few dazed moments, struggling to bring himself back to the stage, to the reality that waited for him.

And then the applause started. A roar from the managers, from the cast, whoops and hollers from the stage crew. Hands slapped him on the back, someone started plucking at his arms and legs as they took his measurements as hurriedly as possible. Everything was a whirl of color and noise around him, and all he could think was that he wouldn't get a chance to tell Melody before he went on that night. Oh, how he wanted to let her know that he'd be performing, and that it had all happened just as she'd predicted.

"…need to get the costumes altered…"

"…change the marquee, announcing an understudy…"

"…need Little on the elephant with Stig, and make sure we get one of the other hands to work drop four in act three…"

"It's Krol. K-R-O-L."

"We're saved, Fred! And you were worried. This will be an amazing night!"

Chapter 8

The stocky stagehand, Stig, passed within inches of her, hidden in the shadows only by the folds of her voluminous cloak. Melody held herself as motionless as only she could, watching as he leaned over the edge of the catwalk to call down to those below. "It musta been the ghost!"

Of course it was the ghost. She'd been their ghost for years, and the performers had always accepted the story Gilbert had concocted to explain her stealthy comings and goings. Better to be thought a phantasm than what she actually was. As a ghost, she was not apt to be destroyed on sight.

There was a commotion going on down below, but she could not afford to pay attention to the chaos she'd sewn. Stig was returning, peering thoughtfully at the pulleys where she'd sliced the ropes just moments before. His gaze was piercing, trying to see through the shadows and darkness above the stage. Trying to find her. She shifted her weight subtly, just enough that she could move quickly if she had to. She could not be discovered.

The blond stagehand prowled across the catwalk toward her, each step bringing him closer to her hiding place. "Come out, come out, pretty lady. I know you're here…"

This was going to be unfortunate. She liked the cheerful little man, and Tony was fond of him. A twitch of her wrist freed her hand from her cloak, still hidden from sight, but where she could easily reach out if she was forced to. The pair of heavy shears she had used to cut the ropes bent ever so slightly in her tense grip.

Not two feet from her, Stig abruptly turned and looked back at the stage. "Well holy crow..." With a grin, he scampered back to the catwalk, leaning over to watch what was happening below.

Only then did she hear his voice, Tony's voice, rising pure and true out over the auditorium. Tony was singing, in front of the entire company. As she'd instructed him, he managed his breath, poured his emotion into the heartbreaking aria. His sweet tenor tones rested easily on her senses, everything humming behind her ears like a purring engine. She closed her eyes, concentrating only on the sounds of her student's glorious voice.

My Tony... The odd thought made her pause, drew her out of her pleasurable daze. How truly strange, to think of him in a possessive fashion. Those such as her had no possessions, no belongings, and to think that a person could be such...

"Mine! She's mine, Papa! She's so beautiful!" The little girl's voice came out of nowhere, and seemed to go nowhere as well. Melody blinked her eyes open, daring to move her head enough that she could glance around the cast on the stage. There were no children present, no one to call out those words. And yet, she was so certain she had heard them, spoken as if from just below her... It was so familiar, and yet she could not place why... For a moment, she forgot herself, and leaned forward, trying to find the source of the child's voice. Her cloak gaped open, exposing the soft rose velvet of her gown.

The applause from below startled her back to the present, and she only had a moment to freeze into stillness again before Stig came pelting past her. The pale fabric of her dress shone against the shadows around her, but the stagehand was too distracted to notice. He thundered down the stairs without a single glance. "Tony! Bravo!"

Yes, bravo Tony. This is what pride felt like, she decided. It was the only thing that could explain the odd swelling feeling in her chest cavity. He would perform, finally, as she had planned for months. She made a note to herself to wear something truly fine that night for his debut.

With Stig safely on the stage, congratulating Tony in the center of the crowing, shouting throng, she finally moved, slipping down the stairs herself and into the recesses of backstage. Now, she needed to speak to Gilbert. He had to explain to her the happenings of the day. She was most disconcerted about the events that had taken place today, though she'd only arrived at the very end. *In time to stop Simon's dreadful debacle of an aria.*

The opera house was old. That much was well known. Older than her, actually, but she had spent decades discovering most of its secrets. She knew the hidden passageways, the dark corners, the secretive little nooks where one could stand and still hear everything as though they were right in the middle of the stage. The building itself was an acoustic marvel.

She found Gilbert in the lobby, his personal effects packed in a leather case as he tried to make his swift departure. "What is happening, Gilbert?"

He froze instantly, his head swiveling this way and that as he attempted to locate her disembodied voice. It echoed throughout the cavernous room, the source impossible to discern. From her hiding place on the second floor, she could see him clearly, but he would never find her.

Finally, he sighed, setting his case on the floor. "We have new owners."

"I am aware of that. What does this mean?"

"It means that I am leaving. I will not be running the opera house any longer."

This was going to be troublesome. She could already anticipate that. "The new owners. Have you informed them of the ghost?"

Gilbert snorted, taking his glasses off his sweaty head to polish them, his nervous habit. "I think you did that, when you tried to kill Simon."

"I wasn't trying to kill him. I just wanted him to stop producing that horrid sound."

"Well you accomplished that right enough." The former manager tucked his glasses away in his breast pocket, and picked his case up off the floor. "I am leaving now. What happens to you after this point is up to you. I wish you all the best."

"Gilbert, you must stop. You must speak to me—"

"Mr. Chalmers!" Melody shrank back into her concealing shadows as the new owners appeared from the auditorium. "Oh good, we were afraid you'd left."

Gilbert looked around the room for a moment, then pasted a smile on his face, straightening his shoulders. "I was just about to depart, actually. Is there anything else I can do for you, before I go?"

Mr. Thomas twisted at the waxed end of his moustache. "What is all this nonsense about a ghost that they're all prattling on about? A ghost? Seriously?"

Gilbert's eyes rose again to the upper reaches of the lobby, searching the shadows on the second floor. For just a moment, Melody was certain he spotted her, his eyes lingering on her hiding place for long seconds, before he moved on. "There are…things that happen here, sirs. Unexplainable things. It has been going on as long as I've been with the opera house. No doubt, once you are settled, the ghost will introduce herself to you."

Mr. Strang snorted. "A cordial sort of phantom, is she?"

Gilbert fixed him with a flat stare. "No. No, she is not. You saw what she did today, and that was just a small tantrum. The opera house will be run to her standards, sirs, and box seven will be left empty for her use at every show. I pity you if you do not abide by her wishes."

He turned to go, but Mr. Thomas caught his elbow, stopping him. "You expect us to believe that there is a ghost here that has a preference about opera? Be honest.

You're just having a go at us, as the new managers."

Gilbert eyed him for long moments, showing more spine than she'd ever remembered him possessing. "Believe what you wish, but do not say you were not informed. Gentlemen, if you need me, I shall be unavailable." He extracted his arm from Mr. Thomas' grip, donned his hat with a polite nod at both gentlemen, and strode out the door.

"Oh for pity's sake… A ghost of all things." Mr. Thomas, the dark one, threw up his hands in exasperation. "Of all the addle-brained ideas."

Mr. Strang, on the other hand, let his gaze wander around the lobby again, following the path that Gilbert's eyes had taken. Again, he seemed to look straight at her for a moment, before moving on. "I don't know, Reg. Things happen in old places like this. And someone cut those ropes on that drop."

"It's sabotage, Fred, plain and simple. Someone with a grudge against that puffed up prat, LeClerc, no doubt, and who could blame them if that's how he conducts himself all the time? We'll find out who did it, and we'll sack them, and then things will be fine." Thomas thumped his partner on the shoulder roughly. "Now come on, we've opening night to prepare for, and an outstanding new tenor to debut. The papers will eat this up!"

Mr. Strang allowed himself to be led away, but not without a few backwards glances.

This was a discouraging development, Melody decided. Mr. Thomas plainly did not believe in ghosts, and therefore would try to discover her at every opportunity. Obviously, she was going to have to do something to make an impression on the two new owners. A note, to start, and if that proved insufficient, she would have to do…something else. She couldn't just leave the opera behind, after all. Where else would she go? What else would she do?

It would wait until the morning. Tonight would be

Tony's night, and she couldn't interfere with that. Not when she had worked so very hard to set the events in motion.

Slipping from the theater was easy, despite the fact that the place was buzzing with activity. Everyone was so rushed to make the changes needed for the night's performance, to finish costumes, to touch up set pieces or rehang the fallen drop, that no one noticed an extra body moving through the bowels of the opera house.

The city too was bustling, everyone out and enjoying the unseasonably warm weather. An early spring was in the offing, the almanac predicted, and if the buds on the trees refused to present themselves for fear of one last snowfall, well, that much could be ignored. Basking in the bright sunlight, in the gentle breeze off the lake, no one paid any mind to the cloaked woman who brushed past them on the street, her face hidden within her deep hood.

The house was quiet and dark when she let herself in, as expected. It had been decades since anyone but her had occupied the structure. The houses on either side had changed hands multiple times in the passing years, and the new occupants never thought to question the silent comings and goings of their seldom-seen neighbor. They left her alone, and that was all she'd ever needed.

Her skirts brushed aside the thin layer of dust on her path from front door to bedroom, her oft-travelled trail indelibly etched in the hardwood floor after so many decades. She rarely ventured into the other rooms of the house, the kitchen, dining room, and wash rooms being of no use to her at all. There, the floors and furniture were covered with a thick layer of dust, like soft gray velvet, whatever colors they once possessed smothered by the years.

The bannister on the stairs was burnished smooth by her frequent grip, the carpets worn in the very center where her boots rested on each riser. She had claimed the bedroom at the far end of the second floor, simply because that's where the gowns were. A matter of expediency and convenience, rather than any personal preference. The other doors on that floor had been shut tight for years, untouched, unopened. She had no need of them.

"Papa, make her sing for me again!" With her hand on the door knob, Melody froze, slowly turning to look behind her for the source of the childish demand.

There was, of course, nothing there. Only the trail through the gathering dust where she herself walked on a daily basis. The house itself was still, even the creaking of its settling foundation silent for the moment.

But no, she had heard it clearly, the same little girl as at the opera house. Her ear could not mistake the distinct timber of a person's voice, and every human had their own particular way of speaking. It was the same child.

Perhaps…perhaps the child had snuck in behind her? Ducked into one of the closed rooms? Turning back on her path, Melody retraced her steps to the first room next to the stairs, hand hovering over the doorknob in uncertainty. The dust was thick on the brass knob, undisturbed for possibly decades, but after a moment, she grasped it, turned it. The door swung open.

It had been a child's room, obviously. A little girl's room. The walls had been pink at some point, before the predations of a determined sun faded it into a barely discernible peach color. The bed was covered in a lacy duvet and an extraordinary amount of crocheted pillows. Dolls lined the shelves, their hair and clothing all a uniform shade of gray under years' worth of dust. Cobwebs waved lazily in the corners, stirred by the door's opening.

A hobby horse stood in the corner, and for one moment, Melody was certain she saw it rock slowly back and forth, and a childish giggle echoed through the room. A music box played at the far reaches of her hearing, a cheerful tinkling too faint to even identify the song. An instant later, all was still, even the dust motes sullen in their drifting dance around her feet. The hobby horse hadn't moved, of course, its dust-dulled eyes staring into space as it had for years.

Gripped by a sudden fear she had no name for, Melody withdrew, pulling the door shut firmly behind her. So firmly, in fact, that the knob bent and crumpled in her fist. She stood, staring at the closed door for long moments, but nothing further occurred. The child, if there had ever been one, was gone.

"I will find some boards and some nails. I will seal the door." It sounded better, said aloud. More decisive. Never mind the ridiculous need to board up an empty room, full of dust and forgotten toys.

Tomorrow, though, it would have to wait until tomorrow. Tonight, she must return to the opera house to hear Tony sing. She would need to choose a gown, fitting for his debut, even if he would never know that she was there. Blue. Tony liked blue, she recalled, though why he'd offered that information to her she could not remember.

Opening the wardrobe, she located the gown she had been thinking of, a blue damask creation with age-yellowed lace around the neckline and sleeves. She'd never worn this particular one before, but she knew it would fit. They all fit her perfectly, though she had no memory of being measured for any of them. They had just always been in the wardrobe, as she had always been in the house, and she did not question such things.

Holding the gown up against her in the mirror – though the glass was going mildewed around the edges, she noticed, and that would have to be repaired soon – she finally nodded her approval. It would do quite nicely.

Chapter 9

"You know, you're rather comely. You'd make a pretty good girl."

Bess eyed her friend's reflection in the mirror with a raised brow and a smirk. "Nah. Girls are too prissy and they cry all the time." A throw pillow hit her in the back of the head. "Hey! I just got my hair up like this! Do you know how long this took?"

"Exactly forty-five minutes, because Andrew has been checking his watch every five." With a chuckle, Susan entered the room, eyeing Bess up and down with a small smile. "But in all seriousness, you look lovely, dear."

Looking herself over in the mirror one last time, Bess was inclined to agree for once. Her wealth of golden curls was piled atop her head with enough pins to tack down a tarpaulin, but it fell down her bared neck in wispy little curls that were oddly appealing. The gown, a stunning confection of cream and gold brocade, had been a gift from Susan and Andrew for Christmas, and the neckline was low enough to be suitably daring, but not immodest enough to cause a scandal. Her only jewelry was a small crystal heart pendant on a delicate gold chain, one of the last birthday gifts she'd received from her mother. She hadn't had occasion to wear it, until now, but this was as good a reason as any.

"I suppose I do clean up well. A far cry from heat, sand, and camel spit." Though Susan made a face at that, Bess felt the familiar longing well up at the very thought. The wanderlust was rearing its head again, and only the fact that she had no idea where she wanted to go had kept her in one place these long months.

"You miss it so." Susan smiled, reaching to take her friend's hand. "I can see it in your eyes. Even when you're talking about camel spit." They both chuckled, and the dark-haired woman shook her head fondly. "I know you've only stayed this long because I asked. If you need to go, Bess, I truly will understand."

Bess looked herself over in the mirror for a moment longer, then shrugged. "And where would I go, Sue? I want to be on the move again, but I've no idea where to go. It's like…" She frowned, trying to wrap words around the intangible feelings. "It's like I'm waiting for something, but I don't know what it is. When I find that thing, then I'll know exactly what I'm supposed to be doing."

"Well, as much as I will miss you, I hope you find it soon. I so want you to be happy." The two women shared a long embrace, before Bess drew away, tucking a strand of Susan's raven hair back into its perfect coif.

"Let me get my gloves, and we'll go. No doubt Andrew has steam coming out his ears by this point." Given her preference, she would have chucked the elbow-length satin gloves out the window, but it seemed that current fashion demanded opera gloves to attend the opera, and so she was forced to encase her hands in the shiny fabric that ensured she would never be able to draw and fire a pistol with any speed. Which may have been Susan's intention, after all. She had to wonder if her dear friend knew that she was once again wearing the Derringer in her garter.

She linked her arm through Susan's as they descended the stairs, and Sue gave her a happy smile. "I've always wanted to go to the opera, but we've never really had the time." Or the funds, Bess knew, but she would never embarrass her friend by saying so.

Contrary to expectation, Bess' conduct at the Worthys' Christmas party had not resulted in social suicide for her dear friends. Instead, it had earned her – and by extension, them – a certain notoriety among Detroit's elite that had resulted in many more social invitations that would have otherwise been closed to them. For example, this night's outing to the opera was courtesy of one Mr. and Mrs. Mason, a senior partner in a law firm that did business with Andrew's bank. They had so conveniently obtained a few extra box tickets to the opening night of *The Maharajah*, and had inquired if Andrew and Susan would like to attend. And they should bring their interesting friend, of course.

Normally, under such circumstances, Bess would have told them to go stuff themselves, but Susan's eyes had nearly glowed at the idea of attending the opera, and so Bess could do nothing but agree. Thus, they found themselves seated in the Masons' barouche, the men riding at the front with the driver, leaving the three women to chat amongst themselves as they wended their way through the city.

Mrs. Mason, one of those rare women who managed to look stunningly fashionable long after her years dictated she should have retired into dowdiness, kept up light conversation without being tiresome, and Bess found to her great surprise that she was actually enjoying herself. At one point, the elder woman leaned across the carriage to pat Bess on the knee with a smile. "You don't worry about what those old biddies think of you, dear. They're only jealous that they didn't have the stones to take off like you did."

"Mrs. Mason!" Susan stared in amazement, but the older woman just laughed.

"Oh now hush. After all these years, if I want to say 'stones', I fully intend to. Life is too short to censor oneself." With a content sigh, Mrs. Mason settled back in her seat. "Such lovely weather tonight. It's the first time we've been able to put the top down since winter, and being able to watch the people along the way is always one of my favorite parts of any outing."

Bess opened her mouth to answer when the carriage gave a sudden lurch, nearly depositing Susan in her lap. The horses gave bugles of fright, and some type of horn blared out its irritation. Craning her neck, she spotted one of the new horseless carriages as it whipped around the startled beasts, its owner laying on its horn for all it was worth, cursing and shaking his fist at the Mason's driver.

"You all right, Sue?" Susan nodded, carefully collecting herself out of the floorboards, while Bess turned fully around to look at the men. "For God's sake, Andrew, what are you doing up there?"

"Nothing to worry about, ladies!" Andrew turned in his seat to give them an encouraging smile, pretending that his face wasn't ashen white under his dark mustache. "The horses are just a bit skittish is all, the driver is settling them now. Everyone all right?"

"We're fine, Andrew. No harm done." Susan gave him a smile from her seat, and for a moment Bess felt uncomfortable. It was like peering in on a scene where only the two of them belonged. Her friend was so very much in love with her husband, and Bess felt a tiny pang of loneliness. She hoped that someday, she would find someone for whom a single smile meant as much as an entire conversation.

Mrs. Mason snorted quietly. "For heaven's sake… If they don't get this thing moving again, I'll go up there and drive myself. Henry! Jackson! We'll be late!" There was a chorus of "yes mums" from the front, and after a few more moments, the driver climbed back into the seat and they were off again.

"You know, this may be evidence of my ever-advancing level of experience – I refuse to say that I'm getting old," Mrs. Mason mused, "But I dislike those new steam contraptions everyone is speeding around in, of late. They're going to kill someone, one of these days."

Bess spotted another of the conveyances further down the street, watching as it swerved in and out of the slower-moving carriages and pedestrians. "Oh, I don't know. In the right hands, I think they might be fun. Perhaps that's what I'll learn to do, I'll pilot one of those auto-mobiles."

Susan chuckled. "If anyone would, it would be you, Bess. But not I. They make me nervous, thinking about all that could go wrong. Rather like that fellow a few years ago who thought he could teach automatons to drive carriages. Such horrid events." She gave a little shiver, drawing her lace shawl around her shoulders.

Bess tilted her head curiously. "This must have been while I was out of country. What happened?"

Susan only shook her head, but Mrs. Mason had no such qualms. "Oh it was ghastly, my dear. You see, an automaton is a mindless machine, it has no concept of strength, or gentleness or the fragility of other creatures. So on the first few attempts, it snapped the horses' necks on the first jerk of the reins. Just dropped them in their tracks." Bess made a face, and the older woman smirked, leaning forward to impart the rest of the story. "Oh, it gets worse. On the last attempt, the machine had been wound so tightly that it actually ripped the beast's head right off. Sprayed gallons of blood all over the crowd, it was perfectly horrendous."

Susan's face looked faintly green. "Someone took pictures, and the newspaper actually published them. Can you imagine?"

Bess was forced to admit that it was probably a rather gruesome scene. "Automatons are wonderful, when used correctly, but I worry that we'll all forget how to do for ourselves, the more we come to rely on machines. In Cairo, only the truly wealthy have them. Everyone else just makes do with man- and animal-power, like we've done for thousands of years."

"This coming from the woman who gallivants across the

globe on those rickety airships?" Sue gave her a wry grin.

"I said I worry. I didn't say I wouldn't use them to my advantage."

"Yet another contraption you won't find me on. My feet are unsteady enough on solid ground, I've no need to go flinging myself into open air." Mrs. Mason gave a very firm nod.

"They're quite safe now, you know," Bess offered. "There hasn't been an accident in almost three years now."

Mrs. Mason sniffed. "Just means they're due."

"Oh Bessie! Look!" Susan leaned forward, pointing ahead of them, and they all turned to see the opera house coming into view.

Bess had to admit, it was a breathtaking sight. The building itself was a vision, the golden status that flanked each window gleaming in the setting sun's light. A red velvet carpet had been rolled down the entirety of the marble staircase, inviting guests in, and posters for the opera had been hung from the very roof, covering all four stories to the ground. Men in their dapper tuxedos and women in shimmering gowns in every color imaginable made their way up to the doors, glittering like a crystal chandelier.

On top of that, the entire square had been taken over for the night's opening show, torches flickering along the streets and bright silks draped over every window that faced the street. Performers put on small displays on the sidewalks, everything from fire breathers to snake handlers to dancing girls clad in nothing much more than their hair and a smile. Automatons, polished to a high sheen, slowly pushed carts of delicacies around the square, the aroma of the exotic food adding to the heady atmosphere. Music bubbled up into the air, and the entire place felt like a street party in India, which was no doubt the intent.

India. Perhaps that would be her next destination. Perhaps this was the inspiration she'd been waiting for.

She'd been a small girl the last time she'd visited that continent, and her memories were fond, if dim.

"It's so beautiful! Oh Bess, look, a snake charmer!" Susan, handed down from the carriage first, disappeared into the crowd immediately, despite Andrew's call for her to wait.

Bess chuckled at him as he lifted her from the carriage and set her on her feet. "Oh, let her enjoy herself, Andrew. When's the next time you'll be able to do something like this?"

"Well, yes, I know, but… Sometimes I forget how very much like you she truly is on the inside." Before Bess could decide if that was a compliment or not, Andrew had pelted off in search of his wife, leaving Bess with the Masons.

"Well come, dear, let us get to our box." Mrs. Mason gathered up her skirt and marched through the crowd, expecting them to clear a path for her and thinking nothing of it when they actually did. Mr. Mason offered Bess his arm, which she took with a chuckle.

They fell into the queue of people filing into the opera house, the babble of excited conversation filling the small pauses in the music around them.

"Oh look, Henry, they're to have an understudy tonight. That's a pity," Mrs. Mason pointed out as they passed through the open doors into the lobby. "LeClerc is such an outstanding tenor, I had hoped to hear him tonight. I do hope his ailment is temporary."

It seemed that everyone attending the opera that night knew the Masons, and by the time they'd finished greeting everyone in sight, and introducing Bess as if she was their dearest friend in the world, Andrew and Susan had caught up. "And he walked right over the live coals, Bess! In bare feet!"

Susan's excitement was infectious, and Bess found herself leaning over the railing of the box right alongside her best friend, pointing out faces below that they knew, waiving to acquaintances across the auditorium, marveling at the size of the orchestra as they filed into the pit. The conductor took his place at his podium, and the crowd in the auditorium slowly began to settle down, muffling their conversations as the orchestra began their warm-ups. The lights began to dim as the uniformed ushers made their way through the auditorium, dousing the lamps one by one.

Finally, only a lone beam of light remained, focused on the red velvet curtains across the stage. After waiting a few moments for the audience to fall silent, a single man in a fashionable tuxedo appeared, giving a low bow to those watching. "Ladies and gentlemen. I am Reginald Thomas, one of the new owners of the opera house, and I would like to thank you all for joining us on this most exciting night!" A small smattering of applause answered him, then died down. "In addition to the opening night of our new production of *The Maharajah*, I would also like to announce that the role of the Maharajah will be sung tonight by our new debut tenor, Anton Krol."

"What??" The word jumped from her lips before she realized, and the loud exclamation earned Bess some withering looks from the neighboring boxes. She could care less.

"Bess? Is everything all right?" Susan whispered at her in concern, but it would have to wait. It had to wait until she was sure.

Surely, it was a common name. It was some other Anton Krol, because Fate would never be so kind to her as to place her at *this* opera, on *this* night, otherwise.

The music came up, the curtains parted, and the chorus went about its work of laying out the premise of the story, a young pauper who had grown up on the streets of Delhi, keeping a charitable nature despite the hardships of his youth.

For Bess, the introduction seemed interminable. All she

wanted to see was the lead tenor. If she saw his face, even under the costuming and makeup, she was certain she would recognize him. And then the music swelled, the spotlight focused into a narrow shaft, and there he was. *Tony...*

He sported loose white trousers and an open vest, leaving his chest bare for all to see. His dark hair was mostly hidden under a winding white turban, and his skin had been darkened to a bronze with makeup, but it was him. There was no mistaking him, even if she'd last seen him at age twelve.

Susan squeezed her arm, giving her a concerned look again. "Sue...it's him! It's Tony!" Bess did her best to keep her voice to a whisper, but it was difficult. That was Tony down there on the stage! And when he opened his mouth, the voice that emerged was surely one directly from an angel. He was amazing. At one point, she even managed to forget that it was her dearest childhood friend down there, and lose herself in the music, wiping tears from her eyes after the most beautiful aria she'd ever heard in her life.

The rest of the opera could have consisted solely of Tony alone, and Bess would have been quite content. The intermission was agonizingly long, and once the curtains had come down on the last of the bows – and Tony got the lion's share of the applause, Bess was proud to note – she couldn't get out of the box fast enough.

"Where ever are you going, child?" Mrs. Mason asked.

"I'm going to see him, obviously."

"I don't think they just let you wander around backstage, Bessie."

Bess threw her best friend a wink. "If you walk like you know where you're going, no one stops you. I'll catch a cab home later. Wish me luck!" And with that she was off, hiking her skirts up so she could wind her way through the crowd as quickly as possible.

It was easier to slip backstage than she'd expected. She was not the only admirer intent on paying a visit, and the back halls of the theater held all the decorum of a coalworks brothel. Bess couldn't begrudge them that. The night had gone off without a hitch, and they'd earned the right to celebrate. Bottles of alcohol were passed from hand to hand, costume pieces tossed aside all willy-nilly, and very little attention paid to one more person slipping through the press.

The dressing rooms were obvious, the one belonging to the star soprano surrounded by eager young callers with arms full of roses and gifts, while the girl herself held court in nothing but her silk dressing gown. The one next to it then, Bess deduced, must belong to the lead tenor. Only one stagehand was posted outside that door, a stocky blond man who quirked a brow as she walked up.

"He'll want to see me, I promise." She gave him a wink, and he grinned wickedly, having obvious ideas about what her intentions were.

"Oh, I'm sure he will. G'wan in."

She knocked lightly, then opened the door.

The dressing room itself was opulent to say the least. Rich fabrics, dark cherry woods on the furniture, numerous posters on the walls for productions of the past. The man sitting before the dressing table seemed out of place there, and rightly so she surmised, if this room belonged to the regular star. Tony sat with his back to her, his head in his hands and so absorbed in his thoughts that he hadn't heard the door open and close at all. Freshly scrubbed of his makeup, his skin gleamed in the lamplight, and Bess let her gaze wander over the play of muscles in his back for long moments. *Oh Tony, you grew up good.*

"Hark hark, the dogs do bark…" A child's rhyme, and one they'd sung often enough together. Would he remember?

His head snapped up, staring at her reflection in the

mirror. After a moment, a slow smile spread on his face. "The beggars are coming to town."

She walked toward him, and he turned to face her, holding his hands out. "Some in rags, and some in jags."

"And one in a velvet gown." His hands were calloused as he took hers, but warm, and he squeezed them hard. "Dear God… Bess!" His dark eyes were wide with wonder, looking her up and down, and she did the same to him, trying to memorize everything about this moment. After a moment, they both burst out laughing, and he stood up to sweep her into his arms, spinning her in a circle with her feet clear off the ground. "I can't believe it's really you!"

"You can't believe? I nearly fell out of the box when they announced your name!" When he sat her on her feet, she swatted his shoulder playfully, but couldn't bring herself to step from the circle of his arms. "It's so *good* to see you!"

"And you. You have no idea." Finally, he seemed to realize that he was standing there with his arms around her, and he stepped back, blushing faintly. "I've thought of you often, of late. For a moment, I thought I'd conjured you here."

"Well, whatever brought me here tonight, I will be forever grateful. You were wonderful, Tony, truly wonderful. I would come back a million times to hear you sing again."

He chuckled a little and ran a hand through his damp hair. "Well, this may be the only chance I get. If Simon comes back…"

"So what if he does? After tonight, any theater company in the world would have you. You truly have no idea how magnificent you were." She tilted her head, an idea forming. "In fact, we should celebrate."

"What?"

"Come. A late supper, my treat. Surely some restaurant

must still be open at this hour, and if not well…we'll find some seedy pub down in the coalworks if we have to. We have years to catch up on." She took his hand and managed to tug him a few steps toward the door before he resisted.

"I can't go out like this." He gestured to his bare chest.

"Fair enough. You change, and I'll go hail a cab. You meet me out front in twenty minutes." He was going to hesitate again, she could tell, and the best thing to do in those circumstances was remove the chance for protest. "Twenty minutes, Anton Krol, and don't you dare be late!" With a grin, she picked up her skirts and sauntered out of the room, ignoring his call of "But Bess!" behind her.

Her steps felt lighter, she realized, as she marched her way out of the opera house and down the marble stairs to where the cabs were standing in wait. *Holy Hell…of all people! Tony…* Perhaps this was what she'd been waiting for all along.

Chapter 10

Surely, it was all a dream. An exquisitely beautiful dream, but a dream nonetheless. Tony sat at the dressing table, staring at the door, still dazed by all that had happened that evening.

To perform before a full house and receive such thunderous applause was unbelievable in and of itself, but then to have Bess just saunter through his door like they hadn't been parted for the past fifteen years… He'd known her at once, of course. No longer the eleven-year-old tomboy that she'd been, but there was no mistaking the shape of the girl in the beautiful woman that stood before him.

It occurred to him, after a few moments of staring into space, that he was wasting the twenty minutes she'd given him. "Oh Hell." His clothes were there, of course, but they were his work clothes – his only clothes, truth be told – and the threadbare trousers and patched elbows on his shirt made him cringe inwardly. Dressed as Bess had been, why in the world would she want to be seen with such a ragamuffin as him? Maybe he could send Stig to make his apologies, bow out…

It's Bess, you idiot. His inner voice made him chuckle a little. Of course, it was Bess. She'd never cared about the difference in their stations as children, he could only hope that she had kept that quality as an adult.

His shirt buttoned and his hair combed, he sat down to pull on his worn boots, humming faintly under his breath with a happiness that simply could not be silent.

"You cannot go with her."

The voice came out of nowhere, giving his heart a jolt in surprise. Standing, he turned a slow circle around the room, but he was well and truly alone. He knew that voice, though, as well as any he might hear in this opera house. "Melody?"

"You cannot go with her. I require your presence tonight." Again, the voice came from nowhere and everywhere, filling the small dressing room without a visible source.

"She's an old friend. I'd like a chance to catch up with her." It was becoming more than eerie, having a conversation with an invisible companion. He checked behind the dressing screen, with no luck, and even opened the door to peer outside. It seemed that most of the raucous party had moved on, and the backstage area was quiet. He closed the door again, encasing him in the room with Melody's voice.

"No. You must come with me instead. We have things to do, after this night. Important things."

"Can't it wait until tomorrow?"

"No!" There was a sharpness to her tone that he'd never heard before. For all her firmness in her teaching, she had never gotten short with him before. "You will come now!"

Having exhausted all possible hiding places, he finally had to ask, "Where *are* you?"

A soft hiss of sound came from behind him, and he turned in time to watch the full length mirror on the opposite wall slide open, revealing a stone hallway beyond, and Melody silhouetted by some faint light further down. She was dressed in opera finery this night, a blue damask gown under her normal heavy cloak, her beaded veil still firmly in place. She held her gloved hand out to him imperiously, the bracelet he'd given her dangling against the lace on her cuff.

"What in the world…?" Coming closer, he could see

the pipes framing the now-revealed doorway, carrying the steam that would power the movement of the secret mirror door. "This is how you get in and out. Secret tunnels in the opera house?"

"Yes. No one else remembers them. They are mine to use as I wish. Now come." Again, she gestured for him to take her hand, and after a moment, he placed his in hers. Her grip was cold, even in the glove, and he felt no softness beneath. If she noticed his look of startled surprise, she didn't address it, merely drawing him into the hallway until she could close the door.

"Where are we going?" he asked, as she began leading him down the dimly-lit tunnel.

"I thought perhaps…you would like to see my home. We have much to discuss, you and I." Her steps never faltered on the roughly hewn floor, and Tony noticed when it began to slope downward, leading them into the depths under the opera house.

"Your home, is it far?"

"Beyond the coalworks. It will be a bit of a walk."

"Can we not take a carriage?" To walk all the way to the coalworks, and beyond, at this time of night seemed ludicrous, and more than a bit foolhardy.

"No." And that seemed all the discussion she was willing to entertain on that topic.

At one point, as the floor beneath them became slippery with a trickle of water, Tony nearly lost his footing, but when he attempted to free his hand and regain his balance, her grip tightened, painfully so, and he winced. "You're hurting my hand."

"Oh. My apologies." Instantly, the pressure eased, but she still refused to relinquish his hand back to him. "We are almost out of the tunnels. Your footing will be surer, once we're outside."

Indeed, after one more turn in the labyrinthine tunnels, they found their way blocked by an immense steel grate, tall enough for a man to walk through with little difficulty. Only then did Melody let go of Tony's hand, and turned her attention instead to the obstacle. Before he could offer to help, she took hold of the grating, and lifted it out of its moorings with little to no effort. "Come."

Slowly, he made his way outside into the alleyway, watching in astonishment as she fitted the grate back into its slot. Seeing the look on his face, she seemed to duck her head in embarrassment. "It is not as heavy as it appears." Once more, she reached for his hand, claiming it in a death grip.

They started down the alley, but Tony glanced back at the steel grate more than once. He'd heard the scraping of the iron bolts into the stone wall as she settled it into place. There was no mistaking the immense weight that she had moved without a second thought. *What are you?* He didn't dare ask, not just now, not when she held so tightly to his hand. *Not when I can't get away.*

Immediately, he chided himself for the thought. This was Melody, not some stranger. They had spent nearly every evening together for months now. She had always been slightly odd, but that did not mean that she was dangerous. And to top it all off, he owed her, more than he could ever hope to repay in five lifetimes. *Bess...* Bess would have to forgive him. Surely she of all people would understand.

His course decided, he quickened his pace to keep up with his mysterious escort, her strides moving them both much faster than a comfortable walk. When she glanced at him, he offered her a small smile, and something in her demeanor seemed to relax.

The city was not asleep, even as late turned into early. Especially as they drew nearer to the coalworks, there were more voices, more shadows moving at the far ends of blocks, or hoofbeats and carriages echoing from many streets over. At any time, Tony knew, he could call out to them, raise an alarm, free himself from Melody's vice-like grip. He did not. What would he say, after all? She'd offered him no harm, and helped him more than any single person in his life to that point. And so the pair of them made their way through the city, their pace dictated by the cloaked woman, who seemed not winded at all, though Tony was developing a stitch in his side.

He had also forgotten his coat, and though the day had been lovely, the night had brought with it the last of the winter chill that refused to let go. Nearly running, his strides were so long, he sweated and froze at the same time, the muscles in his jaw aching as he clenched his teeth against shivering. "Is it far?"

"No. Not far now." She tugged him down a street, an old one judging by the state of the cobblestones, with tall houses looming over them, silhouetted against the night's stars.

At one time, it had been a nice neighborhood, perhaps even affluent. The houses still remained, attesting to that, but they had fallen on hard times of late. Shutters dangled by corners, roofs were missing shingles. Fenced gardens had become overgrown, thorny vines reaching out to pluck at the sleeves of passersby. A few of them felt lived in, had obviously had some semblance of maintenance performed, but most looked abandoned, their owners moving on to better lives, ones that weren't constantly choked in the coalworks' soot and ash.

"Here. This is my home." Only then did Melody release his hand, opening the wrought-iron gate that lead up to an equally vacant and decrepit two-story house. The fence itself had been torn down in several places, no doubt the iron stolen and sold to scrap metal yards. What remained was coated in thick rust or entangled with weeds that might have once been rose bushes.

Melody swept down the broken walk like a queen in a throne room, obviously not having a care in the world for the sad state of her affairs. Tony followed - because what else could he do? – but he was very perplexed. This was not at all how he had imagined Melody's life.

She produced a key from her sleeve, unlocking the front door, and stood aside to let him enter. Tony took a few steps into the foyer, and drew up short, unable to suppress the cough that rose at the strong scent of dust and mice. While the building was dark still, it was easy to see the thick layer of gray silt that coated everything, the voluminous cobwebs that waved serenely in every corner. Nothing had been touched in this house in years, if not decades.

There was, however, a very clear path across the floor, leading directly to the stairs, and as Melody slipped past him, he could see that it had been cleared by the sway of her skirts, over how many trips in and out of the house? Never deviating from her course, never straying into the sitting room, or into the unseen back of the home. Always to the stairs, and back.

"Come inside. Please." She waited for him at the bottom riser, one hand resting on the bannister. Slowly, he tried to follow, only to bark his shin painfully on a bench set near the door. He rubbed his leg with a soft hiss, but was satisfied to find it not bleeding. "Oh. I should light a lamp, shouldn't? I use them so rarely myself. Wait there."

It was cold in the house, colder even than the crisp night outside the door. Apparently she didn't stoke the furnaces either, or the quaint fireplace he could see in the drawing room across from him. There were pictures hanging on the wall in there, but they were so covered with cobwebs and dust that their subjects were impossible to discern. Part of him wanted to get up, go brush off the pictures to see what secrets they could impart to him about this cold and dark residence. The other part was gripped with an irrational fear that if he explored outside Melody's well-swept path, something dire would occur.

"Is this better?" Melody's return was preceded by a warm yellow glow, though it flickered as the lamp wick sputtered and spat. How long had it sat unused? "Should I turn it up?" If she turned it up, it would start to smoke and gutter, which anyone over the age of twelve should know. How was it that she did not?

"No, no it's fine. Here, let me carry that for you." Tony met her halfway up the stairs, taking the lamp from her so that she could see to her skirts. The stairs themselves were warped bowed in the middle of every riser as though some immense weight had rested on them for years. The carpet, the color long faded and pattern lost, had nearly been worn through there, only a few frayed threads keeping up the valiant effort of covering the wood beneath. "You live here, Melody?"

"I have always lived here," she assured him as she turned to again climb the staircase.

"Alone?" Surely she was alone now, because he could not imagine someone else allowing the house to fall into such a state of disrepair.

In mid-step, she paused, not even setting her raised foot down for long moments. Her head tilted to the side, as though listening to something he could not hear, and she remained motionless for long enough that he started to become uncomfortable. Finally, she put her boot down on the next step and continued her climb, as though she had never been interrupted. "I have been alone for a very long time."

At the top of the stairs, they turned right, passing by several closed doors without even a pause. One of them, Tony noted, had been damaged somehow, the brass knob crumpled into a lump of useless metal. Only the door at the end of the hallway stood open, leading into what looked to be a lady's bedroom.

Once, it had been decorated in laces and pastel colors. There was a beautiful dressing table with an enormous mirror against one wall, next to a wardrobe with beautifully carved doors. An embroidery hoop stood in the corner, long neglected by the looks of it, and there was an afghan draped over the foot of the bed that had obviously visited by mice many times. In fact the bed itself didn't look to have been used in decades. Tony raised the lamp higher, trying to banish the sad air of abandonment, even as he tried to fathom how a person could live in such circumstances. Even at their poorest, he and his mother had kept a clean home.

Melody paused in the middle of the room and glanced around, as though she'd forgotten why she came in there in the first place. She canted her head back and forth, as though trying to clear her ears of some obstruction.

"Melody?" His voice startled her, judging by how quickly she whirled to look at him. "Are you all right?"

After a moment, she nodded. "Yes. I am well." Seeming to remember where she was, she gestured about the room. "This is where I spend my time when I am not at the opera house."

Tony looked around obediently, but couldn't figure out just what to say that could be both truthful and polite. Finally, he settled on, "This is a large house, for just you all alone. Does no one visit you here? No friends, or family?"

"I –" Again, she paused, frozen in mid-sentence for long moments, before continuing. "No. No one visits me here."

"Why have you brought me here, then?" He moved to set the lamp down on the dressing table, and Melody only turned her head to watch him pass. Even in the lamp light, the veil across her face concealed it completely. He could not fathom her expression.

"I…do not know. I wanted… I thought…" Again, she whirled in a circle, as though trying to catch the shadows that danced around them in the dark room. "I do not *know*."

"Hey…easy there." There was no mistaking the

confusion in her voice, the frustration. "It's all right, I'm happy to come."

"But I do not understand *why…*" Her hands clenched into fists, and Tony reached for one of them, taking it in his.

"Whatever you're feeling, you can tell me, you know. You're my friend, Melody. You can trust me." Under the glove between his hands, her fingers felt stiff, rigid. Cold.

She finally turned her head to look directly at his face. "Do you hear it?"

"Hear what?" He heard nothing, aside from their voices, the sputtering of the ancient lamp, and the faint creak of the garden gate outside as it swayed in the night breeze.

"The child…the little girl… I know she's here, but I cannot find her… I have looked everywhere." Her hand turned in his, suddenly grasping at him with desperation. "Can you find her? Can you make her show herself?" Her grip tightened on his hand to the point where he felt his knuckle bones grind against each other.

"Melody… Melody, you're hurting me!" She didn't respond, only pulling him with her as she once again darted across the room to peer under the empty embroidery frame. "Let go!"

"Damn you, why do you not just show yourself!" That corner deemed clear, she dragged him across the room to the wardrobe, throwing it open to reveal what was once a fine collection of gowns, now faded with age and frequent washings. With her free hand, she frantically sorted through the hangers, one after another, searching for…something. "No…no, she is not here…"

Spots started to dance before his eyes, and he knew his hand was going to be well and truly broken if she didn't release him. "Melody!" Only when he raised his voice could he get her attention, and she finally acknowledged his presence again, staring at his face in a very odd sort of stillness.

"You are hurting me. You have to let go. My hand, Melody, let go of my hand."

Very slowly, her head turned to look down at their joined hands, and after a long moment she released him. Pain rushed in to replace the throbbing numbness, and Tony's head swam. Putting out a hand for balance, he caught the edge of her hood, yanking it down. The beads on her veil caught on the fabric, and came away, tumbling to the floor in a faint rattle of crystal.

Melody gasped and froze in place, but there was no way to conceal her face any longer. Even the wavering lamplight could not keep the secret she had tried to hide.

Tony stared, caught somewhere between amazement and horror. She wasn't a woman. She wasn't human at all. Oh certainly, she had the shape of a human, and someone had put some artistry into her creation, but instead of skin, her face was covered in finely beaten copper, and her eyes were glass orbs, lit from within by tiny bulbs. A thin shield of copper moved down and up once, a precise mechanical blink. Her mouth was a hinged construction, allowing minimal movement, the opening serving merely as a conduit to emit sound from some internal voice mechanism. The dark curls he had so admired were part of a wig, now askew on her head, revealing the seams of the metal plates that made up her skull. One side of her metal head had gone tarnished, fingers of green creeping across the copper like the moss that encroached up the side of the house.

"You're…you're an automaton!" How was it even possible? The dumb machines were incapable of carrying on even the most basic of conversations, let alone mastering complex pieces of music, or…or anything that Melody had done. Automatons that developed even a slight sense of self had their aether cores destroyed immediately. They were never allowed to be…this.

"No! Do not look at me!" She collapsed to the floor,

scrambling to find her veil, trying in vain to keep her face covered with the other hand.

Tony stepped back as her frantic motions threatened to knock him from his feet. "I don't understand. What…what *are* you?"

She did not appear to hear him, only moaning "no, no, no" as she crawled about on all fours, the fabric of her gown ripping under her careless movements. "No! No, you go away! I don't want you here!"

"Melody?"

"Get out! Get out and leave me!" It wasn't him she was screaming at, he realized, but the phantom child she had searched for earlier. "GO AWAY!"

Still, with his hand throbbing and the obviously rogue machine becoming more erratic by the second, Tony took his chance and bolted, nearly falling down the stairs in his haste. Behind him came the sound of shattering glass, and a large boom as something heavy hit the floor. "GET OUT! GET OUT!" The front door slammed as he tore through it, and the garden gate screeched in protest as he nearly tore it from its hinges in his efforts to get out.

Cradling his broken hand against his chest, he ran, through the dark night, expecting at every moment to feel her steel grip clamp down on his shoulder. He ran until his side ached, until his lungs burned and his head was spinning with pain and fatigue. He had no idea where he was going, but still he ran, and her last cries echoed in his ears, spurring him on.

Chapter 11

There were large pieces of the night that she could not recall, which was a very odd sensation. That was her first coherent thought in hours. She remembered arriving at the house with Tony. She recalled the terrible moment where her veil had come away and he had looked upon her face with horror in his eyes. She could still hear the laughter of the mysterious little girl, though it was fainter now. And she knew that the sun had started to peek over the horizon hours ago. What had occurred between those tattered remnants of memory, she could not say with any certainty.

She could, however, see the chaos left behind. Her beautiful damask gown was shredded beyond repair, though she couldn't say how it had happened. The large mirror on the dressing table was in jagged shards all over the floor, and the wardrobe had been smashed to kindling. Some of the gowns within were likewise destroyed, though she thought a few might be salvageable with proper attention.

She plucked one out of the pile of splinters, knowing that she had to make herself presentable once more. She had to return to the opera house, she had to find Tony. If she could just explain to him, perhaps he would understand. And if he did not? She refused to think about that.

It was more difficult, she realized, moving amongst the oblivious crowds on the street. She had been revealed, her face seen, and it made her vulnerable, despite the fact that once again she was sheltered inside the deep hood of her cloak. At every turn, she expected someone to call a warning, to hear footsteps descending on her. They would crush her aether core, she knew. They would destroy all that made her what she was, the very essence of her. That was what they did to machines that learned to think. The deranged ones, the dangerous ones.

No one shouted. No one even looked at her twice. She slipped through the grate into the sewers below the theater, and felt a weight lift from her shoulders. Here, she was safe. Here, where only she knew the secrets.

At the door of her forgotten storeroom, she stood listening for a very long time. There were sounds on the other side, people passing to and fro in their daily duties. They had nothing to do with her, certainly, but the very thought of their presence held her frozen in fear. Had he told them? Did they know?

It finally occurred to her that her hesitation was reaching ridiculous proportions. She could not remain in the storeroom for eternity. Waiting for a clear moment, she slipped through the door and made her way through the forgotten passages toward Gilbert's office. *No. Not Gilbert's any longer. The new men, their office now. What were their names?* She had written a note, introducing herself, and offering a few helpful tips on the current production. It must be delivered. After that, she would search for Tony. Where in the world had he gone?

The tunnel she traversed passed behind the wall of the director's office, a small vent near the top positioned perfectly so that a piece of paper slipped through the slats would tumble gracefully onto the desk. There was no one in the office, but her missive, signed with a simple quarter-note, would be found soon enough. She retreated again, intending to find a way into the workshop. Surely, Tony would have returned there. He had no other dwelling, after all.

There was a door that should have opened into the catwalks above the stage, and from there she could have made her way into the rafters above the workshop. To her great surprise, however, she found it locked. Perplexed, she pondered the knob. It would be nothing to break it, of course, her strength could easily overcome the basic little mechanism. But the damage would provide evidence that *some*one had been here. And who, she wondered, would lock the door? Who even used it, besides her?

Even as she debated her options, something moved on the other side of the door, and the lock rattled as someone inserted a key. Glancing around, she realized there was nowhere to hide in this hallway, no concealing shadows to lose herself in. She had no option but to turn and flee, only her great speed allowing her to round the far corner just as the door swung open.

Yellow lamplight flooded the hallway, and she edged back away from it as though the light itself could harm her. "Here, pretty lady... I know you're in here... Saw the note, I did..."

Stig. The blond, cheerful stagehand. Curse him. He was not in pursuit of a rogue automaton, she knew, but hunting his lady ghost as he often did. He had set small traps for her before, though they had been so easily avoided as to be laughable. Trays of powder for her to walk through and leave prints. Strings tied across walkways that would ring small bells if disturbed. Small things. Petty things. But this time... This time, he'd found one of her doors, guessed at one of her escapes.

The booted footsteps advanced down the hallway, one slow thump at a time, and she withdrew from the growing circle of light. *Please stop. Please stop.* She found herself repeating it over and over, and wondered oddly if this was what humans did when they prayed. She prayed for Stig to stop, for him to turn around. She did not want to do what she must, if he caught her.

She pressed herself against the wall, hearing his breath as he halted not two feet from her. He was still, too, listening for her to make a sound. If she had been a living, breathing creature, she would have given herself away easily, and even confident in her silence, she started to worry that he would hear the whirring of the gears inside her chest, the very power that animated her form. She could not stop that motion any more than a human could have stilled their heartbeat. The longer they stood there, frozen in silence, the louder the sounds of her mechanics seemed to her, until it nearly thundered inside her skull. How could he not hear it, only inches away?

Finally, Stig sighed, and the circle of light shrank as he retreated. "Don't worry, pretty lady. We'll see each other soon enough." The door at the end of the hallway shut, and locked, but she remained pressed against the wall for nearly half an hour after that, too afraid that he would come back the moment she dared to move.

There would be no searching for Tony in the workshop, she realized. She could not get close enough without the persistent little Swede dogging her every step. Nor could she hope to catch him outside the opera house. He seldom left, and even if he did, the danger of discovery was too great. She could not risk approaching him when he could call out to others, raise the alarm. Her only recourse would be to wait until nightfall, and try to get to him through the dressing room mirror passage. It would be the only time she could catch him alone.

Until then, she would find a place in the theater to hide, and wait out the day.

Passing near one of the places where the sound carried from all corners of the theater, she paused, listening to the agitated male voices coming from the lobby.

"*Her* opera house! *Hers*! Of all the gall, Fred!" Ah, that would be the dark one then, Mr. Thomas. "And whoever heard of a ghost that writes?"

"She seems rather adamant about her demands, Reg. And I checked the records, they really have always left box seven open for her. They don't sell those tickets."

A snort echoed. "We've a full house, and the mayor wants to attend tonight. He will by God have that box."

They wouldn't dare! That was her box, the only one she could reach without being seen!

"And the rest? She obviously expects us to have Krol performing again."

"Well, as he has now disappeared as well, that's going to be a bit difficult. At this rate, you and I are going to wind up on that stage, singing for pennies."

Disappeared? He hadn't returned to the theater? Now she was truly concerned. Something had happened last night, as evidenced by the destruction in her room. Had…had something happened to Tony? *"Melody…you're hurting me!"* Tony's voice came back to her, real enough that she looked about her secret hallway, expecting to see him standing near. But no, he was no more there than the phantom child that dogged her every step now. *What have I done?*

A crash came from the lobby, the French doors slamming open with force.

"Ah, Mr. LeClerc! So glad to see you have returned!"

"Indeed! You're looking well today!"

Oh blast and damn. She had hoped Simon was well and truly gone.

"Would one of you be so kind as to explain *this*?" The sound of paper rattling.

"Oh yes, the Times' review. Wasn't it rather splendid?"

"Anton Krol? Who in the hell is Anton Krol, and why was he singing my role?" She could envision the red flush creeping up Simon's neck into his face, and she was a bit sorry she was not positioned to actually see it.

"Krol… Well, he was a stagehand, has been for months as I understand, but he has quite an amazing voice and—"

"A stagehand?! You replaced me with a stagehand?! Are you out of your minds?" He paced the length of the lobby, she could hear his fine leather shoes squeaking on the floor. "Chalmers was a daft fool, but at least he had some idea of how to run a theater. You two are jokes! Absolute jokes!"

"Now Simon, it was just a temporary solution..." Ah, the little soprano, Caroline. Always at LeClerc's heels, until she thought he wasn't looking, and then she trailed a harem of suitors behind her like some bright celestial body passing through the atmosphere.

"Bah! These two idiots are going to run this place into the ground. Obviously, I will need to return, even at the risk of my own life. This is what one does for their art."

The two new managers set up such a chorus of clucking and gratuitous bowing and scraping that she thought she might be nauseated, if she were capable of such. And over that, a feeling of heat settled somewhere behind her eyes, a faint sheen of red tainting the faint light in the hallway. They were going to put Simon back up on that stage, despite her orders to the direct contrary. They were going to give away her box seat. They obviously did not understand what she was capable of, if disobeyed.

Again, the front doors opened and closed, quietly this time, and whoever it was nearly made it into the back hallways before they were spotted.

"Ah! Mr. Krol! Nice of you to return, finally."

Tony! Tony had returned! A sense of relief ran through her every gear and cog, to know that she hadn't harmed him after all.

"Mr. Strang, Mr. Thomas. My apologies. Something came up that required my attention."

Simon snorted then, she would know that sound anywhere. "Brawling like a coalworks rowdy, no doubt?"

"Is it broken?" Mr. Strang, at least, sounded concerned. But what was broken?

"No, just badly bruised. I'll be fine."

"You'll have to have both hands to work the drop ropes,

you know." Simon's pronouncement was met with long moments of awkward silence, before Tony finally replied.

"If that is where the managers need me to be."

"Well, hang on there, Krol, we need to talk about this matter of you just disappearing last night, and most of today I might add…"

This was the moment, she realized. This is when he would tell them, and then they would hunt for her. Before her fate could be sealed, however, the door opened and closed once more, and a female voice interrupted the conversation.

"Tony! Thank God, I got worried about you."

"Bess!" There was some startled murmuring that she couldn't quite catch, and then Tony spoke again. "Gentlemen, this is Elisabeth Barstow, a very old friend of mine. Bess, this is Mr. Thomas, and Mr. Strang, the new owners, and Mr. LeClerc, and Miss Smythe, our stars."

They made the general "pleased to meet you noises", no doubt bowing and kissing hands and such that humans did.

"Miss Barstow? Not Abner Barstow's daughter, by any chance? I'd thought you were living abroad, by all the tales. A globe-trotting adventurer, or some such."

"Yes sir. I've only been back in the city for a few months. I was fortunate enough to be attending the opera last night, and realized that your new tenor was not a new face to me at all. My thanks for enabling me to renew my acquaintance with Tony. It has been years since we've seen each other."

Her. It was her, the woman from last night. That much she remembered, the golden woman in the pale gown. The one that Tony was going to meet.

"Well we are pleased that you enjoyed the performance, Miss Barstow. We were just thanking Mr. Krol here for being able to step into a last minute role, as Mr. LeClerc was under the weather."

"But feeling just fine for this evening's performance, I

assure you."   There was a smirk in Simon's voice, satisfaction coating his words with machine oil.

"Mmhm. Mr…Strang, was it? Perhaps another time, I could speak to you about making a donation to the opera house. Knowing that Tony is employed here, I'd like to contribute something myself. And my mother always did love the arts."

"Oh! Oh of course, Miss Barstow, any time you wish to discuss it."

"I'll make an appointment then. Now, if you will all excuse me, I'd like to speak to Tony for a moment."

"Oh yes, yes of course…" Footsteps retreated, voices in hushed conversations.

Caroline, obviously unaware that her voice carried, whispered to Simon, "What on earth is she *wearing*?"

"Breeding can only account for so much, my dear." Then they passed beyond the area that could be heard from that particular hiding place.

Still in the lobby, Tony started, "Bess…"

"What happened to you last night? Dear God, Tony, your hand! Have you had that looked at?"

"Jack patched me up, it's nothing. Just bruised."

"It looks terrible."

"Bess, look, about last night…"

"I waited for you."

"I know. I… Something came up and I couldn't get away. I… I hope you're not angry with me."

She sighed. "Well… I was, you know. Angry, and hurt. But after seeing that lot of popinjays you work for, and with, I have a feeling that you vanishing had more to do with the politics of this place than any disdain you held for me."

Again, this is where he would betray her, confess her existence, and then the hunt would be on. Instead, he let the chance pass. Again.

"Forgive me?"

"Of course. But you owe me dinner. And now it's your treat."

Tony chuckled quietly. "All right. I'll see what I can do."

"Here. This is where I'm staying. Susan is a dear friend of mine from college, and I know she'd love to meet you, so come by any time." She started to depart, her steps striding confidently toward the doors. "And don't you stand me up again, Anton Krol. I carry a gun, and I know how to use it."

At that, he outright laughed. "Yes ma'am. So noted."

The doors closed, and Tony's steps carried him toward the workshop, until she could hear them no longer.

No. No, this was not how it was supposed to be happening. She stayed in her listening post for a long while, the events clicking through the gears of her mind.

Simon was not supposed to be singing. The pompous ass was not supposed to be in her opera house at all. Tony was not supposed to be hauling set pieces and working the drops. He had far better things ahead of him than that. The managers were supposed to be listening to her advice, as Gilbert had always done, and that little blond tart was not supposed to be distracting Tony from his calling.

This was all going so very wrong, and she knew she had to correct things before they got too far off course. Obviously, notes were not going to be enough. Now, she would have to take action.

Chapter 12

Bess had every intention of going home after seeing that Tony was indeed all right. But, as she stood on the steps of the opera house, watching the daytime crowds wander about on their mundane tasks, she realized that as much as she adored Susan and her family, she just couldn't stand to be shut in that house any longer. More than that, she couldn't bring herself to walk away from Tony again. What if he disappeared again? How many more years would go by?

Turning on her heel, she headed back inside, striding through the theater as though she owned the place. Not one person thought to stop her, though she did get several startled looks from the maids as she passed through. A result, she knew, of wearing trousers and boots instead of a more appropriate dress. At least she wasn't wearing her Colt. And the Derringer was tucked into the inner pocket of her vest, where no one could see and panic.

The performers barely glanced at her as she proceeded backstage, more interested in their costume fittings and rehearsing. She kept an eye out, peering up into the catwalks above the stage, but when she was unable to locate Tony, she continued deeper into the theater, easily finding the immense workshop at the very back. It was there that she located her friend, surrounded by his coworkers as they examined his injured hand.

"Damn, man. It's swole up like a sausage." A stocky blond man shook his head with a disapproving tsk. "What in the nine hells did you *do*?"

"It's fine, really. Jack's sure it's not broken, and I can still move my fingers. At least it's not my strong hand." Tony demonstrated, wiggling the fingers of his left hand with a cautious wince. Through his twitching fingers, he finally spotted her, standing at the edge of the shelves. "Bess!"

The men there turned as one, and she saw the grins spreading on every face. Tony would not soon live this down. "Am I interrupting anything?"

Tony hopped down off the table. "No, no, not at all. Come in. Bess, this is Stig, and Big and Little, and the kid back there is Franco. Guys, this is Bess, a very old friend."

The stocky blond man, Stig, she recognized from outside the dressing room the previous night. And the pair of obvious brothers, Big and Little, just made her smile at the sheer ridiculousness of their chosen monikers, seeing as how Big was barely her height, and Little towered over even Tony. The boy in the back waved to her shyly, and immediately blushed bright red when she smiled at him in return. "It's a pleasure to meet you all."

"What are you doing back here? I thought you'd gone."

"Well, I was going to." She glanced around, but the stagehands obviously had no intention of departing so they could have a private discussion. Oh well, so be it. "Then I thought that if I let you get away with the promise of 'another time', you'd be just as likely to disappear on me again, so I returned. I thought we would go to lunch now."

Tony blinked, and his cheeks colored faintly pink as the men around him chuckled. "I… I've been gone all day, Bess, I kind of need to work before tonight's show."

"Nonsense." Another man appeared from the rows and rows of looming shelves, lugging a plaster cast of an urn with him. "You need to rest that hand if you want to be able to run the ropes tonight."

"But Jack…"

"No 'but Jack'. Go on, go." The man set his burden

down on the table, and offered his hand to Bess. "Jack Kelly, ma'am, stage manager."

She shook it, pleased to note that he offered a good strong grip even though she was a woman. "Bess Barstow. A genuine pleasure."

Tony sighed. "Jack, it's not fair if I go—"

"I decide what's fair. And the guys don't mind none, do you fellas?"

A chorus of negatives surrounded them, and suddenly the stagehands remembered that they too had duties to attend to, scattering to the far corners of the workshop. Jack chuckled and clapped Tony on the shoulder. "Go on, man. As I understand it, the two of you have years of catching up to do." He winked at Tony when he thought Bess couldn't see, and she hid her smile in a polite little cough.

"If you say so, sir." Tony shrugged his shoulders at Bess. "I suppose I'm all yours. Where did you want to go?"

Bess pursed her lips as she thought for a moment. She'd told him it would be his treat, mostly as a teasing comment, but she knew that he couldn't possibly be making a good wage at what he was doing. She also knew that if she took it back and insisted on paying, she'd hurt his pride. "Hm. You know, the weather's nice again today, and there's a lovely little café down by the lake. We could take a cab down there and be back in time to get ready for tonight. If that's all right with Mr. Kelly."

Jack waved his hand dismissively. "I said go!"

Tony chuckled and offered her his arm, which she took while being mindful of his injured hand. It truly did look terrible, all swollen and bruised in mottled shades of black and purple, going yellow already around a few of the edges. She cast a concerned look at him again, but he shrugged sheepishly, offering no explanation.

They got more attention, passing back through the

theater together, more than one person stopping to see the woman on the stagehand's arm. The whispers sprung up behind them like escaping steam, and Bess could only chuckle. "Theater folk. They would wither away without their little scandals and intrigues."

"It's the truth." Tony looked her up and down, and raised a brow. "Which, I think, was your purpose today?"

She sniffed. "I wear them because they're easier to get around in than corsets and hoop skirts. Men don't realize that they seem to have cornered the market in comfortable fashion."

"Of course we do. That's why we do it." He grinned, and she swatted his shoulder, the two of them dissolving into laughter as they stepped outside into the sunlight.

It was easy to hail a cab at this time of day, and the ride down to the lake shore was pleasant on this early spring day. More than once, though, she caught Tony staring off into space, a furrow between his dark brows. She reached over and touched his arm lightly, and he almost flinched. "Hey. You want to tell me what's going on in that busy head of yours?"

With a faint smile, he shook his head. "No. No, I really don't."

At their destination, he did her the courtesy of *not* offering her a hand down from the carriage, and she leapt lightly down of her own accord, tipping the driver who very wisely said nothing. "Come on, the café is just over here. Susan says they have lovely pastries."

"Pastries for lunch? You haven't changed a bit."

She cast him a wry grin. "Did you expect me to?" She marched past him, leaving him to trail along behind her, and heard him say "No…no I didn't."

The café had tables all along the boardwalk that lined the shore of Lake St. Clair, affording a lovely view of those adventurous souls who had already taken their boats out of dry dock for the season. Everything from small single-mast sailboats to tiny punts with oars could be seen tracking to and fro across the lake's pristine surface. The larger ships, of course, would be found on Lake Erie, to the south, but for a smaller body of water, the little pleasure crafts were more than sufficient. The blue sky's reflection was so perfect on the water that it seemed the boats were tacking through the clouds themselves.

Bess sighed contentedly as she took a seat at one of the empty tables. "I always loved this lake. Swimming in it was like flying."

"A bit cold for swimming just now, I would think."

"Well, maybe later when the summer heat comes on."

Tony raised a brow at her. "I have difficulty picturing you wearing a swim dress and splashing about in the shallows with all the other proper ladies."

"True. I'd rather just wear nothing at all." She was rewarded with a dark blush in his cheeks, and laughed. "Oh Hell, Tony. We skinny-dipped together how often, when we were children?"

"We were children, Bess. That was a long time ago." He was saved by the arrival of the waiter, who pretended not to goggle at Bess's unconventional attire. "Um…coffee for me, and a raspberry Danish, if you have one. Bess?"

"Coffee for me as well, and cinnamon muffin." The man took down their order and departed without a word. "So, Anton Krol, who I haven't seen in nearly fifteen years. What has your life been?"

Tony chuckled. "Damn, Bess. You ask all the easy questions first, don't you?"

"It's what I do." She settled back in her chair, propping her boots up on the one next to her. "Seriously. What have you been about, all these years?"

"Nothing as interesting as you, I fear." There was a small pause as their order was delivered, and then he shook his head to find himself holding the delicate china cup in his work-roughened hand. "We stayed on the estate, you know, Mother was an assistant to Mrs. Barstow up until… I'm sorry about your mother, Bess. I'm sorry I couldn't be at the funeral."

"I know. It was a small affair, as she wanted. There were many people who weren't there." Even in death, Josephine Barstow had been determined to keep her daughter away from the hired help's son. Bess knew that now, even if she hadn't realized it at the time.

"After that, I worked at odd jobs around town, doing handyman work and the like. I sang at church on Sundays. That was rather the sum total of my activities."

"I'm surprised. I expected to come home and find you married with a passel of children by now." She tilted her head curiously. "I hear no mention of any courting in this tale of yours."

Again, his cheeks colored. "No, no courting. Newport is small, if you remember, and everyone knows everyone… After growing up there for so many years, they all felt like sisters, you know?" He toyed with his coffee cup. "Not that I didn't have offers, mind you… Emily Cooper would have gladly skinny-dipped with me if I'd have just given the nod… Of course, she'd have gone with anyone who nodded, so I'm not sure that was a glowing recommendation."

Bess chuckled, breaking off pieces of her muffin to pop into her mouth. "Have you looked at yourself in the mirror, Tony? I'm quite certain that there was quite a bit of glowing going on, with you around."

He waved her off, trying to pretend he wasn't blushing again. "Enough of me. Your life has to have been much more interesting than mine in the intervening years. Egypt, I think I heard? Africa? Tomb raiders and gunfights?"

"All highly exaggerated, I assure you. Though, I have to admit, I did love Egypt, and I miss it very much. See this coffee? It's like water compared to what I had in Cairo.

The coffee there is thick, and spiced, and sticks to your ribs. Puts hair on your chest!"

"I shudder to think of you with a hairy chest." He tilted his head at her, eyes thoughtful. "So why did you come back? Or rather…why have you stayed this long? You said you've been in Detroit for months now."

"I don't know," she admitted. "I mean, I know why I came back. I needed to be out of Egypt, and Susan had a new baby, and… You'll have to meet her, Tony, she's truly my dearest friend. She was my friend when I sorely needed one, after they shipped me off to school. But as to why I've stayed… I hadn't figured that out until just recently. I told Susan that I felt like I was waiting for something, but I didn't know what."

"And then what happened?"

"And then we went to the opera." She smiled. "And I saw you."

He blinked at her, then looked down at his Danish again. After a few moments of silence, he chuckled. "You know… After knowing you as well as I did, you think I'd be more accustomed to how blunt you are."

"I prefer to think of it as being efficient with my time." Dropping her feet to the ground again, she leaned both elbows on the table. "Am I pursuing something futile? You haven't thought of me, in all these years?"

"God, Bess…" His laugh was faintly strangled. "With your name in every paper in the county, how could I not think of you? It was all I had of you, after you were sent away. Other people's stories." With a sigh, he leaned forward as well and rested his good hand atop hers. "I used to think it was my fault, you know. That you were sent away."

"Why on earth would you think that? I was the one that fell out of the blasted tree."

"Because that day as I carried you back to the house, and you had your arms wrapped around my neck and your face buried in my shoulder, trying your damnedest not to cry… That was the first time that I realized how much I wanted to keep you safe, to take care of you forever. I thought… I thought it must have shown on my face, that your mother must have known, even though I was too young yet to really understand. I was convinced it was my fault.”

He was right, she realized. That was the day, even with her ankle hurting to all blazes, that she first knew what it was to feel safe in a man's arms. Even if that man was a twelve-year-old boy, and she herself only eleven. “I don't know that you were wrong, but it wasn't entirely you. We were both of that age where things were going to start changing between us. Mother knew that. She was never going to let that happen.”

Turning her hand, she laced her fingers through his, feeling the work-roughened callouses against her skin. “I was angry with her for a very, very long time after that. But, age brings perspective, I suppose. She was trying, in her own way, to make sure that I would be happy. She loved my father very much, you know. In her mind, the only way I could possibly be happy was to live the same life she had, with balls and proper suitors who had appropriate careers. Children and needlepoint and maybe a small garden. She didn't understand that it wasn't the life I wanted, and…oh, I hated her for that, for a long time. I spent a lot of years just…angry at the world for not letting me be me.”

“I was angry for a long time, too,” Tony murmured. “I thought I'd broken my promise.”

“What promise?” Bess tilted her head curiously.

“Don't you remember? Together, or not at all?” A ghost of a smile crossed his face, though his eyes were focused on their joined hands as if he'd never seen such a thing in his life. “We swore with blood from pricked fingers, solemnly, that no matter what happened, we would go together or not at all. I didn't get to keep that promise, once you were sent away."

Bess chuckled. "We were children, Tony. You can't expect to keep promises from childhood."

"No, those are the promises that *should* be kept. Those are the ones we actually mean. Every child believes that they will be able to keep the promises that they make. Only as adults do we learn the folly of that."

"I never blamed you for it. It wasn't like we had any control over our own lives, back then."

"And now? Here we are, two grown adults who don't really know each other, despite what old memories we might share. The wealthy steel heiress, Elisabeth Barstow, and the poor stagehand, Anton Krol."

"The debut tenor at the world-renowned Detroit opera, Anton Krol," she corrected, and he shook his head.

"You and I both know that was a one-time fluke. I give it two weeks before Simon finds a way to have me fired. And then…" Something dark crossed his face, something she couldn't quite define. Despite the warmth of the day, his hand grew cold in her grip, and he shivered slightly.

"I don't care if you're a singer, or a stagehand, or if you sell candied sweets from a cart on the street. In fact, the candied sweets might be an asset." She squeezed his hand, trying to get a smile out of him, but at best what flickered through his eyes was a pale imitation of one. "I was so very fond of Anton Krol, the boy. I want the chance to get to know Anton Krol, the man. Will you at least give me that, before you vanish again?"

His eyes came up at that, surveying the crowd around them. Whatever he saw, some of the color left his face and he quickly extracted his hand from hers. When she turned to look, all she could see was a woman passing nearby in a dark cloak, though the stranger was fully engaged in talking to her escort and didn't notice them at all. Bess turned back to Tony, frowning a little. "Is there someone else?"

"I…no. Not like you're thinking. I have this…teacher. Singing teacher. She is…very demanding of my time. I worry that things will not…be as easy as you'd like."

"Who is this teacher?"

He shook his head with a snort of bitter laughter. "I thought I knew. I really did." He ran a hand over his face, scratching at the faint stubble on his cheeks. "Bess… Have you ever felt like you were walking through a dream, one that was at turns amazing and then terrifying to the very core of your being? Only then you realize that it's not a dream at all, it is life, and there is no waking up from it?"

"No. I can't say that I have." She frowned. "Tony, if you're in some kind of trouble… I can help. I still have connections, I have funds…"

"No. Not that kind of trouble." He smiled, finally, but it was pasted on, a shadow of his usual self. That thought made her chuckle inwardly. As if she knew what was usual for him, after all this time. "Don't worry about it. It'll all come out in the wash, as Mother used to say." The bell on the church nearby tolled the hour, followed by a rolling wave of pealing across the city. "I should go. No matter what Jack said, they need me before tonight. We've got some props to repair and a few…things."

"All right, well after tonight's performance, I want to take you out for our proper dinner. Wonderful pastries notwithstanding, this is hardly a decent meal. Please?"

After a moment, he relented, nodding his head. "As you wish. I'll meet you out front."

"Oh Hell no. You tried that last time, and I got stuck with a cab for one. I'll come backstage and find you myself." She gave him a grin to show there were no hard feelings, but for a moment, she thought he might balk again.

"All right. I'll get free as quickly as I can." He stood, tossing down a few coins for their meal. "I'll walk back, so you can head on to wherever you need to be next."

"I'll see you tonight." She watched him walk away, his hands in the pockets of his coat, an odd hunch to his shoulders as though he expected to be hit at any moment.

Before he rounded the corner of the building, he turned to look at her once more. "Bess, if I haven't said it yet… I am so *very* glad to see you again."

"And I you." There was something oddly final about that, and for one moment, she thought about hopping to her feet and jogging after him. But no, she let the urge pass, afraid to press him any further. There was something going on with her childhood companion, something he was reluctant to tell even her. Justly, no doubt, considering that they truly didn't know each other any longer. Perhaps she was being presumptuous, expecting them to simply resume their friendship where it had ended fifteen years ago.

"Well, Mother didn't call you a stubborn horse's arse for nothing, did she?" Bess mused aloud, and chuckled to see a few startled looks from the patrons nearby. *You can play coy all you want, Anton Krol, but I am not some fainting violet, used to being trampled underfoot.* She fully intended to be at the opera that night, and he would come out to dinner with her if she had to rope and hogtie him herself. That image amused her all the way home.

Chapter 13

It was difficult, remaining motionless for hours on end. It should not have been. She had no muscles to cramp, no need to relieve herself. But in the small closet where she'd chosen to take shelter, there was nothing to focus on, save the small sliver of light that surrounded the ill-fitting door. Nothing to distract her from the thoughts that worked round and round through the gears of her mind until she was certain she'd wear the teeth smooth.

But at least, alone with her thoughts, she had time to plan.

It had been very clear from the discussion in the lobby that Simon would be singing tonight, unless she could find a way to stop him. The simplest way, of course, would be to approach him from behind and snap his neck. She was fairly certain, however, that such an act would cause some concern amongst the rest of the company, and they might cancel the show, so it wasn't a viable option. She needed him ill, not dead.

No doubt, there were plenty of supplies in the theater's workshop that she could pilfer in order to effect such a result. Once the orchestra started warming up, all of the cast and crew would be onstage, ready for their cues, and she would once again be free to roam the recesses of the opera house. She could fetch the needed items then. Simon may begin the performance, but he would not be finishing it.

The second matter that would need dealing with would be box seven. If the new owners truly had the gall to give her seat away, she would ensure that no one would ever want to sit there again. Being a "ghost" had its advantages, after all, and with Stig captive to his duties in the riggings above the stage, there would be no one stalking her every move.

And the third matter… There was a third matter, was there not? The thought flitted in and out of her mind like a well-oiled spring gone astray. A golden spring… A golden curl of hair… Ah yes. This Bess. This strange woman who held some sway over Tony. It could not be allowed, of course. Perhaps she could be frightened away too, and if not… Well, there were more final ways to remove obstructions.

It did occur to her, at some point during the day, that perhaps she should be concerned about her own willingness to so easily end a human life. *I protected, once, did I not?* But she couldn't remember when, or who. Only the faintest of urges was there, the need to prevent harm to…someone. *Tony, then. I will protect Tony.* In the tight little closet, where there was no space save for herself and a few tattered mops, a little girl giggled.

"Go away," she whispered to herself, daring that much noise even in her concealment. "Leave me in peace." Perhaps the phantom child heard her, because it made no further sound.

She did have some concern that, in her confinement, she would not be able to hear the strains of the orchestra as they began to tune their instruments, but her auditory receptors were as keen as always. It was the high pitch of the flutes that reached her, buzzing uncomfortably behind her jaw, but on this occasion she didn't mind.

It was time.

The trip to the workshop was swiftly accomplished and proved fruitful. She found exactly what she needed, and deposited it somewhere that Simon would be certain to discover it in a most unpleasant fashion.

Marking her time by the orchestra's place in their warm-ups, she waited just behind the servants' stairs, and when the audience began applauding as the curtains parted, she used the noise to cover her ascent, not to the viewing boxes, but to the storage level above them. There were places there, like in the rest of the building, where one could hear…and be heard. This particular one she had discovered by accident one night while attending the opera, only after two of the company had decided to have a rather noisy tryst in the storage room above. She was fairly certain that such activities were not supposed to be overheard by others, but she had learned much that night.

It took her a few moments of moving about the dusty alcove before she could find the precise location where the sound would carry. For a few moments, she stopped to listen to the chorus as they sang out their introductions, but once Simon's voice echoed from the stage, she forced herself back to her purpose. She wanted to be in her box when things went wrong for him. She wanted to see.

In the box below, she could hear several people shuffling their programs, fidgeting with their opera glasses, rustling their skirts, and whispering amongst themselves. Noisy creatures, humans. How they could hear the opera itself over all their own racket, she would never understand.

"Excuse me." Her voice bounced off the bare wooden walls around her, but she knew that down below, it sounded perfectly clear to those in her box. All sounds of motion stopped, and then the murmurs began as they tried to find the speaker. "I believe you are in my seat."

"Who is that?"

"I don't know, I can't find anyone…"

"Ellis, is that you? It's not funny."

She waited for a few moments, until it became clear that they were not going to depart, and then tried again. "I said, you are in my seat. Could you please depart?" She was being polite, was she not? They worried so about manners and conduct.

"I'm getting the manager, this is ridiculous."

"John, it's nothing, just stay…"

"If this is some kind of prank, I am hardly amused."

They fussed amongst themselves for long moments, their voices carrying well beyond their own box now, and no doubt disturbing the other patrons. *How rude.* She was offended, she decided. Offended that they refused to relinquish her rightful seat, and that they were ruining the production for others.

"I said, GET OUT!" Certainly, she said it louder than she'd intended, but it fell during a lull in the music, and echoed around the confines of the little alcove, amplifying her irritation. To her great satisfaction, that exclamation finally earned her several startled cries from below, and the sounds of thumping feet as the occupants fled.

There. That was better, and just in time for her to see most of the first act. She had only to wait out the inevitable investigation that would ensue after the opera patrons made their complaints to the management.

As she'd imagined, it was a short time before she heard voices below again.

"I assure you sir, there's no one here. Look." Mr. Thomas, she thought, attending to his duties as owner.

"I don't give a tinker's damn if there's anyone there, I want a different box, or my money back."

The sounds of placation died away as the irate patron was escorted back downstairs, and only then did she leave her tiny alcove to take her seat in the now-empty box. Of course, there was the chance that someone would come again to investigate, but she knew just where to sit that a cursory glance from the doorway would not reveal her, wrapped in her dark cloak and still as death in the shadows. She had been at this for years, after all, and she was not so easily discovered.

Stig would not stop at cursory. Well, no, she knew that,

but he was working the catwalks above the stage, with the rest of the crew. He wouldn't have time to chase her until much later.

Settling into her customary place, she concentrated on the drama unfolding upon stage. Simon's maharajah was about to discover the truth of his birth, that he was indeed royalty… And his change in station was signified by the donning of a glorious new turban, one bedecked with jewels and gold chains. And a small gift from an unexpected patron.

Nothing happened immediately, as she'd expected. The opera went on, the chorus dancing and singing their way around the newly crowned Simon. It was only upon his next aria that it became apparent that something was distracting him.

It was a quaver in his voice at first, which grew into an odd tick to his shoulder as he tried to alleviate some discomfort while remaining in character. At the part of the choreography where the crowd was supposed to swell around him, he frantically tried to adjust the turban on his head before he was revealed again. That effort only made things worse, as he began to flex and wring his hands at his sides, willing away whatever sensation he was feeling.

This was satisfaction, she decided. If she were capable of smiling, she thought she might even try a smirk. The situation seemed to call for it.

Finally, even Simon's years of training could not override the agony he found himself in, and with a yell, he ripped the jeweled turban off his head and threw it across the stage, then proceeded to savage his own head with his fingernails, scratching like he would dig right through his skull. The orchestra stuttered to a stop, and the dancers finally faltered as well, unsure what to do.

Perhaps realizing at last that he was in full view of the audience, Simon rushed off stage, cursing loud enough to be heard in the lobby.

"Curtain! Close the curtain!" That was Mr. Strang's voice, rushing onto the apron from the wings as the velvet curtain slowly closed. The ruddy-haired man's face was almost as red as the curtains behind him. "Ladies and gentlemen, our apologies. There has been a small mishap… Um… The opera will continue in approximately ten minutes, where the role of the maharajah will be played by Anton Krol. Until that time, please enjoy the ballet from Act Three."

"What?!" That from the maestro, who had obviously not been informed of the change in plans, and then the orchestra scrambled to bring forward the proper music, even as the curtain opened on a frantically preparing cast.

The dancers were only half dressed in the correct costumes, the set pieces drifted in haphazardly as the stage crew struggled to make the scene change on short notice and off schedule.

Hm. Not *quite* what she'd intended, but as long as Tony got his place on stage… Perhaps she should check on him, make certain that his preparations were not being hindered. And making sure that he did *not* put on Simon's turban, no matter what.

From the servants' stairs, she made her way into the catwalks above the stage. There were several levels of them, and the crew should all be on the ones directly above the stage, unlikely to encounter her passing above them.

It was easy to locate Simon, who was near the dressing rooms, ranting at full voice. "Sabotage! Outright assault! I want the constable! I want him fired! Her too! She is in collusion!" Mr. Thomas and Mr. Strang tried to soothe their distraught star, even as the costume mistress stood with her face in her hands, weeping, and Tony tried to shed his normal clothes for his own maharajah costume.

"Mr. LeClerc, Krol wasn't able to tamper with your costuming. Mr. Kelly says that if anyone else had touched it, the ground glass would have affected them too, and no one else is itching."

"Well *someone* put it there! It didn't just *fall* in accidentally!" Angry welts were raising on his cheeks and shoulders where he'd been scratching, and his hands were already swelling and red.

Yes, she should like to learn to smirk. There were always broken pieces of glass lying about, and they were generally thrown in the bin in the workshop. It was nothing for one of her strength to take some of the shards and pulverize them into powder. Laced into the folds of the turban, the tiny granules would work into every crevice, every crease of skin, and the itching would drive one mad.

"The first person who says ghost is sacked!" Mr. Thomas warned the onlooking crew, who scattered immediately. "Krol, get on stage. We'll have to deal with the rest of this later."

"Yes sir." Tony dashed for the stage, but before she could move to follow him, the catwalk she stood upon shuddered.

Curiously, she turned, and was horrified to see Stig step onto the far end. Granted, he was across the stage from her, but the fact that he'd ascended to this level meant only one thing. He had no reason to be up there, save that he was looking for her.

She could freeze, motionless, and hope that he gave up, but if he crossed the walkway, he would come face-to-face with her. And if she moved, it was very likely that the simple motion of her cloak would draw his attention. She was trapped.

Move it was, then, because she could not be seen. Not now. Not when everything was starting to proceed as planned. Whirling, she grabbed for a nearby rope, one that she knew would support her weight, and slid down it to the catwalk below. Not easily accomplished in her gown and cloak, but she hadn't time for grace. She landed with a thump that was lost in the low thrum of the bass from the orchestra, and the dancers didn't notice if dust sifted down onto their performance. She froze there, waiting for long moments, to see if she was followed.

Just as she was about to count herself fortunate, a blond head poked over the edge of the walkway above, and Stig grinned, looking directly at her. "There you are."

No. Oh no. He hadn't seen her face yet, she knew that much, and she could not afford to let him catch her. Moving as fast as she dared on the rickety boards, she made for the far side of the stage and the stairs. The catwalk jerked as weight landed behind her, and she knew that Stig had slid down the same rope she had, pelting after her on the shaky walkway.

As she reached the staircase at the end of the catwalk, shadows below told her that there were people ascending. Faced with a split-second decision – face an unknown number of humans below, or one single man here above the stage – she whirled to face the blond stagehand. *So be it.*

Stig grinned when he saw that she'd stopped, advancing slowly. "Here now…No need to be afraid…"

Her hood still shadowed her face, but she knew it wasn't going to be enough this time. He would know, and he would not be as content to keep her secret as Tony appeared to be. "Come closer. You've chased me for so long."

The bolts that held the catwalk to the far walls shook in their moorings as her weight, coupled with Stig's, strained the fastenings to their limits. Below them, on stage, Tony's voice rose to the rafters, soaring high and pure above the orchestra. It soothed her, she realized. No matter what was to happen in the next few moments, at least Tony was singing.

Step by step, she moved to meet Stig at the center of the walk, her gaze focused on the scene playing out below. The dancers moved with such grace, and Tony fit the part of the newly crowned maharajah so well. They threw their bodies about with such abandon, and for one brief moment, she wished that she too could move so freely. But no, a construct of solid metal and stiff joints could not dance, no matter how she wished to.

Nor could she escape. Not this time.

Stig hesitated, just outside of her arm's reach. "I knew you were real. Let me see that pretty face."

"If you wish to see it, step closer. You have earned it, have you not?" She held a gloved hand out to him, and tried not to look at the crystal bracelet dangling from her wrist. Tony would have to understand. He would have to forgive her.

Stig, trusting fool that he was, put his hand in hers, and in a flash she closed her hand around his, yanking him into the circle of her arms where her mechanical embrace pinned him with no hope of wriggling free.

Eyes wide in surprise, his nose mere inches from her own, his gaze met hers so deep in her hood. For long moments, she let him look upon her, upon the horror that time was making of her once-beautiful construction. She knew what she looked like, she could use a mirror the same as any human. The dark patina crept over the right half of her face, marring the glossy finish, making it appear crumpled and deformed against the unmarred opposite. The light in her eye on that side flickered a little, the wiring not nearly as secure as it had been at the time of her making.

"Wh…what are you?"

"A secret." She tightened her arms around him, squeezing the air from his lungs so that he could not call for help. "The last secret you will ever know."

He did try to free himself, a futile struggle at best. Human strength was no match for an automaton's, one of the very reasons the machines had been created to begin with. One of the reasons their existence was so very closely governed. She felt the ribs begin to crack, one by one, followed by the vertebrae in his back, crushed in her powerful embrace. He fought for air until the kicks he aimed at her legs became spastic drumming. She was looking right into his eyes as the inner light dimmed from them, and a bubble of frothy blood burst from his mouth with his last exhale.

So easy. So easy to end a human life. They were frail creatures, delicate to the extreme. One small rupture on the inside, and they would cease to function so quickly. It never failed to amaze her that these poorly constructed beings were considered her betters.

She was left, then, with the dilemma of what to do with him. She could simply leave the body on the catwalk and retreat. She could, but… It was not going to be enough to dispatch with the persistent stagehand, she realized. The owners still had to understand the consequences for disobeying her. Had they simply followed her orders to begin with, none of this would have been necessary. They must learn.

Nearly as fast as thought, she snatched one of the hanging ropes nearby, and wound it around Stig's neck, then heaved the body over the catwalk railing. It plummeted, lifeless, toward the stage, stopping with a snap of broken bone not two feet above the oblivious dancers below.

The first screams came from the audience, followed by shrieks of terror as those on stage caught sight of the macabre decoration swinging back and forth above them.

"Get him down! Big, Little! Grab him!" That was Tony, rallying the stage crew to aid their fellow. They could not know that he was already dead.

Agile Tony, he climbed the false rocks of the set, wrapping his arms around the swinging body's legs. "A blade! Toss me a blade!" Someone did, and he sliced through the rope, dropping Stig down into the waiting arms of the crew.

There was chaos all around them, women screaming, men yelling, the performers and audience dashing in all possible directions, much like butchered chickens would dart about without their heads if allowed. It was an odd spectacle, and she found herself fascinated by it. They could not find the danger, and so they would simply pelt about willy-nilly until they ran headlong into something that would not be moved.

Only one person remained still, and as she looked down, Tony's gaze rose to the rafters to lock with hers. He knew.

Chapter 14

The moment he grabbed hold of Stig's swinging legs, Tony knew the stocky little man was dead. The living, even unconscious, held a sense of being about them, a force that animated even a body at rest. He felt none of that as he lifted, trying to take the pressure off the rope around his friend's neck. It could have been a tailor's dummy, for all the life he felt in it.

Still, they had to try, and he slashed through the rope with Jack's borrowed blade, depositing the body into the arms of the stage crew below them. He watched as Big pressed his ear against Stig's chest, noted the way the blond man's head lolled on his broken neck, saw the bright red froth of blood around his still lips. There was nothing to be done. Nothing at all.

Dreading what he would see, he turned his eyes upward, following the path of the severed rope up into the catwalks above the stage.

Melody was there, watching him in return. He realized that he had known she would be. He had known, perhaps since the very beginning, that his strangely reclusive teacher and the opera ghost were one and the same. Known, and shoved it into the recesses of his mind where he would not have to think about all that it implied.

Now, high above the stage, she gazed down on him, her metal face no longer hidden behind a veil. The tarnished half of her skull painted a snarl on the unmoving copper visage, the darkness displaying the anger her face never could.

He opened his mouth, to…do what? Call out to her? Call an alarm? Before he could decide, she whirled and was gone in a swirl of dark cloak and shadow.

"What do you see?" Jack's voice was loud in his ear, to be heard over the chaotic sound of panic all around them. "What's up there?"

Tony flinched, nearly knocking them both from the precarious perch atop the faux rocks of the set. "Nothing. There was nothing there." Looking down, he found Little laying a piece of scavenged cloth over Stig's staring eyes. "He's dead, isn't he?"

"Yes. Though between you and me, I don't think the fall killed him." Jack's eyes swept the catwalks, then came back to look Tony squarely in the eyes. "Are you sure you saw nothing. Absolutely certain?"

Lies had never come easily to him, especially not to people he respected. "I…don't know. There could have been something. A dark cloak, maybe."

The stage manager sighed. "Guess Stig finally caught up with his ghost after all. Damn." Hopping down, he waved to Mr. Thomas. "We gotta lock the place down, sir! The killer could still be in the building!"

That thought sent a chill through Tony. That was exactly what had happened, he could see it all clearly now. Stig had gone up into the rafters to try to chase down his ghost, and he'd found Melody instead. Melody, who would apparently kill to keep her secret safe. Jack was right, she could indeed be in the building still, her methods of going to and fro known only to her. And if she was willing to kill Stig, who else might she find a need to dispose of? "Dear God… Bess…" Melody hadn't wanted him to go with Bess, the night before. If she knew now that Bess was here, and waiting to take him out…

Though he hadn't seen her yet, Bess had promised to attend that night, and knowing his childhood friend as he thought he did, she would not have fled with the rest of the audience. No doubt, she was even now trying to work her way through the crowd to reach him. If she made it backstage, she would be in Melody's domain, and in very real danger.

He leapt down from the rocks, shoving past the few onlookers who had come to view the macabre scene. The wings were crowded still. A constable had arrived, and was doing his best to create order, but the dancers were hysterical despite Mrs. McRory's commanding presence, and the members of the chorus were scattered about in states varying from numb shock to jagged weeping. Men in tuxedos and women in evening gowns blundered through the darkened wings, either confused and lost, or come to look up on the spectacle of the dead stagehand. If Bess was among them, he could not see her.

"Bess! Bess, do you hear me!" Just as he was about to feel foolish – and very relieved in truth – to find that she had departed after all, he heard his name yelled from near the dressing rooms.

"Tony! Over here!" She was a vision, dressed in an emerald green gown, her golden curls artfully piled atop her head to spill down her bared neck. He realized as he rushed to take her hands that she could have been dressed in coalworks sackcloth and he would still have thought her the most stunning creature on earth. "Oh Tony, what happened? Is he…?"

He clutched at her hands, perhaps tighter than he meant to, ignoring the pain in his still-bruised fingers. "He's dead, Bess. And we have to go. We have to get out of the opera house right now."

"What? Why?" She frowned, her blond brows drawing together in puzzlement. "What's going on?"

"No time. It isn't safe here for you." He could feel eyes on him, boring into his shoulder blades. Flickering, automaton eyes. He darted looks around, but could find nothing in the shadows. The dressing room, though. The mirror door. They were too near Melody's entrance there for his comfort.

"You're making no sense. Please, what's happened?"

"Do you trust me?" He gripped her arms, bending to look into her eyes. "Please, Bess, do you trust me?"

She hesitated for a moment, then gave him one slow nod. "Yes. I do."

"Then we must go now. I promise, I will explain everything, once we are away."

She wanted to tell him no, the stubbornness rising in her green eyes just as it had when they were children. Her gaze searched his, weighing her answer, and finally nodded. "All right. Let's go."

Without waiting for more, he took her hand and turned to make a path through the crowd, only to be brought up short when she resisted. "Let's go out the back way. There are too many people going out the front, it's a madhouse."

Out the back. Out into the dark alleys where no doubt, Melody would be waiting. "No. No, out the front. Stay in the crowd. Stay with people, Bess. If we get separated, stay in the crowd. You should be safe there, surrounded by people. Don't be alone, whatever you do." Surely Melody wouldn't risk exposing herself to a large audience.

"You owe me a grand explanation after all this, Krol." She grabbed her skirts with her free hand, hiking them almost all the way up to her knees, and nodded for him to continue. "Go on, break us a path out of this lunacy. What else are those big shoulders for?"

The audience members, those who intended to depart, were largely outside the building already. The ones still blocking the hallways were the looky-loos, the ones there for the scandal of it all. Their gazes followed Tony and Bess as they wound their way out to the lobby, with many murmured "pardon mes" and more than one viciously thrown elbow. That was always from Bess, proving that she didn't find her short stature to be any kind of disadvantage.

The square in front of the theater was jammed with cabs and carriages as everyone tried to leave at once, and though Tony tried repeatedly to hail a cab, they were finally forced to take shelter at the bottom of the stairs and simply wait their turn.

"There's a cab stand about three blocks from here. We could just walk and try to catch one there," Bess suggested.

Tony eyed the dark mouths of the streets around them, and shuddered. Dark for them, yes, but Melody was plainly in no need of light to make her way. "No. No, stay here, in the light. In the crowd."

Bess tilted her head to look up at him, then took his chin in her hand, tilting his face back and forth. "Hell's bells, Tony… You're white as a sheet under all that makeup. And you're freezing."

Belatedly, he realized he was still shirtless, wearing only the white linen pants of his costume and a thin vest. With a frustrated growl, he swept the turban off his head, leaving it to fall to the sidewalk. "It's not that cold. I'll be fine once we get in the carriage."

"Is that when you're going to tell me what the Hell is going on?" He tried to look away, and she forced him to meet her eyes again. "That stagehand… You don't believe his death was an accident, do you?"

Tony glanced around them, then drew her around the side of the stairs, finding a small respite from the crisp night breeze in the shelter of the marble construction. "I know it wasn't."

"How do you know? Tony, if you know something, you must tell the constables." She reached to take his hand, mistakenly grabbing the injured one, and he winced, jerking out of her grasp. She winced too, in sympathy.

"I'll tell them. I'll tell them whatever they want to know, but I have to get you away from this place first." But would he? *I owe her.* He squelched the voice in his head. He couldn't think about that now.

"Why?"

"Because I'm afraid she'll come for you next."

"She…? A woman murdered that man?" She raised a brow at him, her skepticism written across her pretty face.

Tony shook his head. "No. Not a woman. Not… Later. I'll explain later, but right now, she could hear. She could be very near, and we would never know it."

Bess snorted, and reached a hand into the daring cleavage of her gown, producing a pearl-handled Derringer. With an expert hand, she checked the load, finding it to her satisfaction. "I can take care of myself."

"Not against this. You must trust me, Bess."

"Why would she come for me, then? Who am I to her?"

"It's not who you are to her. I fear it's who you are to me." He leaned against the wall behind them, ignoring the cold against his skin. "I fear that she will not want you near me."

Bess laughed, startling him. "Oh dear… A jealous female? However will I contend?" Her smile faded, though, when he failed to return it. "You're serious. You truly believe this woman will try to kill me?"

"I think she will try to remove you in the most expedient way possible. I fear that's what happened to Stig. He was just…inconvenient."

"And am I inconvenient?" There was something in the tone of her voice, something that told him his answer was vitally important.

"Not to me. Surely you know that."

She pursed her lips a bit, then motioned for him to wait a moment as she checked the line for the cabs. Returning, she shook her head. "Another ten minutes at least before we'll have a clear way out."

Ten minutes seemed like a lifetime. Tony slid down the wall and dropped his head into his hands. "This is my fault. If I'd… If I'd sounded the alarm yesterday.

Or…this morning or… This is all my fault."

"Tony, unless you threw that man off the catwalk – and since I myself witnessed you on stage singing, I highly doubt it – you have no fault in this." Bess crouched down in front of him, heedless of the damage she might be causing to her lovely gown. "But whatever is going on, you're shaken. I don't ever remember seeing you scared, even when we were children, and quite frankly, that alone is frightening me."

He managed a weak smile. "I didn't think you were afraid of anything."

"Very little." She brushed his cheek with her gloved fingers, and he flinched again, reminded abruptly of Melody's hands, steel under satin. His bruised hand throbbed at the mere thought of the automaton's vice-like grip, and he flexed his swollen fingers gingerly. Bess gave him a thoughtful frown. "I know what we'll do."

"Do?"

With a plop, she sat down beside him, managing to arrange the hoops of her skirt so she wasn't flashing her skivvies at the world. Tony had the odd thought that she probably wouldn't care if she did. "They're going to close the opera house. They'll have to, to investigate. Maybe a few days, maybe a week or so… But while they're doing that, we're going to go away. We'll go somewhere that this mystery woman cannot find us."

"I can't just run off, Bess."

"And you're not. You'll leave contact information with a trusted friend where you can be found, and then we'll just go. Not far. Maybe just across the lake. We still have the house on the other side. No one is there now, so we wouldn't be bothered."

He shook his head, amused despite the horrible images still playing through his mind. "Did you just ask me to come away with you, without the benefit of a chaperone?"

She snorted, flipping blond curls out of her eyes. "I

think that ship has sailed, don't you? But yes. Come away with me. You're worried about me, I'm worried about you, so we'd both be safe and worry-free." When he hesitated still, she set her small pistol aside and lifted his injured hand gently in her own. "You need a place to heal. Not just from whatever did this to you, but from what you've just seen. It may be for only a few brief days, but it would be better than trying to stay here, surrounded by all…this."

Her hands were so small, he realized. So tiny compared to his, even if one of them wasn't swollen twice its normal size. How could such tiny hands hold such strength?

"All right. I'll go. For a few days." Slowly, he pushed himself to his feet, then offered a hand to draw her up as well. "I'll tell Jack where I'm going, if they need me for anything."

Bess nodded firmly, a grin splitting her face. "Perfect. We can spend the night at Susan's, then we'll leave word in the morning and be off. I have a friend who pilots an airship, did I tell you? Just local runs. He can whisk us off across the lake faster than you can say Bob's your uncle."

Shock and horror slowly fading into distant numbness, Tony just let himself be led by the hand as Bess guided him back toward the waiting line of cabs. He was fairly certain that they one she urged him into was not meant for them – there seemed to be a rather put out gentleman on the steps with his lady in tow – but he was too tired to question Bess' ways.

She gave the driver an address, then climbed in to sit across from him, rapping smartly on the roof to indicate their readiness. Sadly, with the line being as it was, they would be going nowhere for a few minutes more still.

When she would have drawn the curtains down over the windows, Tony stopped her, leaning his head against the frame to look at the opera house. The lights were still gleaming brightly through every window, and he found himself searching each and every glowing square, afraid he would find a hooded silhouette there, watching. But no, they remained empty, and the lights themselves seemed harsher, a mocking cheerfulness on such a grim night.

The carriage gave a small jolt as the horses were coaxed into motion, and as they circled the square to find the correct street, he slid across the seat so he could still watch the opera house.

What in the world was he going to do now? He had been so close to having everything he'd ever dreamed of. Melody had placed it all within his grasp, like a feast on a silver platter. *Melody...* She wasn't human. It was a fact. And while he had never seen an automaton as advanced as she appeared to be, no one would wait to find that out once they discovered her secret. Especially not now, when she'd done murder. They would remove her aether core and destroy it. Anything that made her what she was would be gone in a flash of blue gases and shattered glass.

I owe her. All he had to do was say the right words to the right ears. He thought he could find her home again, and he knew at least one of her passages in and out of the theater. They would hunt her, they would find her. *But she gave me everything.* And killed Stig.

As the carriage rounded the fountain at the center of the square, a flicker of motion caught his eye. Looking up, he thought he caught the wave of a dark cloak, silhouetted against the night sky, a figure watching from the roof of the opera house. It was gone when he blinked, and though he craned his neck as they left the theater behind them, he couldn't say if he had truly seen something, or if his terror-wearied mind was playing tricks on him.

Interlude - Lake House

Chapter 15

"Are you sure we're supposed to be out here?" Tony had to yell to be heard over the engines, and had to wipe away the moisture from his watering eyes, stung by the strong wind at that altitude.

Bess only flashed him a wicked grin, her curls flying about her head in mass of golden tangles. Dressed in her trousers and vest again, it was easy to see that her reputation as an adventurer wasn't entirely inaccurate. She looked like a pirate, he decided. An air pirate, about to grab a rope and swing through the windows behind them with guns blazing and a blade between her teeth. "Don't you like it?"

"It's…brisk. Definitely brisk." She laughed at him, and he also decided he would probably do any asinine thing she asked, just so he could hear that laugh again. Still, he made sure he had a firm grip in the airship's railing, and only took a few cautious glances over the side.

Below them, the calm surface of Lake Celeste looked like a piece of glass, and Tony could even pick out their own distant reflection, scuttling across the mirror like a tiny insect.

"Oh look! You can see the house from here!" Bess lunged past him to point at a small speck on the far shore of the lake, and he grabbed at her belt instinctively, pulling her back from the railing. Inadvertently, it brought her into his arms, and she gave him another wicked grin. "We'll pretend I was going to fall, and you just saved my life, shall we?"

He felt the heat rise in his face, and released her, but she firmly took his arms and put them back around her waist, leaning against his chest as the airship puttered along through the sky. "This will do quite nicely, actually. You're warm, and there's a chill at this height."

What could he do but acquiesce? He rested his chin against her pile of wild curls, and tried not to think about anything else. For a few days, at least, there was no opera, no Melody, no Stig, no Simon LeClerc. There was only Bess, and him, and whatever it might be that was growing between them.

Growing was perhaps not the most accurate term. It had always been there, he'd realized of late. He'd been in love with her since they were seven years old, if he were to admit the truth to himself. But that was then, and this was now, and they were both very different people. Whether or not the love of a childhood could survive into adulthood remained to be seen. But he was willing to give it a chance, and so, it seemed, was she.

The airship set down with a not-too-jarring thump at the appropriate landing site, a bit less than three hours after they'd taken off. The same trip around the lake, by road, would have taken the better part of a day and a half, and Tony could appreciate the swiftness of it all, even if the idea of flying through the clouds still baffled his mind a little.

The ground wavered under his feet a little, perhaps annoyed that he'd dared taken leave of it, and Bess chuckled at him as he regained his sense of balance. "It'll pass shortly. Flying is an acquired skill."

She said her goodbyes to the pilot, a swarthy man named Christos, and then they were off again, Bess handling the reins of a small one-pony hack she hired for the duration of their visit. "I don't think anyone has been to the lake house in a decade or more. I hope it doesn't need too much work to make it livable for a few days."

That brought a small smile to his face. "You lived in Bedouin tents in the desert, Bess. How bad does it have to be to be considered unlivable?"

She tilted her head a little, then shrugged. "You have a point there."

Tony settled back against the seat cushion, just watching the scenery as they trotted down the road. This shore was popular with the wealthier families who often retreated there during the sweltering days of summer to take advantage of the breezes off the lake. The road was lined with tall, carefully groomed trees, and the occasional sign post, marking a winding drive that would lead off the main road to some lovely cottage, no doubt boarded up for the winter holidays still. It would be another month or more before the lake houses would be opened again for the season, and so he and Bess would truly be alone.

It wasn't proper. It wasn't done. He knew that as well as anyone and Bess' friend Susan had made it very clear that she was simultaneously scandalized and amused by their planned getaway. But, as with many things involving Bess, propriety didn't seem so terribly important when viewed through her eyes.

And he needed somewhere to retreat to. Somewhere that Melody could not reach him, somewhere that he could still his mind enough to actually think. Somewhere to decide just what he was going to do.

They had stopped by the opera house and spoken to Jack briefly. The police were conducting an investigation into Stig's murder, as it had become clear that he had been crushed to death sometime prior to being hanged from the catwalk. Both of the theater automatons had been confiscated and their aether cores destroyed, but it was merely a precaution. It was obvious that no one believed either machine was the culprit.

Jack had nodded his approval at Tony's decision to depart for a few days. "Nothing you can do here, and I don't fancy the idea of you sleeping alone back in the workshop until we get this mess sorted. I'll send word if we need you to come back early." He'd clasped forearms with Tony and shooed him on his way.

I should have told them. There was that voice again, the one that reminded him constantly that he alone held the key to the identity of Stig's killer. What kind of friend was he, if he let justice go undone? And yet, could he condemn Melody to death as well? So much knowledge and talent inside her metal mind. Her very existence was a miracle. And she had given him everything, and asked nothing in return. What kind of friend was he?

"If you think any harder, smoke is going to come pouring out of your ears." Bess' gentle gibe brought him back to the present, and he gave her a small smile as they turned off the road, passing through the wrought-iron arch that marked the entrance to her family's grounds.

"I have a lot to think about."

Bess drew the horse to a halt in front of the house, hopping down from the little carriage. "This is a good place to do things like that. It should be quiet, this time of year."

He hadn't told her yet. Despite his promises of the night before, he hadn't told Bess the truth yet. Once he did, he knew it was out of his hands. Once she knew Melody's secret, she would relay that to the police, and then Melody's fate would be decided elsewhere. And, once she knew Melody's secret, she would be a target, someone Melody would need to remove to protect herself.

Bess, bless her, hadn't pressed him. He caught her watching him in sidelong glances from time to time, but she was content so far to let him hold his peace. How long that would last, he couldn't say. She had never been known for her patience.

But as she said, he had time here. Time to decide what to do, and time to decide whether or not he wanted to include Bess in those plans. In all his plans.

Bess tossed her trunk up on her shoulder, and offered him her free hand. "Come on. Let's go get this place opened up." After a moment, he grabbed his own meager bag and took her hand, following her into the house.

~*!*~

She waited for two days in the dark house, frozen still in the corner next to the destroyed wardrobe. Mice came out of the walls, sifting through the remains of her clothing to scamper away with tiny treasures for their nests. Dust motes drifted idly through the sunbeams that crossed the bedroom floor with the passing of the hours. Out in the hallway, a phantom child ran up and down, tiny feet coupled with girlish laughter and entreaties to come play. Still, she stood waiting, as still as death, only her innermost workings still whirring along. Waiting to hear angry voices coming up the walk, waiting to hear the front door come slamming open. When, after two days, neither of those things occurred, it became plain that she could not remain there, a prisoner in her own home.

Why hadn't they come? Surely, by now, Tony had given away her identity, her location. What were they waiting for?

Of course. They were waiting for her mechanism to wind down. That was the standard procedure for a rogue automaton. Eventually, the dull constructions would simply sputter to a halt, where they could be safely approached and dismantled. Well, if they were waiting for her to unwind, they would be waiting for a very long time indeed.

When night fell again, she grew bold and gathered up her cloak to again make her way to the opera house. The streets were emptier than she'd expected for so early in the evening, and when a stray breeze blew a newspaper across her path, she picked it up to see what was being said about the death at the theater.

MURDER AT THE OPERA, it read, in large black letters right on the front page. A quick perusal of the article proved that an automaton was suspected in the actual death, but that the police were more interested in seeking out the person who must have been controlling such a device. Names were dropped, motives bandied about, and thinly veiled insinuations made. *And where is the new tenor, who not only disappeared the night after his stunning debut, but has now departed to parts unknown, last seen in company with globe-trotting heiress, Elisabeth Barstow?*

Tony had gone? Gone where? So stunned was she that she missed the approach of a horse-drawn carriage until it was nearly upon her.

"Hey there! Get out of the road, you simpleton!"

Belatedly, she moved to the side of the street, her eyes still fixed on the newspaper in her hands. She flipped through the remaining tattered pages, but there was nothing in any of them to indicate where he had fled to. *No! He can't have just gone! Not when we've worked so hard!*

Perhaps someone at the opera house would know, though according to the newspaper, all productions had been cancelled for the foreseeable future. Surely someone would still be there. She tucked the newspaper into the inside pocket of her cloak, and continued on her journey to the theater.

That excursion proved more frustrating than she had anticipated. While where was little traffic passing through the early evening, there were more constables out, walking along the streets or trotting past on their horses. It took her three times as long to reach the square near the theater as usual, and once there, it was clear she had no way to approach unseen.

Even if there had not been two police wagons stationed at the bottom of the grand staircase, her keen eyesight found the outline of riflemen on the nearby rooftops. Most of them were relaxed, only barely attending to their watch, but the sheer fact of their presence kept her concealed in the shadows. The rifles could not hurt her, but once they knew what she was, there were other ways to disable her.

As she slowly retraced her steps, withdrawing from the lighted square, she heard footsteps come pelting down the street toward her. Toward her, through her, past her, the tiny patter of a little girl's shoes disappearing into the night. *"Look Papa, she sings pretty like me!"*

The voice had become familiar to her now, no longer so startling though the sheer fact of its existence still rankled. Who the child was, she could not remember, though she felt she should be able to. Did she belong to the small room in the house, filled with abandoned toys and forgotten frocks and stockings? If so, why was the little girl suddenly haunting her? She'd done nothing to warrant it, nothing at all.

As if to prove that even ghosts have purposes, the invisible child followed her all the way home, scampering about her, giggling, dancing. She didn't sound like a vengeful spirit, that much was true. She was always laughing, always singing. Always pleading for someone to come play with her.

"Just leave me alone," she whispered as she shut herself in her own room once again. "I have nothing for you." Nothing, now that Tony was gone. Gone with the golden woman, according to the newspaper. *My Tony...* The golden woman had taken him away, stolen him from right under her nose.

There was a silence pressing on her ears that seemed greater than an empty house could account for. A silence left by the absence of Tony's beautiful voice. Even his spoken words had been exquisite, and he so often smiled for her as they worked together. He had a very small dimple in his left cheek. Did he know, she wondered?

Should she tell him?

No, she could not tell him, because he was not there. Gone gone gone… Stolen away… Secreted away where she would never be able to see him again, never be able to hear his voice as it soared to shake the very chandelier of the opera house. Something felt too tightly wound within her chest cavity at that thought, and she paused in mid-step to let the sensation subside.

How could he do it? How could he simply vanish without saying a word to her? Were they not friends, as he had claimed? So easily his head was turned by golden curls and soft skin, things she would never possess.

With a cry, she yanked the dark wig from her head, throwing it against the wall where it fell to the floor in a forlorn pile of black curls. Bending, she snatched a shard of broken mirror glass up off the floor, trying in vain to fit her whole face within the small surface. Only one side or the other would be revealed at once, though, and she was left to stare at her unmarred copper face, or the filthy patina that disfigured the opposite side. Of course he left. Who would want to look upon her as she was?

"No!" Her voice beat against the faded walls, nothing left to soften the harsh tones. "Tony has a kind heart, and a gentle spirit. He would never scorn me for my appearance." She believed this, she realized, wholeheartedly. Tony was not the type of man to shun her, despite their…differences.

Then why had he gone? The answer was obvious, when she calmed enough to think on it. She had never told Tony that she had possessive inclinations toward him. Whether or not it was what the humans bantered about as "love", she could not say, but surely, once Tony knew, he would return such feelings. It was not his fault that she had not been honest with him from the beginning, and for that, she would have to ask his forgiveness. But how? When?

Removing the paper from the pocket of her cloak, she

examined the article again. The owners assured everyone that they intended to resume activities as soon as possible, hopefully in time for the annual Founder's Day masquerade ball in three weeks. There. That would do. She could not find Tony, not now, but once the opera house reopened, she would go there, and she would speak to him. Everything was going to be fine.

~*!*~

"Bess! Come look at this!" Tony called to her from the water's edge, and with a chuckle, she trotted to catch up to him. Proudly, he showed off a tiny mound of water-logged sand, the edges of it dissolving in the lapping water even as she watched. "A sand castle."

She couldn't help but laugh. "Is that what that is? It seems to be under attack."

"I didn't say it was a very *good* sand castle." With a chuckle, he stood up, wiping his sandy hands off on his trousers. "I recall this looking more impressive when we were about eight."

"Indeed." A breeze kicked up off the lake, and Bess tugged the fur collar of her coat higher around her neck. "The almanac says that it's supposed to keep getting warmer, but I'm not sure that winter is done with us yet."

Tony frowned in concern. "Do you want to go back up to the house?"

"No, let's walk a bit farther. I'm not ready to go back yet." She held her hand out to him, and he took it without the slightest hesitation, lacing their fingers together.

The week had gone well. Better than she'd hoped, actually, for all that she'd had very little actual plan in mind when she'd made the offer. The weather had been lovely, and they had taken walks through the neighborhood, along the beach, into the small village nearby for dinner supplies. When the sun set, they played cards and board games in front of the small drawing room fireplace, often retiring – to separate bedrooms – well after midnight.

The dark cloud that had followed Tony from the opera house had lightened, if not lifted entirely, while they'd been there. He had still not offered any information about the danger he believed her to be in, or about who he thought was responsible for his friend's death. She knew, with their departure looming on the morrow, that she must press him about it tonight, or not at all, but that was hours away still. It would wait.

To the great delight of them both, they had discovered that the remembered friendship of their youth had not faded over the intervening years. Even more, Bess found that Tony, the man, was thoughtful and intelligent, willing to discuss with her anything she liked, and quite pleased to hear her own opinions on the same. They spent hours talking about…well, everything. Reminiscing over their childhood memories, catching up on the years they had been apart, hashing out everything from current events to world politics.

He was still more staid and proper than she'd ever been, and she was rather surprised to discover that she liked it. He had always been the voice of reason to her spontaneity, the calming factor to her recklessness. It felt good to think that once again, she had someone who could counsel her when her plans outgrew her abilities. It had been known to happen. Not often, but occasionally.

He was the one who insisted on separate sleeping arrangements. He was the one who took three days to be comfortable holding her hand as they walked, though he was obviously as attracted to her as she was to him. On the fourth night, she had asked him why.

"Because you deserve someone who is willing to wait for things to be right."

Sprawled on the floor in front of the fireplace, eyeing him over their chessboard, Bess had raised an eyebrow.

"What do you consider 'right'?"

"Right is a wedding ring on your finger, Bess. Any man who wants you to settle for less isn't any kind of gentleman." She could see the color rise up in his cheeks, despite the dim, flickering light.

"Why, Anton Krol. That was almost a proposal." That got a full blush out of him, and she giggled. "And what if I don't want to ever get married? What then?"

"It's not marriage you object to, you know."

"No?"

"No. It's marriage to the wrong person." He reached out and with a deft flick of his fingers, put her king in check. "Marriage to the correct person wouldn't trap you, or confine you. It wouldn't force you to be anyone other than yourself."

She'd had to admit that he was correct, and it had forced her to think over the few days since. Marriage had always seemed the final punishment, the moment where she gave up the ideas and activities that made her happy in favor of raising a family, creating a stable life. But if Tony was correct, the right person would never require that of her, unless she herself wished it. Why had she never realized that before? She didn't object to marriage, it was true, she just objected to the wrong marriage.

Was Tony the right marriage? She couldn't say, just yet, and he hadn't asked. So there was that. But if it wasn't Tony, she decided she wanted it to be someone like him. Someone who could see all of her, and smile. Tony was a rare breed, though, in this day and age. She didn't hold out hope for there being more than one of him.

He was staring at her, she realized, though how long he'd been watching her wander through her thoughts, she couldn't say. She gave him a small smile, and squeezed his hand. "My mind was wandering off again."

"So long as it always wanders back, I suppose that's all right." He gave her a smile in return, then his gaze went past her to the far side of the lake, where the smoke from the coalworks hung like a floating island in the air above the city. "Your friend is coming to pick us up tomorrow."

"He is." She stopped to, turning to look across the mirror-like water. "Are you ready to go back?"

"As ready as I'll ever be, I suppose." With a sigh, he slipped his arm around her shoulders, and she nestled against his side happily. "I'll have to find a room to rent. I can't stay in the opera house anymore, even if they've finished with their investigation. Until then, I am willing to bet that Jack will give me a place on his floor."

"You could come stay with me at Susan's."

He chuckled, his gaze still focused on the city across the lake. "I would not do that to your friend. I think you are more than enough scandal for her, I wouldn't want to add to it. And her husband might have apoplexy. I couldn't be responsible for that."

Bess chuckled. "Andrew is timid, but he loves her, so I cannot fault him."

"I could see that, the night we stayed there. They are very much in love."

There was an opening there, she knew, a moment where she could ask about many things, including love. It hung between them like the coalworks smog, then dissipated on the wind as they let the moment pass. With another sigh, Tony turned and kissed the top of her curly head.

"Thank you, Bess."

"For what?"

"For…all of this. For being you, for letting me be me… For not pressing, even though I promised you answers." He ran his free hand through his hair, setting the raven locks all a-tousle. "But, before we return, you need those answers. You need to know what's there, and what we may be facing."

"Tony, you don't have to."

He turned to look at her, grim certainty in his eyes. "I

do. If I intend to ask you to stay with me, going forward, you need to know enough to say no."

Her heart skipped a beat, and on some level, she scoffed at herself for such a typical female reaction. Her self-scorn, however, was lost somewhere under the thundering of her heartbeat in her ears. "And do you intend to ask me to stay with you?"

"I suppose that depends on whether or not I think you'll say no, after all is said and done." He took her hand again, and they started retracing their footsteps up the beach.

"I'll tell you a secret, Tony."

"Hm?"

"I don't intend to say no."

ACT III

Chapter 16

The theater was decked in lights and streamers and every bright adornment they could produce. Crystals and metal discs were dangled on garlands from the ceilings, reflecting the light into a host of tiny stars. The windows on the elegant edifice had been thrown open, inviting the refreshing spring breezes to dance through the building, and allowing the sounds of music to spill out into the square, voices and instruments vying for the title of most joyful.

It seemed the whole of the city had turned out for the annual Founder's Day masquerade ball, those with too little income to purchase a ticket holding their own dances and festivities in the square, while the wealthier attendants ascended the marble staircases in their gowns and top hats, glittering with as many jewels as the opera house herself.

Bess let her gaze sweep over the crowd as she was handed down from the carriage, then chided herself for foolishness. What did she think she was going to see? Everywhere she looked was mask after mask. Cats and jesters, Egyptian queens and ravens. Anyone could be anyone, in this crowd.

She herself was dressed as a lithe cheetah of the African savannah. The mask that framed her eyes was spotted, and came down to a point just above her nose where delicate whiskers quivered. A net gathered her hair into a manageable mess, jet beads gleaming darkly against her golden curls. The gown was done in tawny brown with the same beads of jet sown into the cloth, and the skirt itself was split entirely in the front, revealing her slender legs clothed in dark trousers and knee high boots. The gloves on her hands, spotted like her mask, were fingerless, thanks to a pair of sharp scissors. Knowing they were coming back to the opera house for the first time, she didn't want anything to interfere with her shooting ability. Her Colt rested heavily against her thigh, hidden by the folds of her skirt but easily accessible. It was not the ideal place for it, but she refused to carry only her little Derringer into this situation. And unbeknownst to anyone, the skirt itself would tear away with a good sharp tug, should she find it cumbersome. Which was already happening.

Turning to look up at her escort, she forced a smile for him. He was nervous enough as it was, he didn't need to know that she'd planned this night fully prepared to go into battle if need be.

Tony, dressed as an archangel in gold and white with feathered wings trailing down his back, gave her a return smile, then turned to help Susan down from the carriage as well.

Susan and Andrew looked charming, dressed as the king and queen of hearts, though in truth, Andrew looked extremely uncomfortable in the doublet and hose. Sue grabbed her friend's hand, eyes alight behind her white domino mask. "Oh Bess, it's just beautiful! Look at all the lights!"

As usually, Susan's excitement was contagious, and Bess couldn't help but chuckle. Tonight would be fine. She had to keep telling herself that.

They had returned from the lake house two weeks ago, and there had been nothing. No more notes, no more sightings or visitations, and most importantly, no more progress on the investigation into Stig's murder. Though, after all that Tony had confided in her, she hadn't expected there to be. The police had no idea what they were after. It was a thought that they could not even expand their minds to contemplate.

Still, in the absence of any further harassment, even during the hours that Tony returned to the theater to help with the masquerade preparations, they had started to believe that perhaps the mysterious automaton had indeed gone, no doubt unwound somewhere in a dark passage, or in the decrepit house she called home. Perhaps, Melody was gone.

Just in case, though, Bess was armed. A good shot could go through an eye socket on an automaton and shatter the aether core. It was truly the only way to stop one, so long as it was still tightly wound.

Inside the opera house, the lobby had been turned into a grand performance area, the central statue replaced by a podium for the orchestra conductor to stand upon. The musicians were scattered about the immense room, across both levels, and all around the maestro, the opera dancers whirled in their costumes and glamor. Even those members of the company that were normally never seen, the stage crews and cleaning staff, had been invited to attend, and it was impossible to say who was who behind all of the masks.

"Oh, Bess, I think that's Mrs. Mason! I should go say hello!" And with that, Susan was gone, dragging Andrew behind her, though how Sue managed to discern someone's identity in the glittering, teeming throng, Bess couldn't say.

Left alone with Tony – or as alone as they could be in the midst of a grand ball – she linked her arm through his. "Can I ask you a personal question, Tony?"

He smiled down at her. "Of course. Anything." Behind his white mask, edged in gold braid, she could see the uncertainty in his eyes, wondering what she could possibly ask in such a public venue

"Do you dance?" He blinked at her, and she burst out in laughter at his obvious surprise. Finally, he joined her, chuckling softly.

"I do, yes. Not well, but I do."

"Then ask me to dance." Tugging at his elbow, she urged him into the flow of dancers, and felt a tingle go through her as his warm hand settled at her waist. After a second to catch the beat, they fell into the dance, Tony's steps just as sure as hers, as she had known they would be. He was often too modest.

Despite the masks and disguises, it was obvious that most people there recognized Tony, many of them calling out greetings as the couple whirled past. He even earned one disdainful sneer from a cobra that could only be Simon LeClerc with the flighty little soprano on his arm as a harem girl.

It was tiresome, she realized, trying to watch everyone around them, trying to fathom where danger might spring from. Could she not just relax and enjoy the dance, enjoy the company of her fiancé?

Fiancé. Not a word she'd ever expected to use in reference to herself. And yet as she looked up into Tony's eyes, she knew there was nothing else she would rather do with herself. The future was uncertain – and when was it not? – but so long as Tony was at her side, everything would be fine in the end.

He had asked a week ago, and as she had promised, she had not said no. They'd yet to announce it to anyone else, though, not even Susan. Tony felt that the secret would keep Bess safer, at least until they could find out what had happened to Melody. She was not inclined to agree with him, but it eased his mind, so she had let it go.

The ring he had gifted her, his own mother's, dangled on a chain around her neck, hidden under the neckline of her gown. *"Close to my heart,"* she had assured him.

The song ended, and they all turned to applaud the efforts of the orchestra for a moment, before the next selection began. This piece was a choreographed one, for the opera company to perform for their guests, and all those not participating moved to the outer edges of the grand lobby to watch and be enchanted. Susan and Andrew found them again, and the four laughed and gasped at the appropriate places as the singers and dancers displayed their skills with an abandon they normally had to curtail on stage. Tony happily pointed out a few that he could recognize, and at some point, a cunningly costumed fox joined them, and Bess was once again introduced to Jack Kelly, the stage manager.

"Fine turnout tonight," he observed, nodding in time to the music. "At least half these folk came in the hopes that something horrible would go wrong tonight, too."

"It's our nature. We gravitate toward disaster." Privately, Bess had to admit that she herself fully expected something horrible to happen too. That way, she could be pleasantly surprised when the evening passed without incident.

"You should both come into the auditorium when this number is over. There will be another on stage shortly." Jack slipped back into the crowd, moving to take charge of the next part of the production.

"Do you want to go watch?" Tony had to lean down and speak directly into her ear to be heard, but she nodded enthusiastically. For all that she was fighting a feeling of foreboding, it truly was a grand spectacle, the music and dancing showcasing the very best of the opera's talent.

They skirted the crowd in the lobby and made their way into the auditorium, winding their way around people standing in the aisle, between the velvet seats. Paths were blocked by voluminous skirts, costume wings and tails, decorative props. No one minded, and the room was full of chatter and laughter.

Tony managed to get them to the stairs that led up onto the stage, and they found a place in the wings from which to watch, even as the musicians started to slip in from their earlier positions, taking up their new place in the orchestra pit.

Bess watched as the dancers and singers found places amongst the guests, no doubt intending to burst into song throughout the room and draw everyone down to the stage. Above them, in the riggings over the stage, there were several shadows moving around as harnesses were attached, proving that there would be entrances from aloft as well.

She turned to speak to Tony only to find his eyes fixed on the catwalks as well, a grim set to his jaw. Lightly, she touched his hand, now fully healed from the horrible bruising, and he looked down, giving her a wan smile. He squeezed her hand in return, but neither of them needed to say where his mind had gone, just then. Bess too could still see Stig's lifeless body dangling from the rope. It was something she expected to never forget.

A single, pure soprano voice rose out of the seats, and everyone turned to look as the pretty harem dancer – undoubtedly the little star, Caroline – gave the signal for the next number to begin. The brunette was soon joined by other costumed figures, and they danced their way down the aisles, grasping hands to draw the guests to the stage with them, until it was hard to tell just who was a performer and who was not.

Tony guided Bess to the side a bit more, standing well out of the way of the choreography, and they both applauded when the dancers on the catwalks were lowered with wide swathes of silk, tumbling almost to the wooden stage itself before halting abruptly with their bodies in such elegant contortions. When Bess dared to glance up at the man beside her again, she was relieved to see the darkness gone from his eyes. Instead, there was a glow there, a life that had been absent too often these past weeks. Music brought life to him, she realized. It was part of his soul, even if he himself was not performing.

Faster and faster the dancers whirled, and everywhere

was color and glitter and light. Even the chandelier, far overhead, sparkled with a life of its own, giving the impression of stardust sifting down upon the enchanted evening.

At the appropriate moment in the orchestration, the music ceased, and the dancers all crumpled to the ground, leaving only Caroline standing at center stage, illuminated by a single spotlight. She opened her mouth to go into a solo performance, but before the first note could emerge, another voice rose into the silence. Startled, the pretty brunette choked on her words, and even the dancers who were supposed to be frozen in place raised their heads to see what was happening.

The voice was beautiful, ringing out to fill the theater with pure, clear notes, piercing in their perfection. A murmur rippled through the crowd, even the guests realizing that this was an unexpected addition to the performance.

Before Bess could turn to ask Tony what his thoughts were, he gripped her hand, squeezing tight enough to actually hurt, and when she looked up to object, she saw that he'd gone as white as his costume, all color drained from his face. It was then that she realized something had gone very wrong.

From the back of the stage, a cloaked figure emerged, the stunningly beautiful sound obviously originating there. Slowly, step by step, it approached, backing Caroline out of her spotlight by sheer force of presence. No one dared breathe as the mysterious singer raised her hands and dropped the hood back from her face.

The mask itself was a stunning work of art, meant to depict an automaton of course, but one made of pure gold and constructed to be perfectly feminine rather than the carefully blank countenances of most machines. The golden sheet extended down the singer's throat, across her shoulders where her gown of shimmering white bared them, down her arms. Most looking at her marveled at the intricacy of the painting, detailing every rivet, joint and seam.

Bess knew better. Tony's reaction told her that, if nothing else. Only the mask was false, and even its lie was thin. This then, was Melody, the automaton with the voice of an angel, and the capability to do murder without a thought.

"Don't move," Tony whispered in her ear. "If we are still, she may not see us." There was a chance, of course, standing in the shadowed wings of the stage as they were, but Bess thought it a foolish hope. Melody had only one reason to expose herself, and that was to get to Tony.

The aria came to its end, but where the orchestra should have picked up again, stunned silence reigned. The golden mask looked this way and that, the heart-shaped lips curved into a permanently sweet smile. "Good evening, everyone. I am so pleased that you could all attend." Not one person was brave enough to return the greeting.

Bess carefully began easing her skirt aside, her hand slipping along her thigh toward the holster strapped there. If she could just get her hands on her Colt.

"I thought that tonight would be the perfect time to introduce myself formally. There have been some terrible rumors going about, and some other unpleasantness, and I am here to dispel such things." With a flourish, the black cloak dropped completely away, pooling around the golden figure's feet. "If Mr. Thomas and Mr. Strang would be so good as to step forward."

An uneasy murmur spread through the watching crowd as the two owners shuffled their way through the onlookers to the front of the stage. One of them – Bess couldn't tell which was which – was dressed as a peacock, feathers sprouting from the top of his mask, and the other was a boar, the tusks made to look like they were encased in jewels. After a moment of the golden woman staring at them, they thought to remove their headpieces, proving that their faces were as white as Tony's own, though the ruddy fellow had bright spots of red on his cheeks.

"Yes, there you are. Thank you for your prompt response. I would like to address with you the matter of my detailed notes which have heretofore gone unanswered. From now on, I would like my requests completed within two business days, if not earlier. I am certain that this is feasible."

The dark man – she still didn't know if he was Thomas or Strang – nearly choked, his face flushing darkly, but his partner grabbed his arm and pressed him into silence. The automaton seemed to take this as acquiescence, and turned next to fix her gaze upon Simon LeClerc, who was doing his best to melt into the scenery.

"Mr. LeClerc. As your voice has obviously passed its prime, I think we can all agree that it is in the company's best interest for you to depart. However, as you have given many years of devoted service to this opera, I believe it would also be acceptable for you to take a lesser part in the chorus."

Her voice was uncanny, Bess thought. She sounded perfectly human. Too perfect, really, her tones clipped and modulated in a way no human throat would ever manage. Nothing like the scratchy half-words that most mechanical constructions could manage.

Simon himself seemed to have no answer to his abrupt dismissal, his mouth opening and closing like a landed fish, but nothing coming forth. Caroline quailed against his side, but it did not keep the machine's gaze from falling on her. "As for you, Caroline. You have great potential in your art, but you conduct yourself in a manner unbecoming a diva of this company. Please develop a bit more decorum, or you will find yourself dismissed as well."

"Now see here—" Mr. Thomas interrupted, only to have Mr. Strang hiss him quiet again.

"Reg, don't!"

The figure ignored the outburst, her head swiveling on her metal neck in a most unnatural fashion until she fixed her eyes on a certain point in the wings, staring unerringly at Tony. "Anton Krol. Please step forward."

"Don't," Bess whispered, but he was already moving, leaving the shadows to step into the spotlight. Bess gave up the pretense of subtlety and snatched the revolver from its holster, thumbing the hammer back with an audible click. No one seemed to notice.

They stood there in the circle of light, two raven haired figures clad in gold and white, almost as though they had dressed to match. Two angels, one beautiful, one terrible. After long moments of simply looking at each other, the automaton straightened slightly. "I have chosen a new opera for the spring season, details of which have been left for Mr. Thomas and Mr. Strang. You will be the lead tenor. While your voice has made considerable progress over the past few months, I believe that you could be better still if you will present yourself for further instruction. Our usual time and location should be sufficient."

Perhaps Bess moved, and her dressed rustled. Perhaps her breath was simply too loud. Whatever the reason, the machine's gaze was drawn past the man in front of her, focusing on the blond woman in the wings. The masked head tilted slightly, as if weighing Bess, then swiveled to focus on Tony again. "You must also abandon your pursuit of the woman. She is an unnecessary distraction."

"You know I can't do that."

The machine actually flinched, as though his words had been a blow. "You *will* do it. To do otherwise will be to court misfortune."

"Yeah? Try it." Striding forward, Bess brought the pistol level with the automaton's head.

"Bess, no!" Tony whirled, holding his hands out and preventing her to get a clear shot. Behind him, the automaton's glass eyes flared brighter for an instant, and then a loud bang sounded, and the machine dropped through the floor of the stage.

The trap door had always been there, used in a variety of productions over the years, and it was obvious that Melody had staged her appearance on that very spot for a purpose. "Oh no you don't." With a snarl, Bess darted after her, leaping feet first into the dark hole.

"Bess!" Tony's anguished cry followed her into the blackness, and she landed hard enough to jar her teeth in her skull. Before she could orient herself, the door itself snapped closed, and all that was left was the sound of Tony pounding on the stage, and muffled shouts from above.

Ahead of her, footsteps sounded in the tight space, the trap room beneath the stage. It was often used for storage when not in use, and her brief glimpse before the light was extinguished had shown boxes stacked from floor to ceiling. The stack of crates not a foot to her left seemed to form a solid wall, leading…somewhere. She could use it to guide her. Gripping the edges of her flowing skirt, she gave a sharp tug and left the yards of cloth behind her as she followed the sound of the retreating automaton, her pistol at the ready.

Chapter 17

The drop from the stage had damaged a bearing in her left knee joint. That much she knew instantly. It caught and gave in odd jerks, perhaps due to a dent or gouge in the metal. An unfortunate cost, but one that she had known was possible when she planned her escape route. Better a damaged knee than a bullet to the aether core.

That damned woman. She hadn't expected that, hadn't expected the female to draw a weapon. Women did not carry weapons. What kind of creature *was* she?

It took her mere seconds to reach the door of the trap room, but she still heard the thud of boots hitting the stone floor under the trap door. The door itself boomed as it slammed shut, but it was obviously too late. Someone had followed her down. Belatedly, she froze, listening as the echoes of her own steps died away into nothing.

Could it be Tony? Had he come after her? The outlines of the crates that surrounded her were clear to her vision, but any human would have difficulty seeing. Their passage through the darkness would not be swift, or silent.

No sooner had she thought it than the faint scuff of boots on stone reached her ears. The steps were cautious, to be sure, but not hesitant. Someone was coming after her with a sense of quiet determination. The faintest whiff of perfume swirled through the stagnant air, proving that it was most certainly *not* Tony.

The woman, then. This Bess. The woman with the gun. Very well. She was not without resources of her own, and she would be followed at the risk of peril. *"Hide and seek!*

Let's play hide and seek!" For once, she did not disagree with the phantom child. They would play hide and seek.

"Find me, if you can." Her voice was but a whisper, but in the dark and silence, it fairly boomed. She was answered by a quiet curse, the sort of word no lady of any breeding would utter.

"I *will* find you, and I *will* stop you."

"As you will." The trap room was too confined, too cluttered. If this Bess wished to chase her, she would do it through the entirety of the passages beneath the opera house. The door closed behind her easily, and she crumpled the knob in her fierce grip. It would never turn again, effectively locking the door. There. Let her get out of that if she could.

She had no doubt that Bess would escape the trap room. The woman had determination and fire, and would not let something so petty as a jammed door detain her for long. By the time Bess was free, she knew she had to be well into the tunnels, preferably where some of her unpleasant surprises were waiting.

She'd had time to prepare, in the weeks since the incident. Time to secure her territory, to be certain that no one would ever follow her into her passages again. She was done skulking around in the shadows, she was finished flinching at every glance that passed her way. They would learn to do as they were told, or they would be removed.

There was a horrible pounding behind her – boots on the door, she thought – and it finally ended in the sharp crack of a gunshot, no doubt blasting the locking mechanism into useless metal fragments. Her pursuer was coming.

In the past, she had wondered who had constructed the secret passages beneath the opera house. Certainly, the stone-walled sections, the ones that were part of the long-abandoned sewer system, had been there long before the theater itself. But the wooden hallways? The secret doors that connected in forgotten places to the deeper passes?

Someone has anticipated a need for them at one time, though what that could have been was long since lost to the depredations of time. Nevertheless, they were her places now, and she knew them better than anyone else.

Though her choice of path seemed random – a right, two lefts, another right, then a left again and so on – she knew exactly where she was at all times. If the woman dared follow her this far, she would not find a pleasant reception.

And the woman was following. She was making an attempt at stealth, but far back in the passages came the occasional scuff of a boot, the rasp of a fingers trailing against the wooden walls. The sporadic vulgar curses. As humans went, she was making good time through the darkness, no doubt drawn on by the sounds of the damage knee joint as it popped and cracked at inopportune moments. There was nothing to be done about that, she could not stop to make repairs at the present time.

The first surprise she had laid across the floor just where the hallway gave way to stone. The small trip wire would be invisible in the darkness, though she herself could raise her skirts and step over it easily. It would not kill the woman, no. The first few were to dissuade, to encourage someone to turn back before things became worse.

Three turns into the dank tunnels, she paused to wait, wanting to hear what happened when the armed woman encountered her trap. The cautious footsteps approached faster than she had expected, proving that the woman had gained some ground despite being nearly blind in the lightless halls.

There was a faint click as the trip wire snagged, then a crash as the ceiling above collapsed, dropping a heavy bag of sand onto whoever waited below. The heavy canvas bag made a deep thud as it hit the floor and burst, and a string of colorful vitriol followed, any attempt at concealment thrown to the wind. The woman did not, however, sound injured. Somehow, the trap had missed.

"If you come any further, there will be worse awaiting you. Turn back now." She realized that she hoped the woman would *not* turn back after all. Let her come, let her play through the lovely surprises awaiting her. And in the end, she would have the life crushed from her, just like the blond stagehand, and her influence over Tony would no longer be an issue.

"I'm going to enjoy watching while they dismantle you," the adversary hissed back.

She froze for long moments, contemplating that very thing. If she was caught, yes, they would dismantle her. Crush her aether core, part out her gears and springs, melt down her casing. They would never do that to a human. A human would have a trial, would be incarcerated. But she was not human, no matter that she was superior to most of them in every way, and she could not be expected to be treated as such. If they would not treat her as such, then she would not behave as such. "Come then. We've much further to go."

The next trap was also a trip wire, set higher off the floor where it could not simply be stepped over without risk of triggering it. As she passed that point, she turned to rig the line behind her, feeling the tautness of the wire like a humming through the tips of her fingers. Not a full minute later, she heard it spring, a section of the stone wall falling in with a rumble of rotted mortar and damp rocks. For long moments, there was only the sound of pebbles pattering their way through the rubble, then someone coughed.

"You missed. Try again." The voice bounced down the passageway to her, raspy with dust.

Damn! She had been certain that one would at least cause more of a hindrance. She had been so pleased to find the weak point in the wall, the fault in the masonry that she could exploit to her advantage.

They were truly in the bowels of the theater now, an impossible amount of stone and construction between them and the bright lights of the auditorium above. Why, then, could she hear the faintest sound of male voices, calling out? "Bess! Bess, where are you?" *Tony...*

The woman could not hear, not yet. The human ear would never be as keen as her own. However, it was only a matter of time before she realized she was not alone, and no doubt those that followed were bringing light with them. It would remove the one advantage she had, and then they would be after her as she had always feared.

Though she was finding the cat-and-mouse game much to her liking, this had to end, and quickly. "Keep coming this way, you're so close now. Nearly there."

Closer than she had realized, as the growled profanity that followed came from merely two turns back. While she had paused to listen, the woman had continued her pursuit. She had nearly caught up.

Down and down she went, feeling the stones beneath her feet grow rougher, the slope begin that would take her into the sewers proper. The air had changed, growing damper, more stagnant. It always made her think of rust and corrosion, the smell of wet earth and tarnished metal. She always hurried through this section, as if simply lingering there would hasten her own demise.

The tunnel opened up suddenly into a circular area, a hub where many different passages came together, branching off in all directions. She could take any of them, and the woman would be able to follow only by guesswork.

This was where she had laid her final trap, one from which no one would escape. Ducking into the passage to her immediate right, she found the rope tied to the pin, just as she'd left it. She unwound it, carefully taking the considerable weight on the other end upon herself. Somewhere above came the faintest sound of sloshing liquid, and a chemical stench overrode the pervasive aroma of damp and mold.

It was amazing, she thought with a mental smirk that her

face would not allow, what things could be found in the theater workshop, if one knew what one was looking for.

A loose paving stone tumbled out of the tunnel she'd just left, clattering to a stop in the center of the round room. The woman had arrived. Wisely, perhaps sensing the wide open space in front of her, she paused in the mouth of the passage, her head tilting this way and that as she listened for something to reveal her quarry.

Just a bit further. Just a few steps more. The joints in her fingers creaked as she prepared herself to release the rope in her hands.

"Bess!" Foot in the air, poised to step out into her doom, the woman paused as her name echoed around the chamber.

"Tony?"

No, no no no... Too soon! A moment more, even just one!

The woman's form in the darkness was soon silhouetted with an ever growing light, the warm glow trickling out of the tunnel and threatening to expose what lay in wait. There was a moment, only a moment to decide, and ultimately, she had to abandon her plan. With a deft twist, the rope was secured to the metal spike in the wall, and mindful that her damaged knee was clicking audibly, she drifted further back into the tunnel, taking refuge in the shadows once again.

The rescuers arrived in a clamor of footsteps and strained breathing, bringing with them the light of several torches.

"Bess, thank God!"

"Tony! How on earth did you find me down here?" There was the sound of someone swatting at another's hands. "Leave off, I'm fine."

"Boy's like a blood hound, winding down and down into these tunnels." A different male. The stage manager, perhaps. No, she definitely could not risk showing herself when she was outnumbered as she was. "I didn't even know all of this was down here!"

"Here, give me a torch, she went this way!"

Every gear she had skipped a tooth. They would come now, and they would not stop until they found her.

"No." Tony's voice again, sounding thick with some emotion she had never heard from him before. Oh, if she could only see his face, to see what was happening inside his mind.

"What? Tony, she'll get away."

"And we'll let her. You're bleeding, for God's sake. We need to get you up and into the light."

Bleeding. That gave her a small sense of satisfaction. Perhaps her traps had not missed as completely as she'd feared.

There was a long moment of silence, and then the woman cursed softly. "Fine. Do you know the way out?"

"We marked the path on the way down," the stage manager interjected. "Tony's idea."

Slowly, the circle of intrusive light faded with the voices, the trio departing back to the safety of the world above. Left alone in the darkness, she remained still for a long time, contemplating events.

The marked path would have to be erased. That much was clear. No doubt Tony had found the way down through the trap room, or perhaps through the dressing room mirror. Those would not be safe to use again, but she had others. The true blow would be if he revealed her secret grate in the alleyway, her method of getting in and out. Once they blocked that, she would have to take more drastic measures.

Someone coughed nearby, and she nearly popped a spring in surprise until she realized that it wasn't an adult voice, but a child. A small child, coughing. *"But Papa, I want to go back outside!"* The little ghost girl had caught a cold, it seemed. What a very odd thought indeed.

The sound of occasional coughing followed her out of the opera house, and all the way home.

Chapter 18

"Ow! Who taught you to do that, a butcher?" Bess slapped his hand away with a cross frown, but Tony only sighed and continued to dab at the deep cut near her hairline.

"Stop fidgeting and it won't hurt so much." She only sulked, giving him the evil eye, much to his amusement.

It was pleasant to be able to *feel* amusement. Not an hour gone by, all he had felt was terror and sick dread. Venturing down into the passages beneath the opera house, unsure if he could find Bess in time, or find her at all for that matter. Certain that at every corner he rounded, he would find her crumpled on the floor, eyes staring-- No. No thinking that way. It hadn't happened, and he forcefully banished the image from his mind yet again.

"You know, I think you're worse now than you were as a child." The cut as clean as he could make it, he fished in the supplies for some gauze. "You're a terrible patient."

"I'm going to kick you in the shin."

"I rest my case. Hold this." Obediently, she held the padding over her cut as he wound another bandage around her head to keep it in place. Not without sticking her tongue out at him, though.

Cups clattered nearby, and he turned to see Jack arriving with the tea. "Here we are, piping hot. No sugar, but there's cream if you like."

"How about whiskey?"

"Got that too."

Tony rolled his eyes at his fiancée and his boss. "Thank

you, Jack."

They'd found refuge at the stage manager's house, doing their best to keep their voices down in the study so they wouldn't wake the rest of the family. Bess had protested, but when he pointed out that her friend Susan would most likely haul her to a doctor for her injury, she reluctantly allowed him to clean and bandage the vicious cut.

Bess' wound bandaged as well as he could manage, Tony slumped back into his chair, running a hand through his hair. It came away coated with cobwebs and unidentifiable other things, and he shuddered. No doubt, souvenirs of his journey into the tunnels.

Jack pressed a cup of tea into Bess' hands, then offered Tony one as well. Tony took it out of habit, more than any real desire for tea. "Well. Now what do we do?"

"We get the constables, and we head back down into those tunnels, flush her out." Of course, that was Bess' answer. She was still angry about her forced retreat earlier.

"No."

"And why not?" She leaned forward, elbows on her knees, to look directly into his eyes. "What is this misplaced loyalty?"

He shook his head. "No loyalty, not now. Not anymore. But she left traps for you, and you barely escaped them." He nodded to the bandage around her golden curls. "You send more men down there, more people are going to die, and I can't... I can't stomach that."

Jack nodded his agreement, leaning against the fireplace with crossed arms. "Tony's right. Going after her in her territory is just asking for disaster. Hell, a couple of years ago, they had an automaton go wild on the docks, and it killed twelve men before a sharpshooter could get the shot he needed."

Bess grumbled, but sat back in her seat again, sipping at her tea. "Then we have to find whoever is winding her. Someone is keeping her functional."

"Who in their right mind would do something like that?" Jack wondered, shaking his head.

"I think that's the key point. This is someone not in their right mind." Bess finally noticed that Tony hadn't spoken up, and raised a brow at him. "What is this look on your face? You look like you're thinking hard enough to bust a spring."

He gnawed his current train of thought over for a few moments more before answering. "She calls him Gilbert."

"What?"

"Mr. Chalmers, the former manager of the opera house. She calls him Gilbert." Tony looked to Jack. "He's been at the opera house for how long? Twenty years? Thirty?"

"Not rightly sure myself. A long time."

"Long enough that he knows her. She knows him. If anyone is going to tell us anything about her, I think we'll have to start there."

Bess hopped up, reaching for the holster she'd laid aside on their arrival. "Well let's go!"

With a sigh, Tony stood and grabbed her hands, forcing her to be still. "It's the middle of the night, Bess. It'll wait until morning. Besides, I don't know where he lives."

"I do." Jack nodded. "I think it's worth paying him a visit." He pushed off the mantle with a sigh. "I'll get some blankets, you two can bed down here on the floor for the night. When the sun comes up, we'll go."

With Jack gone, Tony tilted his head at Bess. "Are you all right, really?"

She started to scoff at him again, then relented, nodding. "A little dizzy, and jumping to my feet like that was not the smartest thing I've ever done."

Tony traced the faint shadow of bruising that showed at the edges of the bandage. "If you'd have been a fraction of a second slower, Bess, she'd have cracked your skull right open. I thought my heart was going to burst, when you jumped down that hole."

"Then I guess we're both lucky that I'm amazing." She caught his hand, and nuzzled her cheek into his palm. "I'm harder to kill than you think."

"I'd prefer not to think of it at all." She stepped into his arms, and he rested his chin atop her head gratefully. "I can't lose you again, Bess, not after all this time."

"You won't. I promise."

Morning came very early on a night spent watching over an injured loved one. Tony knew that a good knock to the head could be far worse than it appeared on the outside, so while Bess slumbered beside him, he woke every hour or so just to be sure she was still with him. Her soft breath would lull him back to sleep again, only for him to startle awake again and repeat the process. The sun found him bleary, but Bess as well as could be expected.

She borrowed one of Tony's shirts, shedding the last remnants of her costume from the night before, and grinned when she caught him watching her tuck the tails into her trousers. "Tsk tsk."

He blushed, but grinned in return. It faded, though, as the thought of their day's plan intruded again.

"Hey, Tony, here's Chalmers' address…" Struggling to pull his coat on, and talk with a slip of paper between his teeth, Jack only stopped by the study briefly. Tony took the address, and Jack gave him a grateful nod. "The owners are calling a meeting with me and the maestro and Mrs. McRory. Thinking their wanting to discuss whatever new opera the ghost has demanded of us. Otherwise, I'd be going with you."

"It's all right, Jack. Be careful, please."

"Sure thing. And your cab should be here in a few minutes." With a wink, he was gone.

"So, just you and me, hm?" Turning, he caught Bess tying the intimidating pistol to her thigh again.

"Do you really think we'll need that?"

"Nope." She adjusted it a bit, then seemed satisfied.

"But I'd rather have it and not need it, than need it and be without."

"Somehow, I don't see Mr. Chalmers as a threat."

"But we don't know that he'll be alone, do we?" Bess raised a brow at him. "If he's the one winding her…"

"I didn't say that. I just said I believe he knows more than we do."

"Well. We'll see, won't we?"

Jack and his family lived on the edges of the coalworks district, but on the side where the smog and smoke was carried away. Not a rich neighborhood, but neither was it poor, a place for families of modest income. Children played in the streets, rolling hoops or congregating for games of jacks. Tony found himself watching them as the few with velocipedes kept pace with the cab for a few blocks, just because they could. Would this be his life, one day? The thought of a herd of golden-haired children brought a small smile to his lips. When Bess cast him a questioning look, he just shrugged and shook his head. They hadn't discussed things like children yet. It would wait.

The address they'd been given was in an older part of the city, a place where the once-wealthy still clung to their ivy-covered walls and wrought iron fences. The sight of a garden gate, swinging in the wind, gave him a chill, recalling the gate outside Melody's decrepit home. But they were on the opposite side of the city, as near as he could remember, and where her block had been largely abandoned and forgotten, there were still people in this neighborhood. Maids were collecting the morning milk as they passed, or throwing out pails of muddy water after mopping up the night's soot deposits from the floors. Flowers at the fences and hedgerows had been carefully tended, and the occasional dog yapped to warn them off from its territory. This neighborhood was alive, albeit doddering.

Mr. Chalmers' house was simply one house among many. It was remarkable in no way whatsoever, the color nearly hidden by the decades of plant growth that climbed from garden to roof. The gate from the street was white, though weathered, and it swung in silently, proving that it was frequently oiled. As they walked up the path, Bess put a cautionary hand on Tony's arm, the light squeeze saying very clearly "Be careful."

The bell cord produced a jangling sound somewhere deep within the house, but it was followed with nothing but silence. After a few moments, Bess nodded. "Try again." Tony pulled the cord once more, again eliciting the harsh ring inside. He was about to do it a third time when they heard shuffling on the other side of the door. The locks rattled – quite a few more than just the one that was normal – and then the door opened up enough for one bleary eye to peer out at them.

"Mr. Chalmers? It's me, Anton Krol. From the opera house?" The person on the other side of the door was still so long that Tony feared they would slam the door shut after all, but finally it swung open.

"I knew you would come. Well, I knew someone would come. Once I saw the story in the paper, I knew someone would come." Mr. Chalmers did not appear to be…himself. That was Tony's first thought. While the man had often been befuddled, his appearance was always fastidious. His hair combed neatly, his suit perfectly pressed, his shoes polished. A far cry from what Tony and Bess now found before them.

His hair seemed to have gone grayer in the few weeks since his departure from the theater, and it stuck out from his head at wild angles. His face had obviously not seen a razor in some time, the salt and pepper stubble grown in patchy with any refusal to form a proper beard. He was dressed in a moth-eaten dressing gown, one that might have once been a burgundy brocade of some kind, and the strong aroma of whiskey layered over the scent of someone who had not bathed in days wafted through the doorway with enough presence to make Bess cough.

"You may as well come on in. I knew you would come." He shuffled back, allowing them inside, then stuck his head out the door to survey the street for long moments. Apparently satisfied at finding – or not finding – whatever it was he was looking for, he shut the door and motioned them to follow. "Come. I've set up camp in the study. Drink?"

"I think it's a bit early for a drink, Mr. Chalmers."

The frazzled man snorted as he plopped into a well-worn armchair. "Nonsense. Any time is good for a drink. You never know when you won't have a 'later'. Please, have a seat."

Tony looked around and finally cleared a stack of old newspapers off the only remaining chair so that Bess could sit. All of the papers, he noticed, were ones with mentions of Stig's murder at the opera house. There were stacks and stacks of them surrounding Mr. Chalmers' chair, layered with empty whiskey bottles and a few plates of food that were starting to grow green fuzzy things on them. The room itself was stagnant and dark, the only visible lamps being emptied of oil long ago.

Tony found himself a seat on an ottoman after moving another stack of newspapers, and rested his elbows on his knees. "You said you knew someone would come, so you know why we're here, then."

Mr. Chalmers nodded, then leaned alarmingly far to one side as he fished at the side of his chair for his current bottle. Finding it, he held it up in triumph, but his hands shook alarmingly as he poured whiskey into a filthy glass on the table next to his chair. "Of course. Where else would you go? Who else would know? Always had to be me. Knew that. I'd hoped… I don't know what I'd hoped. But I knew. Oh yes, always knew."

"What can you tell us, Mr. Chalmers? About her?" Bess perched on the edge of her seat, trying to touch as little as possible.

He drained his glass completely, and filled it once more, before he answered. "Everything. I know everything about her. Absolutely everything." His voice trailed off into nothing as he stared deeply into the alcohol in his glass, and it became apparent after a few moments that he'd become lost in the swirling, intoxicating substance.

"Mr. Chalmers, please." The inebriated man looked up, blinking at Tony as if he'd only just noticed him. "She's killed one man, and she nearly killed Bess last night. We have to know anything you can tell us."

"All right. For all the good it will do you." The bleary eyes focused on the whiskey, as if seeing days gone by in its amber depths. "It begins almost fifty years ago. Yes…nearly fifty. Almost. It begins with my father. I don't suppose you've ever heard of him? Oliver Chalmers. That was his name.

"My father was a master engineer. If he could dream of it, he could build it, bring it to life. Even to this day, thirty years after his death, almost every automaton you will see is based on one of his designs. He was a genius." Mr. Chalmers gave a small sniff and downed a slug of his whiskey. "I, unfortunately, inherited none of his talent, but that is another tale."

"My father also loved music. You wouldn't think that a man with such a head for calculation would love the creative arts so, but he found pleasure in the numbers inherent in the score. He found math in the music, and it sang to him in a way I cannot even hear. Do you know what it's like, to feel that you are missing something that is so obvious to those around you? That is what it was like, being around my father." Again, his eyes lost focus, no doubt seeing scenes from many decades gone as they played through his whiskey-soaked mind.

"Mr. Chalmers, please go on." Bess' quiet prompting brought him back to the present.

"Ah, yes, where was I? The music. He loved music. When I was…ten? Yes, ten or so. My mother gave birth to a baby girl, and died in the doing. It left my father to raise a boy whose mind was alien to him, and an infant who was…well, a girl. Alien to us both." He snorted and almost smiled at some remembered thought. "All was well, for some time. I grew, she grew, we were a family. Then, for Jessica's – I did say her name, yes? Her name was Jessica – seventh birthday, father decided to build her a gift. A wondrous gift, the likes of which the world had never seen before."

"An automaton."

"Oh yes. But what an automaton. Sculpted as near to human as he could make her, put together with parts so fine that it required tweezers and magnifying glasses. Her inner workings so complicated that she would make the automatons you know look like lumps of lead. And he gave her a voice, such a voice. She was to be my sister's music box, you see. A living music box. Or, as living as an automaton can be." The words trailed off into mumbling for a moment. "Almost alive…"

"And then what happened?"

"She died. Oh…not the automaton, of course. No, my sister died. Nearly three years later. Scarlet fever or some such. I was away at school, by that point, you understand, a young man already, but as it was explained to me, she had gone outside to play in the rain, and took a chill. By the next morning, the fever had come on, and… She was gone before I could even catch the train to come home."

"He never….my father never really recovered from that. He…he never forgave himself for letting her go out, never… I don't…" Finally, he just shook his head and drifted into morose silence, draining his whiskey glass again. When he went to refill it, he found the bottle empty, and sighed.

"I didn't know what he'd done until a few years later, you see. I didn't live there anymore, and I couldn't bring myself to come and visit. It was just too painful, without her. When I discovered what he'd done, I begged him to stop. I begged him to reconsider. It was dangerous, I said! It was going to end badly! But he wouldn't listen."

"What exactly did he do, Mr. Chalmers?"

"Nothing." He snorted softly. "He did nothing. He kept the music box, and he did nothing. It was her memories, you see. The memories she had of Jessica were all he had left of her, and he could not bring himself to destroy that aether core, not when it held the last of his little girl in there."

"Even then, I could see that she had learned. She wasn't like the others, with their scratchy voices and simple obedience. The sum total of what she had learned of the world was building up in that aether core, and it was making her change. She was *different*, do you understand?" He leaned forward suddenly, a feverish brightness taking over his eyes. "I saw it, and God help me, I did nothing too. All that has happened since is as much my fault as it was his. Every bit of blood is on my hands."

"Mr. Chalmers-" Tony began, only to have the agitated man reach out and grasp his wrist in a tight grip.

"You must listen! I must tell someone, before she comes. And she will. I know her secrets, and she will come because the world cannot know. So I must tell you, quickly." His skin was dry and hot where he gripped Tony's arm, a fever brought on by illness or madness, it was impossible to say.

"My father died, nearly thirty years ago, and she was still in that house, forgotten by all but me. I couldn't bring myself to destroy her, you see. Couldn't have her look at me when I came to crush the life and memories out of her very skull. And then, on a whim, I lied my way into the manager's job at the opera house. I didn't know a thing about music, and when it became clear that I was out of my depth, I returned to that house, and I found her there waiting. I asked for her advice, because who would know music better than the creation of a man who prized it above all?

"She gave me advice, the opera thrived, and I invented the story of the opera ghost to explain her comings and goings. For all of these years, she has been the manager of that theater, not I." Finally, he released his manic grip on Tony's arm and slumped back into his chair, as if his brief burst of energy was well and truly spent.

"Mr. Chalmers, there is one thing I do not understand." Well, there were many things Tony did not understand about the fantastic story, but only one that truly needed an answer. "Why, even after all this, do you continue to wind her? If you would just let her wind down, this would all be over."

The drunk man barked a laugh that turned into a wheezing cough, interrupting them for long moments. Bess cast Tony a concerned look, but he could only wait until Mr. Chalmers had recovered himself. "Wind her… I have never wound her. And that's the key to it all… The key! See what I did there! Ha!"

He was mad, that much was clear. Well and truly mad, and Tony could only hope that they could find something useful before he devolved into out and out babbling. "If it is not you, then who?"

"My father designed her for a child of seven. A child that he assumed would not be able to wind the machine herself." Mr. Chalmers leaned forward, beckoning for them to do the same, which they did, reluctantly. "Against all of his usual precepts, against all design parameters that are followed to this day, he built her with her winding mechanism on the front side."

"Dear God," Bess murmured, and Tony too felt a cold chill run down his spine.

All automatons were built with their winding mechanisms on the back side, a place that the machine itself could never reach. They were designed to be wholly dependent on human intervention to keep them functional, knowing that should they malfunction, they had a limited range before their power would simply run down.

Mr. Chalmers nodded, seeing that they understood the magnitude of his revelation. "It is here," he said, laying his hand over his heart. "She winds herself, and she wears the key on a chain around her neck. It looks like a filigree heart. She is never without it."

He had seen it, Tony realized. The delicate golden chain around her neck, the pendant on the end always hidden under the neckline of her dress. She always wore it, at every lesson he had attended.

"She winds herself….she winds herself…" Mr. Chalmers shook his head and repeated the phrase, over and over again.

Bess stood, holding her hand out for Tony to join her. "I think we've learned all we can here, Tony."

With a sigh, he joined her, pausing for one moment to look at the pathetic figure in the chair. "Mr. Chalmers, is there someone we can call for you? The constables perhaps, if you are worried for your safety?"

"No…no constables. If she comes…when she comes… I will have earned the fate that waits for me." He lurched up from his chair suddenly, and Tony took a step back, guiding Bess behind him less the drunk man strike out irrationally. But instead, Mr. Chalmers merely wandered out into the dark house, presumably headed for more whiskey. "It's my fault…it's all my fault…" He vanished into the back of the house, taking his ramblings with him.

"Come on, Tony. Let's go."

Her hand clasped tightly in his, they made their

departure, closing the door on the pathetic creature behind them.

Chapter 19

"What on earth do we *do*?" Mr. Thomas stared around at the gathered theater folk, his eyes wide and showing the whites like a startled horse. "She'll never stop. Never."

A rumbling of male voices went around the room, each of them trying to talk over the last, and Bess rolled her eyes from her place leaning against the mantelpiece. They were going to talk themselves to death before a deranged and rogue automaton got to them.

For fear of being overheard at the opera house, Tony had summoned the theater owners to Jack's house again, all of them crammed into the tiny study where she and Tony had spent the previous night on the floor. There, Tony had imparted all that he knew of the opera ghost and her creation, as well as her one weakness. The telling had taken most of the evening, and the hours were now threatening to pass from late into early, the fire dying down and stirred to life again many times over the course of the hours.

"So long as she has that key, she is unstoppable," Mr. Strang asserted, dabbing at his face with a handkerchief. "We're ruined. We may as well close up shop now."

"Oh for…" Bess muttered, and shoved off the mantel to rejoin the group. "Nothing is unstoppable. One good bullet would end her, we just need a chance to take the shot."

The men – well, most of them – had forgotten she was there, obviously. The dark one, Mr. Thomas, jumped a little at the sound of a female voice, and tried to cover it with a feigned coughing fit. He'd been trying to pretend she wasn't standing in the corner wearing trousers and a man's shirt since he arrived.

Jack nodded his agreement with her. "Yes, a bullet would work, but it's finding our chance that's the dilemma. She's a danger as long as she's in the opera house. There are a lot of innocents there."

Mr. Strang nodded as well. "If Mr. Krol here is correct, she comes and goes as she pleases, by means known only to her. How do you intend to anticipate her movement, in order to lie in wait for her?"

"That's easy." She locked eyes with Tony, seated in one of the arm chairs, and he pleaded silently with his eyes for her to stop there. She couldn't, though. Not when his life was at stake. "We have something she wants, very much."

"And what would that be?"

"Tony." All eyes turned to look at him, and he sighed, dropping his eyes to the toes of his boots. "If he sings, she'll come."

"You don't know that for sure."

"Oh yes I do. He does too, he just doesn't want to say."

Tony raised his head, glancing around at the men surrounding him, and finally he nodded. "I believe she will, yes."

Mr. Thomas stood up to pace, something he'd practiced quite a lot through the telling of Tony's tale. "Wonderful. We know how to get her into the opera house – which is where we do *not* want her, I might add – but then what do we do with her?"

"You leave her box empty, as she requires, and you position police marksmen in the box across the gallery. When she finds her seat, they will have her." It seemed so logical to Bess, why in the world could these men not see it too?

"If they miss, she'll be out amidst the audience in a heartbeat." Tony's voice was quiet, and she could read reluctance in every motion his body made.

"Then don't miss." Ignoring the other men, Bess moved to crouch at Tony's feet, forcing him to meet her eyes on his level. "Tony, you know you have to do this. If she goes on, who knows how many others she will kill to protect her secret? Yes, it is dangerous to try to ambush her. But I see no other feasible choice."

He turned his hands over, and she placed hers in his. His thumb traced over the scrapes and bruises from her foray into the tunnels. They all sat in silence for long moments, waiting for his answer. "What opera did she demand we perform next?"

"Um…Pygmalion." Jack shrugged his lanky shoulders. "We did it just a few years ago, we still have all the props, and it doesn't really require rehearsal."

A faint smile crossed Tony's face. "Of course. About a sculptor who falls in love with one of his creations… It speaks to her."

"Do you know it?" Bess could almost hold her breath, afraid that at any moment, Tony was going to balk at the plan.

"Oh yes, I know it. I could sing it, if I had to."

"Tony, you must. It's our only chance."

He finally met her eyes, and searched them intently. Whatever he was looking for, he apparently found it. "Fine. I will sing." The entire room let out an audible sigh of relief, but Tony held up one hand. "I have one stipulation. I wish to change some of the costuming."

"That's all? Lord, man, you can perform in the buff if you want." Mr. Thomas threw his hands up, and Mr. Strang cast him a chiding look. "Reg…"

"Jack, can you get me some paper? I'll need to make some notes for the costume mistress, and you'll need to scrounge up all the gold leaf you can find in the workshop."

The stage manager nodded and went about producing the required paper and a pen for Tony's use. On their way out the door, both the owners stopped to shake Tony's hand, though he did not seem nearly as enthused as they were. "Good man. You're a good man, Krol. This will all come right in the end, you'll see." They left, making plans to request the constables to attend that night's performance.

"What are you thinking of?" Bess moved to stand behind Tony, resting her hands on his shoulders as he sketched on the piece of brown butcher's paper that Jack had found for him.

"She has lived her life alone, terrified of being seen, and rightly so. It is because of me that she took a risk, exposed herself." Scritch scritch went the pen, and a form started to take shape on the paper. "If nothing else, I need to let her know that I am beholden to her, that I appreciate the gift she risked her life to give me."

"Tony…she's not human. She doesn't have a life to risk."

He raised his head to look at her, the fireplace throwing dancing shadows across his face. "Are you very certain of that? She thinks. She feels. If that isn't human, I don't know what is. And I do not want her to die believing that she was alone."

Finished with his sketch, he passed it across the small table to Jack, who nodded as he pursed his lips. "You're a passable artist, Tony, I'm impressed. We can do this. It will only be a matter of convincing Miss Caroline to wear it."

"She'll do it. She'll do whatever she's told."

Jack stood, gathering his coat and hat from the rack. "I'd better get to the theater then. If we're going to do this tonight, I need to start pulling props and getting things touched up."

"I'll come too, I can help…" Tony started to stand, only to have Jack wave him off.

"No, if you're singing tonight, you need your rest. Ain't one of us slept well in days, and I don't know about you, but I'm not as young as I once was. You stay here, sleep.

Today's going to be trial enough as it is." Jack tipped his hat to Bess. "You keep him here, young lady. Strikes me that he might listen to you, better than me."

"Oh trust me, I'll hogtie him if I must." The front door closed, and they found themselves alone once again.

"You should go back to your friend's house. She'll be mad with worry for you."

Bess snorted. "Not a chance. The moment I left, you'd be haring out of here to that theater, whether you ought to or not. I'll just have to risk what few shreds of my reputation are left and stay here to see to your well-being." When he didn't respond to that playful gibe, she tilted her head. "Are you all right?"

"No." He sighed and ran his fingers through his raven hair, spiking it up at odd angles. With a smile, she began the process of smoothing it down again, tracing her fingers over the furrows in his brow. "They're going to kill her, Bess."

"After all she's done, do you think she deserves to live? Stig was your friend, Tony." Coming around the front of the chair, she slid into his lap, his hands coming to rest on her waist like they had always belonged there. It felt good.

"He was, you're right. A good friend. It's hard to reconcile the Melody who is capable of…that…with the Melody who spent months at a piano, bringing out the best in me. Like they are two different people."

"She is not 'people'. You have to stop thinking of her like that. She is a machine, Tony, and she's malfunctioning in the worst possible way."

With a frown, Tony sat her on her feet, then stood up himself. "You don't know her, Bess. You haven't spoken to her."

"She spoke to me in those tunnels, and she made it very clear what her intentions were." Bess sighed, watching as he moved to lean on the mantle, staring into the dying fire. "I don't wish to quarrel with you."

After a few moments of silence, he nodded. "I know. You're worried, and frightened. So am I."

"What are you afraid of?" She slipped her hands around his waist, leaning her cheek against his broad back, warm beneath his shirt.

"I'm afraid that more people will die. I'm afraid that we're endangering more lives with what we plan." His voice rumbled under her ear, like a distant thunderstorm. "I'm afraid that we will be destroying something amazing, some miracle of life that we didn't even know was possible." He turned, gathering her close, and she snuggled into the fire-heated warmth of his chest. "Most of all, I'm afraid of losing you in this, somehow. And really, that's the only reason I agreed to this. She'd have killed you down in those tunnels, if we hadn't come. I know that. And for that, I cannot forgive her."

Bess looked up to find his eyes dark and shadowed, looking her over like a starving man might eye a feast. He leaned down to press his lips against hers gently, and when he would have withdrawn, she wrapped her arms around his neck and held him fast, showing him exactly what a kiss should be. When they finally parted, his face was flushed, and he gave her a small lop-sided smile in response to her grin.

"I don't want you to worry about losing me, Tony. I feel like I've finally found the thing that I never knew I was looking for, in you, and I'm not so easily driven off." She rested her palm against his cheek, feeling the prickle of his beard stubble. "And when this is all over, we have plans to make, things to do."

"Such as?" He was trying to distract himself, to not think about the night that would arrive far sooner than either of them wished. She was happy to oblige.

"Such as a wedding. Such as a place to live...or not. Such as children... Many things."

"And what kind of wedding would you wish?"

"Oh, the most grandiose, gaudy, horrible thing you can imagine." It wasn't true, of course, and he knew it. A wedding of frills and fripperies would be the last thing on her list of wishes, but he was willing to play the game. "I want twenty-three bridesmaids, and seven flower bearers."

"Only seven? A dozen at least."

"I want an entire orchestra to play, and the mayor himself to give me away."

"Live peacocks to carry your fifty-foot train down the aisle of the cathedral?"

"Albino peacocks. And a flock of doves to fly behind me and carry my veil." That got a chuckle out of him, at least. "And for you, you can ride in on a white stallion that is trained to prance in time to the music."

"That would be a most uncomfortable ride, you know."

"Doesn't matter. It's my wedding, and I'll have what I want."

He feigned a disapproving frown. "Well it's my wedding too. What if I want some things?"

"Such as?"

He had to think about that one. "Hm. Such as… A waistcoat studded with real diamonds and rubies. And a cane with an emerald for the head."

"A cane? Are you infirm, now?"

"It's *fashion*, my dear, where *have* you been?" At the snooty tone of his voice, she couldn't help but dissolve into giggles, and after a moment, he joined her, hugging her tightly. "I love you, Bess."

"I love you too." She smiled up at him, sad to see his own smile flee quickly from his eyes. His mind would not let the events of the day rest, no matter what distractions they played at. "In all seriousness, though, I intend to make plans with you, Anton Krol. Many plans, involving many long, happy years."

"I look forward to it. Whatever you want, Bess, if it is in my power, it's yours. Always." He plucked an errant curl off her forehead and tucked it behind her ear. "If you wish a massive house to live in, I will build it. If you want to gallivant around the world on airships, we'll go. If you want a dozen children, or none at all, it will be as you wish. So long as I can be with you. It is all I want. It is all I have ever wanted."

Tears prickled at her eyes, and she blinked them away, chiding herself for feminine silliness. "We have only to get through tonight, Tony, and it will all be over and we will both have everything we ever wanted. I believe that wholeheartedly."

"I hope you're right. I truly do."

Chapter 20

They thought they were clever. They thought they were subtle. But it was impossible to bring in over a dozen armed constables without her knowledge. This was *her* opera house. Its secret ways were hers to travel, to control, its conversations hers to sift and sort through as she wished. The very air whispered of plots and conspiracies, hissing threats against her like serpents inside the walls. Those responsible would face the consequences of their actions, but that would come later. First, there was a show to put on.

To her very great pleasure, the stage manager had spent the better part of the night pulling and repairing set and prop pieces for *Pygmalion*. He, at least, seemed to be obeying her orders, and for that she intended to send him a note of gratitude when she found the time. Once it became clear that he was performing admirably, she left her secret place above the workshop to observe other happenings in the theater.

The cast began trailing in beginning in the early afternoon. It was notable, though, that the chorus had grown smaller, and several members of the orchestra were remarkably absent. Cowards, the lot of them. Their poor attitude would not be missed in the slightest. The stage crew was all present, though they continually eyed the catwalks above the stage with wary trepidation, and they came and went in pairs, never alone. All in all, they were very subdued, for a performance night. Not the boisterous, carefree lot she was accustomed to.

"I can kiss it and make it better!" The child was always with her now. Humming nonsense tunes in the back of her mind, or dancing about on light feet, pleading with her to sing or play. Sometimes, she was startled by the faint, childish cough, coming out of nowhere, but that too had become almost familiar.

She knew immediately when Tony entered the building, as there was a wave of voices that followed his path from the front door to the dressing rooms. Some called greetings to him, others merely murmured darkly after he had passed. She made note of which were which, when she could tell. There would be notes, and sackings, if she had her way. And she would. Her way was all that mattered now.

One voice, though, one voice stood out to her, and some apparent malfunction in her glass eyes tinted the world red. *Bess.* The golden woman. The bold one with the gun. Still here, still trailing after Tony like a bitch in heat. She had been warned. Now, she would be removed. After the show, though. There would be nothing to interrupt tonight's performance. It would be perfect, despite anyone else's plans to the contrary. The punishment for interference would be severe.

As the cast and crew went about their usual preparations, so too did she. A rope tied just so, a weight balanced on a precarious edge, a pair of shears conveniently misplaced. Other things. Many things. Any who grew curious tonight, or courageous, would find themselves schooled in obedience. She would not enjoy it, no, but she knew it must be done. They were as children, they must be taught. And if rewards did not work, then punishment would.

Once the theater opened to the night's audience, she found herself a place to watch where no accidental trespasser could stumble across her. High above the ceiling of the gallery itself, where the great chandelier hung pendulous and glittering over the crowd below, she settled into a small alcove, watching through a cut-out section of the ceiling. It was invisible from below, any who dared to look up blinded by the dancing lights bouncing off the thousands and thousands of crystals on the chandelier.

She spotted the shadows moving in her box, number seven, and allowed herself a mental smirk. Did they really think she would be there? She was mechanical, not stupid. The shadows departed, and after a time, she could see more of them moving around in box one, directly across the stage. The rounded shapes of bodies were interspersed with the long, angular lines of rifles, no doubt sharpshooters set to fire when she showed her face in her usual seat. A flash of gold caught her eye, and she was certain she saw the outline of a head of golden curls. The woman again, no doubt with her own firearm. They were in for a long, disappointing wait.

As the orchestra began warming up, she closed her eyes and listened to see if the missing members were going to be a detriment. The absent viola would hurt, perhaps, but the flute player was one of seven, and her absence was of negligible effect. Lacking members in the chorus was more likely to cause notice, though this particular opera was not nearly as dependent on them as some others.

She had to admit, if she had a favorite opera, it would be this one. There was something hauntingly beautiful about the man falling in love with his inanimate creation, pining away for the marble perfection that could never return his affections. Only with the intervention of a benevolent goddess in the end could their love ever be truly realized. It made something inside her chest cavity feel too large, like an overheated valve or spring that had come too loose.

Or, perhaps she was simply in need of repairs. She would have to examine her workings later. Most things she could fix herself, but there were a few areas – her faltering, flickering eye, for example – that were simply beyond her capacity. The damaged bearing in her knee had been a simple thing to repair, and she had taken the time to oil and tweak every piece that needed it, anticipating that she might be forced to flee at some considerable speed in the future. It was not outside the realm of possibility.

The lights in the auditorium were dimmed, and with a flourish of his baton, Maestro waved the orchestra into full volume. The red velvet curtains were drawn back by thick golden ropes, and there was Tony on the stage. The first scene was in the sculptor's workshop, where the artist's friends would visit him to try and entice him out of his solitude in the wake of a recently broken heart. All the while, a cloth-draped form took center stage, silent and still.

Beneath the cloth, she knew, would be the little soprano, Caroline, set to play the part of the sculptor's creation. It was a role that most divas loathed to play, because they were not only silent but completely immobile throughout the greatest portion of the first act. Only in the second, when the sculptor slept, were they able to finally meet in the flesh, the statue stepping from her pedestal to dance with her long-suffering love. That, she decided, was her favorite part.

Tony sounded divine, as always. The heartbreak in his voice was convincing enough that the wires behind her jaw ached. Where Simon might have played the role for the melodrama of it, Tony's performance was utterly simple, and perfectly genuine. He loved the being beneath the concealing tarp, and not one person in that theater could doubt it.

At the appropriate time, he took hold of the vast cloth and gave a flourishing yank, finally revealing the creation beneath. If she had been capable of breath, she might have gasped aloud. Many in the audience did.

Where there would usually be a statue, a singer made up in pale draping cloth and alabaster paint on her skin and hair, there instead stood a creature of pure gold, her dress a filmy thing done in the Greek style, and her ebony curls spilling loose down her back to her waist.

Someone had done a fine job on the painting. Even from her seat high above, she could see the lines of seams, the outlines of bolts and screws at every joint. It had been intricately done, and from a distance it was impossible to tell that the figure on stage was, or ever had been, human. Only her eyes gave her away, as no human could imitate an automaton's lighted glass orbs.

For that is what she was. Not a statue and her sculptor, but an automaton of pure gold, and the pining engineer who had built her. A creature of metal and oil, rather than marble, and she shone in the stage lights. No, gleamed, and every eye could not help but marvel, and love as well.

He had done this for her. She knew that with stunning certainty. It was a message for her, and her alone. "Oh Tony…" *Oh, my Tony…* She had to tell him that she had heard, and understood. She had to let him know, somehow, that his message had reached its intended recipient.

But how? She dared not show herself when they were watching so intently for her. There had to be a way, some way she could speak to him before he left the stage. They would never attack her in so public a place. It came to her in a flash of brilliance. Shortly, there would be a scene change, and Caroline would be wheeled off the stage for a much needed respite and to touch up any of her makeup that had run under the lights. That would be her chance, while the soprano was alone in her dressing room. She would have to move fast.

Her entrance into the lead tenor's dressing room was surely known. She had no doubt that Tony had shown them the mirror door when he came in search of the golden woman, Bess. He did not, however, know about the entrance into the soprano's quarters. It was not as cleverly concealed as the mirror door, and so Caroline the soprano gaped in open astonishment as the section of the wall she was facing slid open with a hiss of escaping steam.

It could almost be comical, the expression of mute shock on the face of a golden automaton. Fortunately, the singer's surprise lasted long enough for the true automaton to spring from concealment, mechanical hand closing around the gold-painted throat. Her delicate fingers scrabbled at the vice-like grip, in vain, bits of gold leaf flaking away like glittery snow.

"You have performed admirably to this point, my dear. Unfortunately, your services are no longer required." The green eyes, the only thing human in the faux-metal face, widened for a split second, then there was a muffled snap, and the gleam in them dimmed, the fog of death taking them.

On stage, the players played on, the story progressing on schedule, no one aware of the brief and silent struggle just yards away. She lay the singer's body down gently, tucking her diaphanous skirt modestly around her legs. There was no reason for humiliation upon her discovery, the girl had done nothing to deserve such.

It was easy to appropriate the next costume, she was not so different in size from the diminutive brunette. The gown itself was meant to evoke the image of a wedding dress, though slit up the sides to allow for the graceful ballet that would accompany the dream sequence. She paused to admire herself in the mirror, and if she were capable she would have smiled in amusement at the transparent veil that only just covered her face. Once again into the veil, it seemed, though she was certain Tony would recognize her. How could he not?

Someone tapped lightly on the door, and hissed, "Caroline! Thirty seconds!" It was time.

No one noticed as she passed within touching distance of them, including the two constables who flanked the other dressing room door. As usual, humans saw what they expected to see, and what they were looking for was a cloaked woman, darting furtively from shadow to shadow. They were not looking for an automaton moving among them bold as brass. *As brass...* She could have chuckled at herself, but she would have missed her cue.

On stage, the lights were dimmed as the sculptor-cum-engineer fell into a fitful sleep, laid over his drawing board. Dancers of the troupe flitted back and forth at the upstage level, representing the demons and dreams that warred within the tortured man. Closer and closer to him the tiny battles raged, and he tossed and turned, torn by his powerful emotions even in his sleep. Just when it appeared that the ephemeral war would land right on his head, she stepped from the curtains at stage right, and all the dream creatures froze in place, chastised by a simple look from her golden visage, hidden behind the sheer veil. They cowered from her, slinking and snarling silently as she backed them down with her simple presence, golden against their darkness.

The moment she began to sing, chasing away the devils of the night with the purity of her voice, Tony's thrashing stilled, and as she approached him one graceful step at a time, his head came up slowly, blinking the dreams from his eyes. She offered her hand to him, and slowly, as if he feared to end the dream too soon, he placed his hand in hers.

He knew. She could see that in his eyes the moment his gaze met hers. Despite the lights, despite the deception, despite the thin bit of cloth covering her face, he knew her voice, knew her touch. And still he sang, pouring out words of love and devotion, even as she answered him in kind. Together, their voices wove and intertwined, harmony and melody, back and forth, trading and sparring all at once. It was perfect. To her ear, it was absolutely, blissfully, perfect.

There were other dancers on stage. She knew this, in the back of her mind, as she knew every other minute detail of this opera. But for a few glorious, brief moments, they did not exist. She and Tony moved about the stage, singing the dreamed vows of a wedding that could never be. The beam of the spotlight followed them and only them, and the rest of the world vanished.

The music swelled, the chorus dancers faded to the background, and they were left alone at center stage, caught in the cage of white light. With trembling hands, the sculptor raised his hands to lift the veil from his bride's face. This was the moment, the consummation of the dream marriage with a kiss. The instruments in the pit faded to silence, per the orchestration, leaving the two dream lovers suspended in a timeless moment.

Tony's eyes met hers, bared now for all the audience to see, the unwavering glass orbs of a true automaton. The tarnished half of her face, the half she seldom looked upon herself, faced them, and she heard the startled murmurs go through the crowd. It didn't matter. All that mattered was that Tony was looking upon her, truly seeing her. He gave her a small, sad smile, brushing his fingers over the unmarred side of her face. "I'm sorry."

That wasn't in the script. Caught up in the moment as she was, she failed to react as he dropped his hand and snatched at the key dangling from the chain around her neck. With a sharp tug, the links parted, and he came away with the most precious thing in the universe to her. In shock, she stared at him, only inches away.

"I'm so sorry, Melody."

Somewhere in the gallery, a rifle cracked, and a woman screamed.

Chapter 21

"I'm so sorry, Melody." She stared at him in utter shock, and Tony knew that he should be moving, should be getting out of her reach before she retaliated. Still, his feet seemed frozen in place, the beautiful filigreed heart key dangling from his fingers as he gazed into the glass eyes of his one-time teacher.

The crack of a rifle broke the silence at the same moment that he heard the screaming start, and Bess's distinct voice yelled "No!" from the boxes. Something ricocheted off Melody's metal skull with a whine, and he felt a line of fire sear across his cheek. Raising his hand, his fingers came away bloody, and he blinked in puzzlement. How had that happened?

Melody knew, apparently, and she whirled to face the audience. "How *dare* you?!" Two more shots rang out, the bullets having as much effect as a wad of paper, but causing more danger to those around her than to the automaton herself.

"Tony! Run!" Bess again. With the stage lights shining in his eyes he couldn't see her, the audience just a large formless blackness beyond the end of the stage, but he could hear her berating the marksmen in her box until it was lost in the screaming of the audience as they panicked and fled.

"You will learn your place," Melody snarled, her perfect voice making the vicious words even more menacing. She marched purposefully to stage left, grasping the red velvet curtains in both metal hands. With a shriek of rent cloth, she tore them to tatters, revealing a rope behind them, as big around as Tony's wrist. Twice more, bullets streaked across the auditorium, one of them actually staggering her, but it would not deter her from her intent.

Something landed on the stage with a thud, and he turned to see Bess running at him, having leapt from her box. "Tony, run!" She offered him her hand, her other occupied with the enormous gun she carried.

But no, he had to see what Melody was doing, what was that rope? He'd been all over this stage, and he'd never noticed it before.

The metal woman grasped the thick cable in both hands and simple pulled, the fibers snapping like cotton batting. Above the auditorium, the chandelier gave an ominous shudder.

"No...no, don't!" It was too late. The heavy rope parted in a shower of dust that glittered in the lights, and overhead, parts of the ceiling gave way as the fixtures that supported the great crystal construction snapped under the heavy weight. Those below who had not fled before scrambled for the aisles now, trampling over each other in their panic, but there was no way for everyone to escape. The chandelier glittered cheerfully as it crashed down into the seats, sending crystal pieces rocketing in all directions. Tony wrapped his arms around Bess and sheltered her from the worst of the shrapnel, but bits of it pelted his shoulders hard enough to bruise. Sparks flew, caught, and the first glimmers of fire were born, eating eagerly at the newly upholstered seats.

"We have to go!" Bess yanked on his arm, finally spurring him into motion, both of them knocked this way and that by the cast and crew as they too fled the wings and the walks above the stage. Through the pandemonium, Tony caught one last sight of Melody standing near the severed rope, her face turned toward him, and then he was running with Bess, her hand locked in his grip lest he lose her in the chaos.

Back stage, men and women alike screamed and pushed and shoved to get out, at odds with the constables who were trying to move against the tide, attempting to reach the stage and the monster they had come to destroy. Tony caught one brief glimpse of Simon LeClerc, seated on the floor with a gold-painted Caroline in his lap, his head bowed as he wept over the ominously still form. Then Bess pulled him on, and all he could see in front of him was her golden curls, bouncing as they pushed and shoved their way through the hallways.

Suddenly, they spilled out the doorway into the night air, only to be buffeted and shoved from behind, more people trying to escape the growing fire within. He could hear it above the fear-shrill voices, a crackle that was slowly growing to a roar. Sharp noises came from within, but it was impossible to tell if it was more gunshots, or simple the noises of metal giving way under the heat.

Bess led them to the side of the grand marble staircase where they were less likely to be trampled. "Do you still have it?"

For a moment, he had no idea what she was talking about until she reached for his other hand. There, wound in his fingers, was the delicate gold chain bearing a beautifully carved winding key. He closed his fist around it.

"We have to get you out of here. Somewhere she can't reach." Bess looked around, but the square in front of the theater was a madhouse. Carriages tangled and blocked each other, horses shrieked in terror, their every instinct warning them to flee the growing inferno. Men yelled and came to blows, women screamed and wept, their gowns shredded and bloodstained. "On foot, then. Quickly."

When she would have darted down the stairs, he grabbed her arm. "She's faster than us."

"Then we better get moving. I know where to go." And

then they were running, ducking and weaving through the crowd until they broke free into the dark alleys beyond.

It was comforting, Tony realized, that Bess had a plan. He had none. He wasn't even sure he could have made one, after all that had taken place this night. Dear God, Caroline…all those people…Melody herself… He couldn't even wrap his mind around it.

They ran through the dark city streets, stopping several times as they were nearly mowed down by fire wagons headed toward the theater. Piercing whistles rang out from blocks away, the constables summoned toward the disaster, but no one seemed to notice the couple as Bess took corners and turns seemingly at random.

"Where are we going?" Tony finally asked, his side hurting as he gasped for breath.

"The airfield. Christos' ship. She can't get us once we're in the air, and she'll never find us in time if we can reach the far side of the lake."

"And what if your friend isn't there?"

"Then we find out if I've learned how to pilot for all the times I've watched it done." Tony had no doubt at all that she would try it, and he hope fervently that the pilot would somehow still be with his ship at this time of night. Escaping one fiery death to plunge into another was not an appetizing thought.

The airfield was on the far side of the coalworks, just past the industrial docks. The quickest path, therefore, was straight through the coalworks themselves. Men shouted in alarm as the pair of them plunged through open doors, darting through machinery and equipment. The furnaces roared like great beasts, the heat beating down on them like a physical force. Tony could feel the cloth of his shirt sticking to him, instantly soaked in sweat, and he knew once they were outside again, they were going to freeze in the cold night air. Ahead of him, Bess' back was almost coal black just from the dust sifting into the air, and her golden curls had dimmed to a nondescript dun color. No doubt, he looked the same.

Once, an automaton loomed into their path, its glass eyes flickering erratically. For one heart-stopping moment, he thought it was Melody, but this machine was made of battered, pitted steel, rusting at more than one seam, and its face was only vaguely human, not even having a semblance of a nose or ears. Bess had the same thought, because her Colt was out and leveled at the thing's eye faster than Tony could even see. The automaton itself appeared oblivious to its own imminent demise. The thing's arms were loaded with a heavy crate, and after it took a moment to register the obstacle in its path, it simply stepped aside, continuing on about its assigned duty. After a moment, Bess lowered her pistol, stuffing it back into its holster. She gave Tony a look that said everything he was feeling at that moment. For a heartbeat, their lives had been in very real danger, and the relief that swept in to replace the fear was enough to leave him dizzy.

It took them almost fifteen minutes to navigate through the coalworks, weaving through the furnaces and coal stacks and workers. Tony knew that they'd have had constables on their heels for the intrusion, if all of law enforcement hadn't already been dealing with the chaos at the opera house. He glanced behind them once, in the direction of the theater, but it was impossible to see anything over the pall cast from the coalworks smokestacks. *Please be all right. Please, everyone be all right.* They weren't. He'd seen that as they'd fled. Bodies broken and bloodied, lying far too still... He shut his eyes for a moment, trusting Bess to drag him on, trying to drive those sights from his mind.

The airfield was little more than a large grassy pasture that had been taken over with the new fad of air travel. There were three ships at dock there, two of them quite large and bearing official seals. They took up the majority of the space, school yard bullies shoving everyone else out of their way.

The third was smaller, the balloon a bit more patched, the box below capable of carrying no more than a dozen or so. It was there that Bess led him, banging on the door to the cabin. "Christos! Christos, are you here?"

As they waited for a response, Tony rested, bent over with his hands on his knees. It was the second time in recent weeks that he'd run nearly across the entire city, and he decided that it simply wasn't an activity he enjoyed. His lungs burned, his muscles ached faint protests that promised to become screams once he calmed some.

"He's not here," Bess grumbled, backing up to get a good look at the ship again. No sooner said, than a light appeared in the cabin compartment, bouncing against the windows as it came toward the door.

A very sleepy Christos popped his head out, blinking by the light of the lantern he held. His dark hair stuck out at abrupt angles, and he had only managed to pull on a pair of loose pants before he'd answered the knock at his door. "Bess? What the Hell? Do you have any idea of the time?"

"Why, is your watch broken?" She pulled Tony upright again, flashing him an attempt at an encouraging smile. "We need to get in the air, Christos, *now*."

The swarthy man blinked a little, then his brows drew together suspiciously. "Are you running from the police?"

"No." Bess nodded firmly. "I can honestly say we are *not* running from the police."

Christos sighed. "Damn. That could have been fun. Come on aboard, then." With a gesture, he welcomed them aboard his ship, shuffling ahead of them with his lantern.

Tony was the last aboard, and he turned to look across the grassy field toward the city again. The night was still. The coalworks churned on, and nothing stirred. Still, to be safe, he threw the flimsy lock on the cabin door. It wouldn't keep something like Melody out, no, but… He did it anyway.

"My engineer's gone for the night. Had a lady friend to visit or something. But I can get her up, if you're willing to help me," Christos was informing Bess as Tony caught up to them in the pilot's area. It was merely a small room, crowded with three people in it, at the head of the passenger cabin. From there, they could control the ship's engines and rudders, located in a room below them, accessible only by a trap door at their feet. Tony had spent most of his previous trip aboard this ship outside the main cabin, standing at the railing that surrounded the narrow walkway. They hadn't had time for a tour.

"I'll do whatever you need." Bess took a seat in the co-pilot's chair, looking the controls over eagerly.

"Any idea where we're going? I don't have a lot of fuel. Was getting a delivery in the morning."

"Just across the lake." Tony finally found his voice. "As far as you can get us."

Christos raised a brow, but nodded. "Aye. I can get you across the lake. Probably snag some coal over there to get me back home." He plopped down in his own chair for a moment, identifiable because it was much larger to account for his size. "All right, let's get her engines warming up, then I'll go cast off the ropes, and we'll be up. Bess, you just sit here and when this gauge right here hits one-twenty, you push this red button. That'll fire her up."

"Aye, Captain." She gave him a grin.

"C'mon…Tony, is it? You come down and shovel coal with me."

Obediently, Tony followed the airship pilot down through the trap door, dropping into the close confines of the engine room. There was barely room for the big captain's shoulders on the narrow metal walkway, but he maneuvered in the tight quarters with the ease of long familiarity. "See this one here is Layla." He patted the engine on his right with a fond touch. "Her sister is Frieda. They're my ladies, but they get hungry and they like to be fed."

At the aft end of the chamber was a large pile of coal and a couple of small shovels. Christos picked up one and tossed the other at Tony, who only barely caught it. "Just open up the door there, and shovel her in. You take Frieda."

The furnace portion of the engines was not the raging inferno of the coalworks, but there was still considerable heat from the banked coals as they opened the metal doors and began shoveling the dark rocks inside. In no time at all, the fires were roaring pleasantly, and Christos had to shout to be heard. "There, that should do to take us over the lake. We'll just get her up in the air now."

They climbed up out of the engine chamber, the cooler air in the cabin a blessed relief from the heat below. Christos looked over Bess' shoulder to verify that she'd done as he'd asked, and he nodded his approval. "All right, I'll go cast off the ropes, haul in the anchor, and we'll be off." He started to leave, then paused at the door, giving Bess a stern look. "Don't touch anything."

She chuckled. "Aye, Captain."

With Christos gone, Tony slumped into the captain's chair, dropping his head into his hands. He felt Bess' fingers run soothingly through his hair, and the chain of Melody's necklace pressed into his cheek, still wound through his fingers as it was. "We're almost safe. Once we're airborne, she can't follow us. And even if she could, she'd never make it around the lake before her winding ran down."

"Are you sure?" He raised his head to finger the filigreed key. "I'm starting to think there is nothing certain anymore."

"She's a machine, Tony, not some unstoppable fiend from Hell."

No. That much was true. Not from Hell. Not Melody.

"All right, we're loose and ready to take off, and there's a fellow in my seat for some reason." Christos returned and gave Tony a raised brow until he moved out of the captain's seat. "No offense, friend, but you look like a dog's breakfast. Why don't you go back into the passenger cabin and get some sleep while we're in the air."

Bess nodded her agreement. "Go on, Tony. I'll wake you when we land."

As unlikely as sleep was, it was still worth the effort, he finally decided, and he found himself a place to sprawl across three cushioned chairs in the passenger cabin. He felt the ship give a small shudder as she broke her bonds with the earth, and a slight fluttery feeling in his stomach that recognized as ascending into the air. He lay his arm across his eyes, the winding key held tightly in his fist, and tried to turn his mind off.

Suddenly, the ship gave a lurch, listing hard to the port side, and pitching Tony onto the floor where he blinked in surprise. He was still there when Christos stormed out of the captain's cabin, growling under his breath about a snagged anchor. He had managed to pick himself up by the time Christos stalked back through, still grumbling. "Bess, the pulley's stuck, I'm gonna have to get at it down in the engine room. Just keep us heading out toward the lake, she'll fly even lopsided til I get her fixed."

Tony followed the captain back to the stern, watching as the big man disappeared through the trap door again. He braced his arms on Bess' chair to compensate for the uneven floor. "Never a dull moment, yes?"

"Don't worry, Christos isn't panicking, so whatever it is, it's fine." She smiled up at him. "He says he'll teach me the controls as we cross the lake."

"Wonderful. Next you'll be wanting one of these for yourself."

"We could rappel down into our wedding from it."

They both chuckled, and he bent down to kiss her gently.

With a groan, the ship slowly righted herself, the deck once again level. Christos, however, did not reappear. After a few minutes, Bess leaned over to peer into the open trap door. "Christos? Everything all right down there?" Their only response was the low roar from the engine furnaces, and the persistent growl as the propellers behind the ship turned faster than sight. "Christos?"

"He probably can't hear you. I'll go look, you're flying, remember?" He kissed the top of her head, then climbed down into the engine room.

The only lighting came from the red glow of the furnaces, giving the cramped chamber an aura of some demonic domain, hell fire and stench surrounding him. It had been much more pleasant the first time down, before the engines had come to full function. "Christos? Hello?" There was no answer.

Slowly, Tony made his way down the narrow walkway, the metal grating under his feet no wider than the catwalks above the stage at the theater. Nothing stirred, save the inner workings of the massive turbines on either side of him. Despite the immense heat, he felt a cold chill. Something was very wrong.

The cold chill came again, wafting against his face, and he realized that it was no figment of his imagination, but an actual breeze. Cold night air was gusting in from somewhere. Making his way to the aft side again, he found a door in the ship's hull unsecured, banging open and closed. It was clearly the coal chute, where they loaded the ship's fuel, large enough for a man to pass through if he was careful.

There was still no sign of Christos, however, and swallowing his dread, Tony knelt in the coal dust to stick his head out the portal. Below them, the airfield was shrinking into the night, and a rope dangled like a fishing line behind the ship, fluttering into empty air. But there was no Christos.

The metal grating under his feet, the only floor available in the tight chamber, shuddered as someone stepped onto it, and he turned, expecting to find Bess. "You're supposed to be flying!"

It was not the plucky blonde on the walkway, however. Even in the dim light, he could never make that mistake. The crimson glow from the furnaces reflected on metal skin, and the hair was raven black, a color not even coal dust could achieve in Bess' golden locks. She was still dressed in her costume from the opera, though the once-white wedding dress would never be pristine again, covered in ominous smears and soot, and the hem had been ripped to tatters at some point. The tarnished half of her face gave her a glower that her true face would never possess.

"Melody." He tightened his fist around the key, moving it slightly behind his leg as he stood, where she could not see it.

The lights behind her glass eyes gleamed in the darkness, though one of them flickered from time to time, giving her the impression of a nervous tic. "I did not kill the dark man."

"Christos?"

"If that was his name. I pulled him out of the portal, and dropped him to the ground, but the ship was not high enough to kill him."

Oddly, it was a small bit of comfort. No one else needed to die because of him. "How did you escape?" She stood between him and the trap door, and on the narrow walk between the engines, there was no way to get past her without being in reach of her crushing grasp. With the engines roaring at full power, there was no way Bess could hear him if he tried to call a warning.

"There are ways in and out that only I know. And the men were more interested in the fire, once it started, than in me." She took a step toward him, and his heart skipped a beat. "You have something of mine."

"I destroyed it. I threw it in the furnaces in the coalworks."

"No you did not. You would not." She seemed so confident in him. "I would like to have it back now." She held out her hand to him expectantly.

He flexed his fingers, feeling the edges of the key dig into his palm, and shook his head. "I can't do that, Melody. You…you have to stop. You've been going too long. It's time for you to wind down."

She flinched as though his words had been a blow. "You? Even you? Of all of them, I thought that you would understand."

"I do understand. You are a miracle, something that was never before imagined. But it's gone wrong, somehow. All those people…Caroline…Stig… You killed them. You're not…right. Not anymore."

"I only wished to help you."

"I know. And you have, immensely. But it's over now. It's done, and it's time for you to rest."

For a moment, one long, drawn-out moment, he thought she might acquiesce. She tilted her head as if considering it, the flickering in her bad eye ceasing briefly. Then, she righted herself, and stepped forward again. "If you will not give me the key willingly, I will take it from you."

"Like Hell!" Bess' voice snarled from behind the menacing machine, and Tony caught a glimpse of her, hanging halfway down the ladder, her pistol drawn and aimed.

"Bess no!" But the Colt thundered in the close confines, smashing into the back of the automaton's skull hard enough to pitch her forward onto her hands and knees. The bullet, denied entrance through the metal shell, ricocheted off with a whine, piercing the side of the starboard engine instead. *Layla*, Tony thought absurdly, as a blast of scalding steam jetted from the ruptured casing.

"Tony come on!" Bess scrambled back up the ladder, and Tony only hesitated a second before leaping over Melody on the floor. He took the ladder in two steps, expecting to feel a metal hand clamp down on his ankle at any second, but he reached the top and Bess slammed the trap door down and threw the latch. "Where the hell did she come from?"

"The coal chute. She pitched Christos over when he stuck his head out, then climbed on in." Tony stared out the windows, realizing just how high in the air they truly were. "There's nowhere to go. Can you land this thing?"

Their answer came in the form of a shiver through the ship's frame, the starboard engine giving a wholly unnatural shriek. That was followed by several large bangs that shook the entire structure. The gauges on the pilot's console all pegged into the red section and quivered there.

"I'm not a pilot, but I think the engine's going to blow. Come on, we have to jump for it." Bess grabbed his hand and dragged him out to the walkway, both of them peering over the railing. Far below them, the city slept, the coalworks just below, belching out endless black smoke. To the north, there was an orange glow against the night sky, no doubt the remains of the opera house as it smoldered in its death throes.

They ran the length of the ship, but there were no more pleasant options at the aft end. The ship was drifting aimlessly without anyone at the helm, and it had begun a listless circle as the starboard propeller sputtered and faltered. Another small concussion shook the cabin, and they clung to the railing lest they be pitched overboard.

"The lake. If I can get her over the lake, we can hit the water from there. It's a chance." Bess grabbed his hand, but as they both turned, they found their path blocked once again by the automaton. Lightning fast, Bess had her gun out and pointed again, but Melody reached out even faster and bent the barrel back on itself with no effort at all.

"No!" Tony yanked Bess behind him, putting himself between his love and the angry machine. "No. I'll give you the key."

"Don't you dare!" Bess protested behind him, but he couldn't afford to listen. He couldn't risk Bess, not when he could end this.

Letting the key dangle from his fingers, he offered it to Melody, fully aware that at that range, she could crush the life out of him as easily as she could take the necklace. She eyed him for silent moments, as if waiting to see if he was sincere, then reached her hand out to take the key.

Just as her fingers brushed the delicate chain, there was a deafening boom, and the deck pitched sharply to one side as the starboard engine blew out the side of the hull. The railing slammed into Tony's ribs, leaving him staring down at the city below, but Bess was not so lucky. With a cry, she was flung over the side, and only swift lunge from Tony caught at her flailing hand, leaving her dangling in the night. Her weight wrenched at his shoulder, nearly dragging him over with her, but he gritted his teeth and dug in, holding as tightly as he could.

The ship itself was done for, hemorrhaging black clouds of smoke through its ruptured hull, beginning a slow downward spiral. Bess' nails dug into Tony's wrist, but he had no leverage to haul her back up, and their skin was sweat-slick, starting to slip.

Bess looked down at the ground below, then back up. "Let me go! You'll get pulled over!"

"Never," he growled, and planted his feet against the railing to pull. Every muscle he had screamed, and his grip on her wrist slipped another inch.

"Tony! Let go!" She pleaded with him, real fear in her eyes for the first time he could ever remember. Not fear for herself, no, but fear for him.

"No!" The deck shook again, and the metal railing started to bend under their combined weight. "Together, or not at all. Remember?"

She gave him a small smile, shaking her head at him even in their dire circumstances. "You're a foo- Tony, watch out!"

He had no time to react, and no idea what he would have done if he could. A metal hand reached past him, grasping Bess' arm, and lifted her out of the jaws of death as easily as one might a child. He could do no more than gape in astonishment as Melody set Bess on her feet, all of them braced against the leaning deck. The automaton looked back and forth between them, then backed up a few steps, as if aware that they would not trust her presence.

Bess winced, cradling her almost surely broken arm to her chest, but at least she was alive. Tony gathered her close, holding the woman that only moments before, he was certain he would never hold again. Looking up to Melody, he asked, "Why?"

"I could not bear to see you sad. Her death would have made you grieve." She tilted her head again, somehow the dark half of her face appearing unspeakably weary. "You love her."

"Yes. Very much." The ship shook again, and Tony gripped the railing tightly.

"We still have the small matter of how we get off this ride before it explodes," Bess pointed out. "We're too high to jump."

"Not over the lake." Melody gestured toward the dark waters of Lake Celeste, gleaming in the distance. "I can pilot the ship out over the water, and it will be low enough at that time for you to leap to safety."

The trio stared at each other, until Bess once again spurred them into action. "You heard the lady. Let's find a place to jump from." Too near the aft, they knew, they would be diced to bits by the remaining propeller.

Steering the crippled vessel was haphazard at best, but somehow, Melody got the thing pointed in one direction and managed to keep it on course. More explosions shook the frame, and it was clear that reaching the water before the last catastrophic one was going to be a matter of luck, not planning. Perched on the bow, Tony watched her through the windows as she piloted the ship as though it had been her original function.

"We're almost there… Get ready." Bess had one leg thrown over the railing already, and gestured for him to join her. "Tony, come on!"

"I have to do something first. When we're over deep enough water, go. Don't wait for me."

"Tony!" He ignored her, and returned to the captain's cabin. Melody looked up from her tasks, eyeing him almost warily.

"Here." He held out the key to her. "Take it."

She eyed his offering, then shook her head. "No. You keep it." There was sadness to her perfect voice, and a great bone-deep weariness.

Tony blinked. "But…you'll die."

"Most likely." She nodded. "Perhaps it is time. There is a child's ghost here, and she very much wishes me to come play with her. I think perhaps that was my original purpose." When he didn't move, she looked to him again. "Go. You must live a long, happy life, with her."

"Melody…"

"Go now, please. The second engine will explode soon, if these gauges are at all accurate."

He hesitated a moment longer, then stepped forward, cupping her face in his palm. She watched him, even her glass eyes managing to convey surprise. Leaning close, he pressed a gentle kiss to her metal mouth. "Thank you, Melody."

"Goodbye, Tony."

He left her behind, returning to Bess who had defiantly not jumped as she'd been told. Below them, the mirror surface of the lake waited. Tony took her uninjured hand,

and stepped to the outside of the railing. "Ready?"

"Together, or not at all." With a shared nod, they both stepped out into empty air.

Down and down they plunged, until the cold waters of the lake rushed up to meet them, closed over their heads, disoriented them in a haze of bubbles and darkness.

Tony fought his way back to the surface first, Bess popping up next to him a breath later, and together they watched as the dying airship floated further out over the water. It gave two great heaves, and then the port side exploded in a rain of fiery metal that reached even the two lovers in the water.

"Dive!" Below they went again, and the surface was peppered with screws and bolts and bits of cable, fired like bullets from the exploding engine. Clasping hands, they stayed down until their lungs burned, until the basic need to breathe drove them to the surface again.

Further out over the lake, the remains of the airship slowly plunged into the water, the balloon itself floating like an immense buoy until the lake claimed it too.

Shrapnel rained down over the lake like vibrant stars plummeting from the heavens, going so far as to reach the industrial docks and the coalworks themselves. Most of it was lost to the depths of the mirror lake, however, the surface closing over the wreckage, smoothing away all traces. In the end, it was impossible to say what pieces belonged to the ship, and what might have belonged to…something else.

EPILOGUE

Felicia closed the book, smoothing the brittle pages carefully, then smiled and reached down to stroke the hair of her sleeping son, pillowed on her skirts. Peter had succumbed somewhere near chapter ten, but Josie had listened 'til almost the end before retiring for the night. She had finished the story just reading for Casimir, the two siblings spending a rare moment alone. Very little cleaning had been done, truth be told, but it had been wonderful to be lost in one of Aunt Susan's stories again, and one that involved the beloved family members so recently lost.

Casimir bent down to gather Peter up into his arms, the sleeping boy never even stirring, his body limp with the sleep that only children could manage. "So. Do you think it was real?"

Felicia chuckled softly. "Of course not. Though I don't understand why Aunt Susan never published this one. It was quite good."

"Maybe she wrote it as a favor for Mother, or a gift. I will say, she got her spot on." With a fond smile, Casimir disappeared down the steep stairs, his nephew cradled carefully in his arms.

Felicia sighed quietly, gazing around the dusty attic. So many memories, so much life. The story had depicted her mother in every way she remembered. Loud, joyful, full of life. And her father, the quiet thinker, the gentle hands. They had completed each other, until the last months of their lives when her father had been forced to go on without his beloved Bess. He'd followed her soon enough, slipping away in his sleep. "Together, or not at all."

She brushed a few tears away, mindful that she was no doubt leaving trails of mud across her cheeks. Ah well. The rest of the attic would wait until morning. Josie could sleep in her old room, and Peter could share Casimir's with him. She herself would take her mother and father's room, and sleep there one last time before it no longer belonged to any of them. Tomorrow, they would finish removing all that they wished to save, and then another family would take the house, and would fill the rooms with laughing children and joyful noises.

"Felicia?" Casimir's head appeared again at the top of the ladder, giving her a curious look. "Aren't you coming down? It's too late to keep working now."

"I'm coming. I am. Just… Let me finish this trunk at least, since we've started it."

Her brother clambered the rest of the way up the stairs, sitting in the portal with his legs dangling. "Save that book, will you?"

"Of course. I'd intended to." She laid the brittle manuscript aside where she could collect it later. "You know, if we keep it long enough, generations from now, a great-grandchild will find it, and believe wholeheartedly that it happened. Opera infernos, rogue automatons, a great airship explosion…"

"Who's to say it didn't happen, just like that? We could go research in the newspaper archives, you know. See if we can find some sign. Surely something like an opera house burning down would be recorded."

"Oh Cas. You have always been the fanciful one." She reached out a hand to him, and he stretched to meet her, squeezing three times. "I think the world would be brighter if I could see it the way you do. You have that much of Mother in you."

"Oh I don't know. I distinctly recall a very proper debutante knocking out one of Randall Shaw's teeth at her coming out ball, because he made an improper advance. There's some of Mother in you too."

Felicia sniffed. "That was a thousand years ago, Casimir Krol. You're a beast to bring it up."

Her brother chuckled, and pressed a kiss to her knuckles. "Embrace it, little sister. It's who we are. Now come downstairs. We'll start fresh in the morning." With a light hop, he was gone, simply leaping down the length of the stairs to the floor below.

With a sigh, Felicia scooted over to examine the remaining contents of the trunk. A half-knitted…something, the yard gone all mouse-chewed. A few very old family portraits, obviously taken before either she or Casimir had made an appearance. Those she put aside with the book, to be saved. And deep down, at the very bottom, her fingers brushed across something cold and metal.

"Cas…? Casimir!"

"Hunh? What?" A moment later, he popped back up in the portal, proving that he'd not gone very far to begin with. "What are you squalling for? You're like to wake the house."

"Look." She held out her two new finds to him, and watched his eyes go wide.

The first was heavy, and her arm trembled after a moment to keep it steady. A vicious looking revolver, the steel gone dark with time and age, but at one time, it had been a quality piece. That is, until someone had bent the barrel back on itself, the opening pointing back at the luckless shooter.

From her other hand dangled a delicate gold chain, the links broken near the clasp. At the bottom swayed a beautiful key, shaped like a filigreed heart.

About the Author

K.A. Stewart has a BA in English with an emphasis in Literature from William Jewell College. She lives in Missouri with her husband, daughter, two cats, and one small furry demon that thinks it's a cat.

www.ingramcontent.com/pod-product-compliance
Lightning Source LLC
Chambersburg PA
CBHW061028120726
47910CB00006B/2144